Pieces
Of
Joi

Pieces of Joi is a **So Real Publishing** book, published by arrangement with the author.

Printing History
First Printing: 11/01/2011
Second Printing: 00/00/2017

ISBN: 978-0-9840216-0-4

For information www.sorealproductions.com
Authormikiellos@gmail.com

Printed in the United States of America

Acknowledgements

I'd like to thank my children for helping me become a better man because without fatherhood, I don't know where I would be. You all give me a reason to push through the madness even when I'm ready to give in. The parent-teacher conference is a long way from the streets, and I appreciate you all for showing me the way there. A father is only as good as his efforts and you three make my efforts look unchallenged! I love you all and I dedicate this book to my children, Dayjah Bhadd, Terrel Los, and Robert-Jakwon.

Pieces
Of
Joi

Prologue

Summertime was always the liveliest season in Detroit, and the summer of 1997 was no different. Joi was left alone for the Fourth of July weekend, so like any typical teenager, she decided to throw a house party. House parties were usually rest havens for neighborhood hoodlums, but Joi didn't keep that type of company. D'Vyne, Andre, and Joshua were Joi's best friends. They were definitely in attendance, but Joi's special guest was Major. Major was a guy in the neighborhood who Joi adored.

Being a teenager in the nineties was rough, especially in a city that had been robbed of its culture. Crack cocaine was the greatest heist ever pulled off on people. The little integrity Detroit retained after the heroin boom, crack swept through and vacuumed it away, leaving the city with an illumination of violence. The doo-whopping nights became devils' nights, and the sounds of automatic weapons became a wakeup call in some neighborhoods. However, Joi was given a sense of refuge daily. School was a refuge for most teenagers, but especially for Joi because she found Major there daily.

Major was *that guy* in the neighborhood. He sported all the latest clothes and jewels. Everyone at their high school assumed he was a drug dealer because of his name, his jewels, and his swagger. Major had the bad boy appearance, but Joi wasn't fooled by his façade. Joi knew Major was an imposter posing as a thug. She knew because Major's family went to the same church as hers. Although Joi knew the truth about Major's identity, she never ousted him because she did not believe in hating on players, not to mention Major was always nice to Joi, despite her being an unfashionable social outcast.

Joi was from a middle-class family, but one could never tell because she was a terrible dresser. She was never fashionable and that was an unattractive quality in a city known for its flamboyant nature. So, in Joi's juvenile mind, Major was admirable for accepting her despite her having an unflattering dress code.

On the day of the party, Joi was preparing some things when she heard the telephone ringing. After looking at the caller I.D., she answered. "What, D'Vyne?" she asked as she placed the telephone to her ear.

"You ain't chump-up did you?" D'Vyne asked with a slight chuckle. "I was lookin' for you at the mall this morning."

"It's still on. I already have clothes. I didn't have to go to the mall." Joi cringed after replying because she knew D'Vyne was going to hit the roof.

"OH, HELL NAW!" D'Vyne yelled into the telephone. "I'm on my way over there right now. I swear you ain't fixin' to embarrass me."

The telephone went silent while Joi was still holding it to her ear. Although she was livid about D'Vyne's rudeness, she quickly calmed down because she knew she needed her girl's fashion sense. D'Vyne was like Joi's personal stylist. She met Joi at the entrance of their high school daily and rearranged her clothing. D'Vyne assured Joi she had the shape and the clothing, but she verbally assassinated her for the way she wore them.

Seconds after the telephone went silent, Joi heard her name being called from the kitchen of her parent's home. She walked into the kitchen and playfully rolled her eyes at D'Vyne.

"You're rude, D'Vyne, busting into people's houses, screaming and stuff."

D'Vyne was visibly unmoved by Joi's comments. She brushed past Joi.

"Get outta my way, wench," she snickered. "Let me see what you think you're about to wear." She walked into Joi's bedroom.

Joi followed behind D'Vyne. "GET OUT OF MY ROOM, SLUT," she playfully yelled, rustling up behind D'Vyne.

D'Vyne casually nodded her head and giggled. "I am! As soon as I find yo' country-ass something to wear." She continued rummaging through Joi's closet, then paused and looked back toward Joi. "I thought you were trying to get Major's attention tonight?"

A devilish smirk wisped across Joi's face. "I have his attention already. I'm trying to get something else tonight," she replied with a nod and a suggestive snicker.

D'Vyne laughed. "Yeah right! You're scared of dick, so stop frontin'. You talk that shit, but I know you're perpin'."

D'Vyne was right about what she'd just said to Joi because Joi was definitely afraid. Joi had often pictured herself with Major in the future, but she wasn't sure if he viewed her in the same way. Major gave her signs from time-to-time, but she was still unsure about his intentions.

Major drove Joi to school and paid for her lunch daily, but he hadn't shown her any romantic interest. Although they were only friends, Joi received all the perks of being Major's girl, including the hate which she would have rather done without. All the females at their school, their church, and in their neighborhood envied Joi because of her friendship with Major. Even some of the older women in the neighborhood were jealous because they wanted Major in their worlds, too.

After coming to an agreement with D'Vyne about what she was going to wear to the party, Joi called Andre and Joshua over to help them set everything up. Andre and Joshua were from the same neighborhood as Joi and D'Vyne, but they both went to different high schools than them. Andre went to Kettering and Joshua went to a private school named St Martin de Porres. The two of them were best friends, but you wouldn't know it if you didn't know them. They competed over everything, especially females.

Joshua was the handsomer of the two, but he was a pushover. Everyone in the neighborhood had beaten him up, including Joi, but Andre always came to Joshua's defense. Andre was the typical short guy. What he lacked in height, he made up for with courage. No one in the neighborhood crossed Andre unless they wanted a head-busting. These were Joi's boys, and there was no way anyone would throw a party without inviting the two of them because they were party animals.

Shortly after Joi finished dressing, Joshua and Andre showed up. After entering the house, Joshua stood in front of D'Vyne smiling.

"Vee, tell this fool about Gucci loafers and light-skinned niggaz with dimples because he's sleep." He continued to tower over her, nodding his head in a cheerful manner.

D'Vyne stared up to Joshua with a confused look on her face. "What?" she asked, questioning what Joshua meant by his statement.

"Gucci, light skin, and the dimple are a trio. We gonna knock mo' ho's than . . ." Joshua paused and stared over at Andre, pointing to his attire, "a black-ass nigga and Polo." He patted Andre on the back. "I'm sorry to be the one to break the news to you, but you're a mismatch."

Joshua, Joi, and D'Vyne burst into laughter, but Andre simply smiled sinisterly. He nodded and sucked air through his teeth. "Whatever, dog. You right, you got all that shit, but what them pockets look like?" He chuckled and nodded his head victoriously because he knew he had won that battle.

Joi burst into a hysterical laughter. "He got you with that one, Joshua, but don't trip because Major is going to take all y'all's shine tonight."

Joshua looked up toward Joi. "Damn, Joi! He might need to piss. Give the nigga his dick back."

Everyone belted out boisterous laughter and they continued to bounce jokes back-and-forth to one another while setting things up for the party.

Joi was sure her party would be a hit because she was receiving calls from all sorts of people while she and her friends were setting things up. Guys were calling, saying, "What up, doe? Is it still on?" And females were calling, saying, "Hey, Joi. I know we don't speak, but can I come to your party?" Everyone was trying to be at the party. Joi knew they weren't coming to support her, but she didn't mind because she was finally getting some attention from her peers.

People started arriving at eight o'clock on the dot. They were driving up by the carloads. The DJ had the music banging. Joi was sure people could hear the speakers beating from blocks away, but she didn't mind because her party was jumping. Everyone was dancing. Guys were showing their footwork and females were getting low. People were in-and-out of Joi's home, freely eating and drinking. Joi knew how untrustworthy people were, so she had the upper level of the house locked off. The basement was the only free reign welcome to the party-goers.

Although the party had jumped off from the beginning, Joi was disappointed because Major hadn't shown up. She walked into the basement to check the food basket and quickly became upset. The baskets were empty after only a short time of partying. Joi gathered the baskets off the table and began walking toward the stairs. As she began walking up the stairs, Major was walking down them. Joi's face lit up.

"HEY, MAJOR," she unconsciously shrieked, giving him a once-over glance.

Major was fresh-to-death. He was wearing a powered-blue short-sleeved Coogi shirt, denim Girbaud shorts, and Coogi socks to match his shirt. The diamond bezel on his coin charm, swinging freely from his platinum chain, hypnotized Joi. She smiled widely.

"When did you get here?"

Major smiled. "Why? You been waitin' on me or somethin'?" he asked, grabbing the baskets out of Joi's hands.

Joi's cringed. "No; I just know who was out there when I left and you weren't," she replied, walking up the stairs, followed by Major.

As Joi opened the kitchen door, she playfully snatched the baskets from Major's hands. "Give me my baskets," she said and chuckled lightly.

"Oh, you want me to leave? I'll bounce because I saw a couple of honeys in the backyard. I was tryin' to be helpful, but I can go help myself to one of them because I know they been waitin' on a nigga." He chuckled.

"Pssh." Joi sighed and waved Major's comments off. "If you consider them honey, I wonder what vinegar looks like to you?" she said sassily.

Major looked at Joi and began shaking his head. "For mines. The ungrateful broad I'm fixin' to leave in the kitchen would most likely be the vinegar," he replied, turning and walking away.

Joi was fuming because in all actuality, she wanted to be the honey. She was downplaying the females in the backyard because she wanted Major to herself, but her sarcasm had pushed him into the yard with the scavengers. After briefly sulking, Joi finished filling the food baskets and returned to the party.

Joi walked into the backyard and noticed Major posted up talking to an attractive, light-hued female she didn't know. Joi watched as Major captivated the girl's attention. She was upset. Joi knew Major worked fast because every morning when he dropped her off in front of the school, another female would jump into the car with him as she got out. Joi had put up with that for years, but she wasn't feeling it at her party.

D'Vyne stared at Joi until she gained her attention, then she gave Joi a head gesture to go and interrupt the conversation between Major and the unknown female, but Joi didn't budge. D'Vyne walked over to Joi.

"Bitch, if you don't go over there and get him outta her face, I will! I'm gonna embarrass you, too." D'Vyne stared at Joi, assuring her she was serious.

"You'd better not, D'Vyne! I swear, you'd better not!" Joi threatened.

"Oh, you think I'm shittin' you, huh?"

D'Vyne rushed over toward Major and his female friend. As she approached them, she looked over her shoulder and smiled at Joi teasingly.

Joi watched as D'Vyne rudely interrupted Major's conversation with the girl. Joi's face flushed when D'Vyne pointed Major in her direction. Major said a few words to D'Vyne before walking off in Joi's direction. As Major walked away, D'Vyne boldly began a conversation with the female.

Joi's heart beat erratically as Major approached her showing his pristine smile. "What're you smiling at" she asked, blushing uncontrollably.

"You." Major chuckled. "What, you were too coward to tell me you been feelin' a nigga?"

"No, don't front! You know how I feel about you."

Major burst into laughter. "Goddamn, you're easy! D'Vyne ain't even say that shit. She said you needed some help gettin' food, but I knew she was lyin' because you'd already done it."

"So," Joi replied candidly, although she was unmistakably embarrassed, "now you know. Where do we go from here?" She sassily pursed her lips.

"Nowhere," Major replied. "Joi, you ain't tryin' to-fuck-with this gangsta shit." He chuckled and shook his head in a warning manner.

Joi nodded her head. "Oh, now I see. You're the coward." She giggled.

"Naw, Joi. On some real shit, I got game by the pound and a dick long as the California coastline, so go 'head on before you get hurt." He grabbed his crotch area and smiled devilishly.

Joi's neck snapped back, and she placed her hands onto her hips. "Gangster shit? Negro, please! I know your whole family. From where? Oh, from church. Your mom is the choir director and your father is a deacon. I don't think either of them raised a gangster, but they did raise a coward. Coward!" Joi angrily rolled her eyes at him.

"Coward?" Major shook his head in defiance. "Naw, never that, lil momma." He chuckled, continuing to shake his head.

"Always that, Major. You hide behind your clothes and your looks, but I bet you're a virgin just like me, and the last time I checked . . ." she paused briefly before continuing, "gangsters weren't scared of pussy. Humph!"

"Joi, I will fuck all-the-hell up outta you."

"When, muthafucka? Because I've been trying to push this pussy off on you for over two years now." Joi grabbed her mouth after realizing what she'd said.

Major stared at her in disbelief. Joi was humiliated by her own actions, so she ran off toward the house, seeking refuge. After entering the house, Joi watched the party from the window. She looked on as D'Vyne mixed and mingled throughout the yard as if she was the host of the party. Some people came and others left, including Major. Joi was livid as she watched Major leaving the party with the female he was speaking to prior to Joi embarrassing herself.

Around midnight, the yard was nearly empty, so Joi decided to come out of her shelter and end the party before it got too late. D'Vyne, Andre, and Joshua stayed behind and helped clean up the yard and the basement. Although Joi hadn't got what she wanted, she was pleased with the overall outcome of the party. Throughout the night, there wasn't even one argument and that was rare in a city known for its violent nature.

After seeing her friends off, Joi sprawled out in her living room floor and turned on the television. As she began dozing off, she was startled by the sound of the doorbell. She walked to the window and peeked through the blinds and smiled. After seeing Major's car parked in the driveway, Joi rushed to the door.

"Who is it," she asked, trying to hold in her excitement.

"It's Major." His voice pierced through the door.

Joi opened the door and smiled loudly. "What if my parents were at home, boy?"

"You wouldn't have had that party earlier, that's what." Major walked into the home.

"Whatever," Joi replied and closed the door behind him.

Major wrapped his arms around Joi's waist and palmed her youthfully-firm behind. He began kissing her neck, lips, and face passionately, while caressing her body.

Joi breathed heavily. Major had touched her spot, a spot she herself didn't even know existed. Her body tingled and her womanhood moistened. Just as she began to give in to Major's passion, she remembered he had left her house with another female earlier. Joi pushed him away and placed her hands on her hips, staring at him judgingly.

Major was puzzled by Joi's stare. "What's up? I thought it was on?"

"Pssh! What happened? The trick you left with earlier said no and you thought you were coming back to a for-sure yes?"

"You trippin', Joi." Major chuckled. "That was my thirteen-year-old cousin. I was tryin' to put my check-hand down on her when D'Vyne interrupted me, cryin' about you needed some help with the food, so I asked D'Vyne to talk to her on some female-to-female shit while I helped you out. Then you dipped off in the house, so I dropped her off so I could come back to kick it with you."

"Major, please." Joi turned her lips up as if she didn't believe what he was saying, but she really did.

"Look, Joi, I've been likin' you for a while and I been wantin' to-fuck-with you, but you be turnin' ya nose up at everybody because you're smart and cute, so I'm like, fuck that. I ain't fixin' to put myself out there to be shot down."

"Major, that shit sounded so lame." Joi giggled. "You know you're lying, and I know you're lying, so stop the games."

"Naw, Joi. I really wanna be with you, on some real shit." Major appeared to be sincere.

"Quit lying!" Joi was becoming agitated because she thought Major was trying to run game on her. "I'm ready, Major, and I want it to be with you. You don't have to talk up on it, but you can talk yourself out of it."

"I ain't lyin' though. That's what I'm tryin' to tell you." Major wrapped his arms around her waist and kissed her. "I'm serious." He continued kissing her.

Joi's body stiffened. She was nervous, but she was ready to become a woman. Major walked Joi into her bedroom and laid her across her bed. Joi knew her time had come, so she relaxed and let Major lead her.

That night, Joi became Major's woman. The two of them were nearly inseparable after they made love. Joi thought they would only share a single night of passion, but to her surprise, Major had deep and sincere feelings for her. During that summer, Joi lost her virginity and her name because everyone started referring to her as "Major's girl". Joi believed being Major's girl was a compliment; however, what started off as a compliment soon became an insult.

CB•EO

About a year-and-a-half into their relationship, Major's parents pushed him out of the nest. They allowed him to live with them, but that was the extent of their support for him. He worked a few jobs here and there, but he was unable to maintain stable employment. Eventually Major's parents got fed up with his lazy and unproductive behavior and put him out of their home.

Joi had an apartment of her own at the time, so she allowed Major to move in with her. Joi loved Major and had faith in his ability to get his life together. She knew things would be rough, but she had belief in the strength of their relationship. Joi knew Major had the ability and the intelligence to succeed in life; however, she had no idea about his lack of ambition, but she soon found out.

Major lounged around their apartment for months, jobless and penniless. Out of love, Joi dealt with Major's leeching until she could no longer take it. She realized her man was a bum, almost to the point of abuse. Although she truly loved him, she was at the top of her hierarchy of loved ones; therefore, she dropped him and tended to her own needs. Despite Major being a nice guy and although he had taken the first piece of Joi, it was over between them.

Chapter 1

Joi's life had been good throughout the last few years. She had completed her two-year associate degree in business at Wayne State University, and she had also received her real estate license. Joi was definitely on the path she intended to be on in life, and the woman she intended to become was becoming more prevalent. Although Joi had always been ambitious, she had become stagnated during the time she was with Major. The weight of a grown man was too heavy to carry to the top with her, so she did what she considered was in her best interests and dropped the dead weight.

Shortly after she received her degree, Joi gained employment at Regal Management, a large real estate company in Farmington Hills, Michigan. Her personal time became nonexistent for the first six months or so that she was employed with Regal. Joshua's pet name for her was MIA because of the distance Joi's new career created between her and her friends.

Joi, Joshua, D'Vyne, and Andre had been friends throughout the larger part of their lives, but lately none of them had been communicating the way they had while growing up. Joi had been feeling guilty about her distance from her friends, so after receiving some time off from work, she called D'Vyne and set up an outing for their clique. D'Vyne was ecstatic when Joi called and she assured her Andre and Joshua would be down.

As Joi slipped into her denim True Religion capris, she slowly twirled in front of the wall mirror admiring the way the jean material clung to her forty-inch derriere. Although Joi's hipline was wide for her five-foot-four frame, her twenty-two-inch waist and C-cup breasts created a balance to her pulchritude.

Joi continued dressing. She took time to perfect every detail of her appearance. Being fashionable wasn't a natural ability of Joi's, so getting dressed required a lot of thought. She was usually the worst-dressed throughout her high school years and well into college, but after a few months working for Regal, Joi learned to dress too impress. She was a quick learner, so it was no surprise she had picked up a killer sense of style in impressive time. Joi learned to look like money because she knew she had to look like money or people wouldn't trust her with theirs.

Although Joi hadn't seen D'Vyne in the last few months, she wanted to look her best because D'Vyne was a staunch fashion critic, and she knew D'Vyne would rearrange her clothing if they weren't up to her standards. After dressing, Joi smiled into the mirror and placed a fresh flower in her hair before escaping into the hallway of her apartment.

Joi sashayed through the hallway of her downtown loft apartment in a haughty manner. She smiled as she was greeted by her neighbors, men and women alike. Joi was feeling herself and definitely being felt by others. As she neared the elevators, she saw a younger woman clutch her man snugly and mouth "bitch' in her direction. Joi bravely walked over to the young lady.

"Excuse me?" Joi asked, knowing she'd misread what the woman appeared to have said.

The younger woman stared at Joi in a challenging manner. "Yeah?" She continued to stare, sassily pursing her lips.

"We don't speak to our neighbors like that at the Loft Havens, or any of our other properties for that matter. This is your verbal. Be thankful of this bitch, because it should be your eviction."

Joi spun and walked off with the sway of a super model. Although Joi was a humble woman, she did possess a great deal of power and influence within the company that employed her, and she wasn't afraid to assert it when necessary. She had earned her place within the ranks of Regal Management, and she carried it honorably. Joi knew an educated and soundly-employed black woman had to carry herself with poise. As she exited her building, she smiled because she knew she had done that.

After entering the parking lot, Joi heard someone yelling her name from a short distance. She turned to see where the voice was coming from. As her eyes roved over the lot, she saw a familiar figure descending from an H2 Hummer.

"JOI! JOI!" a man shouted, approaching Joi. He looked debonair and held a handsome smile on his face as he reached her.

Joi smiled weakly. "Hi, Damon. How've you been?" Joi embraced the man and rolled her eyes while her face was hidden in his chest.

Damon smiled. "I was good when it was me and you, but you don't even-fuck-with a nigga no more."

"Humph! You got part of it right."

Joi stepped slightly away from him and placed her hands on her hips. She looked up to him and stared directly into his eyes because she wanted him to feel and understand her fully.

"You're right. I don't fuck-with-you anymore, but there was never an us, and never will be."

Damon smiled sinisterly. "Oh!" He grabbed his chest. "I'm hurt. After all the work I put in on that pussy and all the work you put in for me, you don't want me." He chuckled.

"Whatever, sorry-ass-nigga." Joi began walking away. "Don't front because if you didn't care, you wouldn't be chasing and stalking my building.

Damon grabbed his mouth in a theatrical manner. "Oops, I forgot to tell you: I knocked a broad at Second City last month. Tall, slim, and sophisticated. Y'all ain't-got-shit in common except y'all live in the same building." Damon walked off toward the building, teasingly jingling the keys to his new woman's apartment in the air.

Joi entered her vehicle steaming with hatred for Damon. She had tears in her eyes, which was something she'd promised herself she would never allow to happen again because of Damon. Joi hated to lose, especially to people she didn't like, and she hated Damon! She despised him for everything he'd done to her in the past.

ᚼ•ᚼ

Joi met Damon in 2006 at a real estate seminar. She was seated in the rear of the room, desperately trying to type every detail of the seminar into her laptop computer. As she typed, Damon approached her, flashing his mesmerizing smile. Joi became uneasy because Damon was violating her personal space. She immediately stopped typing and looked up to him.

"Excuse me, sir. I'm working here." She smiled at him politely.

Damon chuckled. "Yeah, I see. Personally, I think you're working too hard actually."

"And that's your business because?" Joi looked to him, awaiting an answer to her glib remark.

"Because I frequent these events. I speak at some and know it's hard to keep all those notes, so I bring one of these." Damon pulled a tape recorder from the inside of his blazer and offered it to Joi.

Joi blushed. She was grandly embarrassed because of her rudeness. "Thanks, but I'm good." She smiled. "Besides, what are you going to use, and you might want something." She began typing again.

"I'm insisting. I have my secretary." Damon pointed to an attractive white woman sitting in the second row of seats. "She's recording and taking notes. I'm just here to network." He passed the recorder to Joi and introduced himself to her.

"Networking? Is that what you're doing with me?" Joi smiled flirtatiously.

"Of course not," Damon chuckled. "I'm flirting with you." They both burst into a subtle laugh after Damon's bold admission.

Joi admired Damon's approach. She was approached by men daily, but she was rarely impressed by her suitors, and never as impressed as she was with Damon. Although impressed, she had no intention of becoming involved with anyone until she was well established, but she did see the potential for something with Damon.

Damon was familiar with the real estate business, and from the looks of the large princess cut diamonds set in his platinum bracelet, Joi was sure he was successful at it. Joi intended to date Damon and learn some loops in the real estate business, but her intentions soon became null.

Joi hadn't dated anyone since her breakup with Major, so the attention she received from Damon was fulfilling to her. He was bold and unyielding in his efforts to win Joi over. He wined and dined her, and showered her with gifts, something Joi was unaccustomed to because her last man was only efficient for her necessities, so the luxury Damon provided her with clouded her judgment and lessened her independence.

After months of dating Damon, things began to get rocky between them because Joi began learning things about him that weren't admirable. She and Damon attended a high school basketball game together, something Damon usually did alone, but they were supposed to go to dinner afterwards, so Joi tagged along with him. Joi assumed Damon was just a fan and supporter of the student league, but as they sat watching the game, she learned different.

Joi had grown up in the hood, so criminal activity was something she could spot from a mile away, which made it easier to see through what Damon was into. As they watched the game, young teenage boys continuously came to the bleachers and sat next to Damon. Joi wouldn't have noticed if the boys had stayed a while, but she became suspicious after noticing a pattern of the young men sitting briefly and leaving. As she began to pay closer attention to what was going on, she was sure she wasn't mistaken about what was happening.

As one of the teenagers was approaching Damon, Joi noticed him reaching into his jacket pocket. The young man pulled out a roll of cash and discretely passed it to Damon after sitting next to him. Although their operation was low-key, Joi had picked up on it. She was livid. She cut her eyes at Damon but said nothing. Her entire mood changed. She remained silent throughout the rest of the basketball game because she didn't want to create a scene and embarrass herself more than what she already was; however, she had every intention to address what she had seen once they left the game.

After the game was over, Joi and Damon were walking toward Damon's vehicle when Joi abruptly stopped.

"Why didn't you tell me, Damon?"

Her eyes vehemently pierced through Damon's flesh as she stood with her hands defensively folded across her sternum.

Damon was confused. He didn't know what he had forgotten to tell Joi.

"Tell you what?" he asked, walking off toward his truck.

Joi briskly followed behind him. "That you sold drugs! That's what! Don't lie either because I saw those kids passing you money in there, Damon."

Damon's eyes roved over the parking lot. He wanted to make sure no one had heard Joi's loud rant about his side occupation. After confirming they were alone, Damon turned to Joi and casually shook his head.

"Now you're overstepping your boundaries. Not about questioning me, because I encourage that, but never accuse me of lying. I ain't gotta lie about shit," he said as he opened the passenger door for Joi.

"Oh, so let me get this right: You do sell drugs, but you'd never lie?" Joi said glibly. "Wow, a drug dealer with morals." She wildly threw her hands into the air as if she was outdone.

After they both entered the truck, Damon looked over to Joi. "Joi, we've been happy. The nature and the direction of our relationship says we don't disrespect one another, so let's not start. I see where this is going, so I'm gonna drop you off at home. If you wanna talk and work it out, call me, but if your mind is made up . . ." he paused and rubbed his chin before continuing, "it's been real."

Damon drove off and the entire drive to Joi's apartment was silent. Damon was content with his words and Joi was amazed by Damon's humble demeanor.

During the next few weeks, Joi was torn between her convictions about dating drug dealers and the feelings she had developed for Damon. She knew his occupation was a dishonorable one she despised, but her feelings wouldn't allow her to discount how good he had been to her. Damon treated her like a queen. He had even handled the situation at the basketball game in a sensible manner, which confused her even more because he didn't display the typical criminal posture, instead he was gentle.

Joi sat in her dining room with the telephone clasped in her palms, contemplating giving Damon a call. It had been nearly a month and she missed him, so she decided to go through with the call. After Damon answered, he and Joi spoke briefly. Joi was surprised that Damon was so receptive of her. He invited her to lunch, and she accepted.

After getting herself together, Joi left her apartment to meet Damon at Pegasus Restaurant in Greektown. She was thrilled about seeing Damon after being away from him for so long but didn't want to appear too eager. After reaching the restaurant, she briefly collected herself before leaving her car and entering the restaurant.

Approaching the table, Joi noticed that, unlike herself, Damon wasn't trying to hide his excitement to see her. As she reached him, Damon rose and embraced her. Joi melted into his chest.

"Hi, Damon." She greeted him in a coy manner.

Damon held his embrace. "Hey, baby. I missed you—a lot, too." He kissed her, gently caressing her hips.

Joi smiled. "Me, too, but we need to talk," she said as they both sat.

Damon nodded. "Cool, but if it's about my work, it wouldn't be good. The less you know, the safer you are."

"But—" Joi began to contest before being interrupted by Damon.

"No buts, baby girl. What is just is but know one thing: Know that what I do won't bleed into or interfere with our relationship." He gave her a reassuring smile. "Trust that and know that."

Although Joi was skeptical about going against her better judgment, she allowed Damon to come back into her life. She convinced herself she was content knowing his business wouldn't interfere with their relationship. Joi believed him and was desperate to make it work.

Shortly after Joi and Damon's makeup, he told Joi they would be going to Miami for the Super Bowl weekend. The Super Bowl was around the same time as Joi's birthday, so Damon also let her know he had a surprise for her, but they would get it once they were in Florida. Joi was elated about the trip. She began shopping for swimsuits and sandals immediately after Damon told her they were going.

One evening after shopping, Joi decided to go to Damon's home and wait for him to return from work. She wanted to model the swimwear she had picked up for the trip. As she lay across the sofa, she was startled by Damon's brusque entrance. Damon walked over to her and kissed her cheek. Joi knew something was bothering him because he had a look of concern on his face, so she asked him what was bothering him. Damon told her he was unable to make the trip to Florida. His tone was empathetic as he explained the situation to Joi. Joi was instantly disappointed because she'd had her heart set on the trip. She hadn't been on a vacation since she'd left her parents' home five years ago, so she'd been looking forward to their Super Bowl trip.

Damon walked over to Joi. "What's wrong with you?"

"I wanted to go. I need a trip," she replied disappointedly.

"I said I couldn't go. You're good. You can take D'Vyne with you if you want to."

Joi perked up. "WHAT?" she screamed excitedly. "Are you serious, Damon?"

Joi was ecstatic. She had never been on a vacation with D'Vyne, so knowing they'd be going to Miami together was amazing.

Damon nodded his head in reassurance as he leaned closer to her and whispered, "You can pick your Beemer up, too." Damon had purchased Joi a 3-series BMW convertible, but she would have to pick it up once she got to Miami.

Joi was outdone. She was overjoyed to have a man who was willing and able to buy her a car, especially a BMW. She modeled the swimsuits for Damon and showed her appreciation in other ways, too. She was extremely happy.

After arriving in Florida and picking up her car, Joi and D'Vyne partied nonstop. They flossed the BMW throughout the city like they were the wives of celebrities and had no cares in the world. D'Vyne continuously complemented Joi about how good she looked behind the steering wheel of the convertible. Joi knew she had a good man. The car said it, D'Vyne said it, and the attention she was getting assured her of it. As they cruised through the strip, men were trying to flag them down and women stared at them with envy in their eyes.

The entire weekend was a blur of excitement. As Joi let the top down and got onto the expressway, en route for home, she smiled at the image of her life. She felt deserving of a man like Damon, and she planned to prove her love for him daily after getting home.

After a two-day drive, Joi made it home. She dropped D'Vyne off and called Damon. He told her to meet him at Glisten, a car wash one of his friends owned. She went to the car wash as Damon had suggested, but he hadn't arrived yet, so she waited out front. After about an hour, Joi was ready to leave. She knew her car needed to be cleaned and serviced after two days on the highway, but she was becoming impatient. Fifteen more minutes passed before an older man appeared from inside the car wash. He approached Joi's car and signaled her to roll the window down. Joi rolled the window down and politely smiled at the old scrawny looking man.

"I'm waiting on Damon."

The man smiled, showing a toothless gum line. "I know, but we're fixin' to close, so come on in and we'll get you out of the way." He turned and walked back toward the building, waving for Joi to follow him.

After driving the car inside, Joi went to the waiting area and began watching television while waiting on them to finish detailing her car. She had called Damon a few times, but there was no answer. She began to become worried until she heard a faint sound of his distinct voice. Joi leapt to her feet and rushed out toward the sound of Damon's voice.

As Joi entered the washing area, her legs nearly gave out on her. Her face became flushed with an array of congestive emotion. Under Damon's supervision, the men who were working at the car wash were pulling multiple kilos of cocaine from the BMW. They removed drugs from the panels, the doors and the gas tank, and from underneath the hood of the car. Joi couldn't believe Damon had used her to transport cocaine from Miami into Detroit.

"MOTHERFUCKER! YOU AIN'T SHIT! I COULD'VE GONE TO PRISON!" She charged toward Damon with hate in her eyes.

Damon stared at Joi in a daring manner. "But you didn't. Instead you got a vacation and a BMW." He smiled as if he was unfazed by Joi's anger.

Joi burst into tears. "It's over, Damon! I mean it this time."

Damon chuckled lightly. "Shit, I figured that much." He paused briefly before continuing, "It was good while it lasted though. Enjoy the car; it's your color." He winked before turning and walking out the car wash.

After that humiliating ordeal, Joi waited for weeks to receive a telephone call from Damon, apologizing for what he had done to her, but it never came. Those weeks turned into months, but she never received as much as a card from Damon.

CԐ•ഌ

After nearly a year, Damon had showed up and humiliated her again. After the showdown Joi had just experienced with Damon in the parking lot of her apartment building, she sat inside her car cursing and wishing bad things would happen to Damon. She hated him.

"Sorry motherfucker!" Joi spat out, pulling Kleenex from her purse. She blew her nose, fixed her makeup, and drove off to meet her friends.

As Joi entered Juanita's Lounge, she noticed Joshua speaking to an attractive, light-hued female. The woman was giving Joshua a courteous smile, but Joi could see the disinterest in her body language, so she decided to rescue him from the disappointment he was surely setting himself up for.

Joshua's back was turned to Joi as she reached him. She tapped his shoulder.

"Hey, Joshua," she said, stepping back. She smiled brightly, posing with one hand on her hip and the other loosely swinging her Gucci purse.

Joshua turned to the sound of Joi's voice and smiled. "Mia, long time no see," he teased before embracing Joi. "Excuse me, I'm being rude. Joi, this is . . ." he began saying as he turned to introduce Joi to the woman he was previously talking to. To his astonishment, the woman had sneaked off while he briefly hugged Joi.

Joi snickered. "What, you were going to introduce me to a ghost?" She continued to snicker, watching Joshua's eyes scan the room, looking for the woman he had been talking to prior to Joi's arriving.

Joshua shook his head. "You're out cold, Joi. You ain't been here but a minute, and you're already scaring off my potential."

Joi giggled. "Boy, that girl was as interested in you as I am in hockey." She thumped Joshua's forehead, continuing to laugh at his misfortune.

"Hate is one of your strong suits. You should work on that, hater."

"Negro, please. Where are Andre and D'Vyne? I thought we were supposed to meet here."

"There they go," Joshua said, pointing toward the ceiling, causing Joi to look up. Joshua laughed. "Oh, you went for that? I see you're still naïve."

Joi pursed her lips. "And you still ain't got no game." She giggled.

"Where is my drink, man? Long Island, top shelf; you know how I do it."

Joshua brushed past Joi on his way to the bar. The space inside of Juanita's was minimal, but it created a personal atmosphere. Most of the patrons who frequented the bar were either acquainted with one another or had some type of comfort level with each other, so in essence, space was a small price to pay for ambiance. Joshua was undisturbed by the small space because Juanita's was his comfort zone. He had been a regular since his return to Detroit.

Shortly after Joshua graduated from high school, he relocated to Alaska to work in the logging industry with his uncle. He and his uncle were two in a very small population of blacks, but that wasn't a problem for Joshua because he was a player, and according to him, "Players don't race hate." There were other factors in his decision to return to Detroit. Joshua had been born and raised in the city. He had never encountered nature's wildlife up close and personal. So, after having a face-to-face encounter with a polar bear, he decided to leave the logging to the lumberjacks.

Once Joshua returned to Detroit, he earned his barbers license and went into business with D'Vyne. The two of them opened an upscale beauty salon. In Joshua's shallow world, Juanita's was his optimal hustling grounds because being a beauty salon owner required networking with women, and there is where he pulled in his best clientele.

While purchasing Joi's drink, Joshua noticed the range of attention Joi was receiving from the other men in the bar. He watched as men came and left the booth as if Joi was giving out a little more than conversation. As he walked back toward where Joi sat, he felt the stares of men impaling his back. Others grunted, letting Joshua know he was interfering with their game. He slid in the booth and passed Joi her drink.

"Damn, Joi, you're almost as popular as me."

Joi gave him a disapproving stare as if he had offended her.

"Don't mistake *sex appeal* with popularity, lil bruh." She giggled before taking a sip from her drink.

"Lil bruh?" Joshua waved her statement off. "You're corny as hell. *Sex appeal* . . ." He mimicked her, giving her a once over. "Pssh! Where?"

They burst into hysterical laughter. Joi was really enjoying herself. She had completely dedicated her life to her career after her trying breakup with Damon, so fun had become foreign to her. As she and Joshua sat around sipping and talking about old times and new ones, men sent loads of drinks to their table for her. Joshua asked her about the breakup between her and Damon, but she refused to talk about it. Joi loved Joshua and he was one of her closest friends, but she wasn't ready to discuss

Damon, especially after what had occurred between them earlier that day.

About an hour had passed before D'Vyne showed up. She walked toward the booth Joshua and Joi were occupying with a subtle bounce in her step. Joi was envious because she was sure D'Vyne's bounce and her tardiness had to do with her getting laid. D'Vyne reached their booth and slid inside.

"Hey, Jigga Joi. Hey, Joshua." She leaned over and playfully slapped the back of Joshua's neck.

"I'm gonna fuck-you-up," Joshua said with a light chuckle, "putting them paws on a player."

"Aww please, boy," D'Vyne laughed. "We've been whippin' yo' ass since . . ." she paused briefly before wildly throwing her hands into the air and continuing, "shit, since forever."

They all burst into laughter.

"Whatever; I just don't hit women . . ." he paused again and turned to Joi, "but I'll hit you, bull dagger!"

Joi playfully punched Joshua's arm. "Negro, you're crazy. This is a man's wonderland." She seductively pursed her lips and pushed her breasts up.

Joshua laughed and slid one of the drinks one of the men had sent to Joi across the table to D'Vyne. "Go ahead and push one of these back, Vee. You're too sober for this content."

"Oh, you buyin' tonight? BALLIN'!" D'Vyne yelled out, trying to emulate Jim Jones.

"Ballin', my ass! That cheap-ass-punk ain't bought shit over here." Joi giggled.

"I ain't got to. Shit, all these niggaz keep shootin' them through here." Joshua looked over to Joi with a sinister stare. "That shit about to stop through." He leaned over and kissed Joi on the lips. "Let's see how many drinks float through here now." He and D'Vyne burst into laughter.

Joi wiped her lips with a napkin. "You're a hater, Joshua. That shit's running all through your veins, putting those blunt tokers on me."

They all began laughing.

Joshua left the table after he saw a few women he knew entering the bar. After he left, D'Vyne and Joi began catching up. Although they spoke to one another weekly, they still had a lot of catching up to do. Both women had demanding lives, especially D'Vyne.

D'Vyne was the co-owner of Perceptions, a beauty salon she had started with Joshua. They'd opened up the shop shortly after Joshua graduated from barber college. It was tough, but with the assistance of D'Vyne's man Demetric, they'd pulled it off and the doors had been open ever since. Demetric was good to D'Vyne. He inspired her and supported her unconditionally. Although he was uncomfortable doing business with friends and family, Demetric had fronted D'Vyne and Joshua some of the money to start up their salon. Demetric liked Joshua, but he had a hard time trusting anyone other than D'Vyne. After a short time, however, Demetric and everyone else involved in the business became slated.

Perceptions was a success from the beginning. Joshua helped out, but D'Vyne put her heart and soul into Perceptions. She worked countless hours trying to make sure Perceptions continued to be a success. Between the business and Demetric, D'Vyne's time was consumed, so she cherished the rare times she could spend with her best friends together.

Joi pointed toward Joshua. "Look at him," she laughed.

"He's leanin' like a mutha."

"Joi, that fool is drunk. Leanin' my ass! He's drunk!" The women touched glasses and laughed cheerfully.

"Here comes Andre," Joi said, pointing toward the entrance.

Andre stopped and briefly spoke to Joshua before walking to the booth where Joi and D'Vyne were sitting. "What up, doe? No hugs, no kisses?" He opened his arms. "Y'all better get up and give me what I've got coming to me." He smiled as both women rose to his demand.

Joi hugged him. "Hey, Andre." She released him and D'Vyne hugged him next.

"So y'all got started without me, huh?"

Andre nodded toward the empty glasses that aligned the table. Both women giggled a drunken giggle as they sat back down.

Andre was charming. He always knew the right thing to say to women at the right time. Charisma is a rare quality in men, but Andre possessed it without question. His charismatic ways and his authenticity helped him become the businessman he was. He had been an entrepreneur since childhood. Andre had kept a lucrative and legal hustle throughout his childhood. He would mow lawns, shovel snow, or whatever else he could to keep money in his pocket.

After high school, Andre decided to skip college and invest in his future in other ways. He took some of the money he'd saved throughout the years and invested in a truck, a generator, and a power sprayer, and started a mobile car detailing business. His business started off slow, but it began to slowly pick up. Eventually, he inked a few contracts with some local car dealerships and later inked some major contracts. Now, four years later, Andre was a very successful business man with a very successful business.

As Andre, D'Vyne, and Joi drank, enjoyed the music, the scenery, and one another's company, Joshua ballroomed in the aisle with woman after woman. Joi loved the company of her loved ones. She started to feel resentment for moving downtown because it secluded her from her friends and family. She tried to hide her sudden sadness, but unbeknownst to her, her feelings were showing all over her face.

Andre lifted Joi's lowered chin. "What's up, Joi? You all right?"

"Yeah, I'm good, Andre. I just miss this; you know, hanging out with y'all. I miss that."

"Don't fuck-the-moment-up then, super-sensitive-ass," D'Vyne said, before giggling and rubbing Joi's back in a comforting manner.

"I feel you," said Andre. "I can't lie to a friend though. Shit, we still party in your absence. See what I mean." He pointed to Joshua as he was doing the hustle by himself.

They all burst into laughter and began cheering Joshua on. Seeing Joshua do his thing was refreshing and brought the cheerful mood back to the group. It was like Joi's emotionally-driven statement had never been made. They all continued to drink and party throughout the night. It was a night that was well-deserved for their entire clique, and they planned to make the best of it because it was a rarity for them. They all knew they would have to return to their tumultuous personal lives the next day.

Chapter 2

Perceptions is off-the-hook Tuesdays through Saturdays. D'Vyne had amazing clientele, including the women Joshua brought in. Although Joshua was a working barber as well, he only came in Wednesdays through Saturdays because he had other barbers on staff in his absence. His main priority was to take care of his clientele and his responsibilities as co-owner. The rest of Joshua's time was spent partying.

D'Vyne pursed her lips into a frown as Joshua walked into the salon. He looked horrible. His appearance said he had left home without taking care of his daily hygiene. Joshua placed his Polo jacket onto the coat rack and walked past D'Vyne on his way to the restroom.

D'Vyne's eyes roved behind Joshua. "I hope you do something with yourself while you're in there because you look like shit, Joshua."

"Whatever," Joshua replied before closing the door behind himself. Joshua had been through a lot of women, but what he had experienced last night was unbelievable for even him, and he was there.

Joshua's Wednesday clientele was primarily slow, so he usually went out after leaving the salon. After closing the salon earlier than expected yesterday, he'd decided to go have a few drinks at Juanita's before going home. As Joshua entered the bar, he was surprised to see so many people so early in the week. Women were everywhere so Joshua's antennas went into the ceiling. He saw a group of attractive women occupying a booth near the back of the bar. One of the women was impressively beautiful. She was a dark hue with a short, bob-type hairdo. Joshua couldn't tell what her shape was like, but by the look of her thick chocolate thigh that peeked into the aisle, he was sure he wouldn't be disappointed once he found out.

After scouting out his prey, Joshua approached the bar area and ordered a large basket of hot wings before walking over to the booth where the ladies were sitting. Joshua smiled as he reached them.

"Hi; how're you ladies doing?" He held his smile, looking at each of the women.

"Fine," the women chimed in together, looking at Joshua as if he was a piece of meat.

"I'm being rude," he chuckled before continuing, "I'm Joshua and I need a place to sit and eat my wings. Can I sit with y'all?"

"Of course, since you asked so nicely," one of the ladies replied, and the rest of the women began bunching together to create space for Joshua to sit with them.

"Thanks; I bought enough everyone. When Ann comes with the drinks, y'all order drinks on me." Joshua smiled and sat at the end of the booth near the woman he intended to get to know.

"I'm Keisha," the woman who had spoken said. "This is Tanya, Alana, and Zoria," she said, pointing to the woman Joshua sat next to last.

"Coincidence or fate that I meet a group of women whose names all end with an A." Joshua chuckled and tapped Zoria's arm.

"Look around. All these cats in here ice-grillin' me. You know why?" he questioned with a giggle.

Zoria snickered girlishly. "Why?" she asked, looking at Joshua in an attentive manner.

"Because all them niggaz wanna be where I am! You feel me?"

"I guess," Zoria replied and snickered as the waitress walked to their booth with the wings Joshua had ordered.

The women ordered their drinks and the chemistry of the group seasoned. Joshua leaned back into his seat and smiled because he knew he had successfully penetrated the women's group. They were all laughing and joking with one another as if they had known Joshua for years. He knew his finesse and comfortable nature in the presence of women was from so many years of friendship with Joi and D'Vyne. Those friendships had definitely groomed him for situations like the one he was in, and it showed because he was working the table like a veteran.

Suddenly, the conversation ceased, and the women's attention changed direction. Joshua noticed the women turned and began pointing toward the entrance of the bar, so he turned as well. As he turned to see why their attention had diverted, Joshua nearly choked on his drink. The women were pointing toward a woman he knew casually, but intimately.

The woman who had attracted the women's attention approached the booth they were sitting in. She was smiling ecstatically.

"Oh! Y'all hoes hangin' out with a bitch, huh?" She playfully swatted Keisha with her purse.

Joshua lifted his head from his drink and smiled coyly. "What up, doe?" He chuckled, looking up at the woman who had just walked up.

She looked down at Joshua and began shaking her head loosely. "Oh, hell naw!" She pointed at Joshua. "Y'all know this nigga?" she asked, before placing her hands on her hips and sassily pursuing her lips.

Zoria looked over at Joshua in a judging manner. "You know my girl, nigga?"

Joshua took a large sip from his drink and sighed. For the first time since he had sat with the group of women, he felt uncomfortable.

"Yeah, I know Jayla. We're cool, I think." He looked up to Jayla for agreement.

Jayla smiled. "He's good people, y'all. It's crowded down here, so I'm gonna sit at the bar." She pointed at Joshua. "I'm sending you my bill, too," she said before sashaying away from the table.

Keisha and Tanya scurried from the table and followed behind Jayla as if she was the queen bee and they were members of her tribe. Alana left for the restroom shortly after them, which left Zoria and Joshua alone at the table. Joshua knew his chances of getting to know Zoria intimately were slim because of his brief fling with Jayla; however, he still decided to take a shot at it.

Joshua discretely passed Jayla his telephone number. "Call me," he requested before sliding out the booth. As he left the bar, he felt Jayla's eyes piercing his back like daggers.

After getting home, Joshua placed a DVD into the player and slouched on the sofa. Just as he began to get comfortable, his telephone rang. He grabbed the telephone from its receiver.

"Hello."

"Hey, Joshua. This is Jayla."

"Oh, what up, doe?" Joshua chuckled. "Zoria must've gave you my number, huh?"

"Yep. So what's up?"

"I was on my way to sleep, but you can slide through here if you want to."

"I've been drinking too much tonight, but you can come to my house." She snickered. "No pun intended."

"Nah, shorty. I ain't on that creepin' shit."

"I live by myself, boy." Jayla gave Joshua the address to her home and an open invitation, but Joshua was still skeptical.

Joshua didn't like the area and he was unsure of Jayla's intentions. He and Jayla had shared a one-night stand after a night of partying at Club Icon. After their encounter, Joshua had promised to call her, but that call back never happened. He had no idea what Jayla's angle was for insisting he come to her house. She could have been vindictive about him never calling her back and wanted to get back at him.

After a few minutes of contemplating it, Joshua decided to take Jayla up on her offer. He got dressed and drove to Jayla's home. He got nervous as he was driving down Puritan Avenue. He knew he was out of place. It was an unspoken rule that eastsiders stayed east of Woodward and westsiders stayed west of Woodward, but Joshua was defiantly breaking the code of the city and he knew it. He drove up in front of her house and called her from his cellular telephone. Joshua wanted to be sure Jayla wasn't playing any type of childish games, like sending him to the neighborhood dope house or just the wrong address.

Jayla answered his call, came to the door, and waved Joshua inside. He turned his car off and walked to her porch. He sighed once he reached her porch because she had on all her clothes. He knew Jayla possibly wanted more than sex, otherwise, she would have been naked or nearly there. Joshua stepped into Jayla's home.

"What's up?" he said and wrapped his arms around her waist and firmly caressed her behind.

"You." She kissed Joshua and closed and locked the door behind him.

"Come in and make yourself at home."

Joshua began taking his shoes off. He had good ghetto etiquette. He knew "make yourself at home" in the hood was a polite way to tell someone to take their shoes off at the door.

"Ooh, those are nice. What are they, Prada?" Jayla gave him a compliment about his shoes as a thank you.

"Nah, these Testoni's." Joshua replied and began walking toward her.

His feet sank deep into the plush white carpet with every step. He sat next to her on her ocean blue Italian leather sofa. Joshua suddenly became apprehensive looking around Jayla's lavish house. He noticed a large plasma screen television hanging from the wall.

"Aw, hell naw! I should probably bounce." He looked at Jayla as he began standing. "Whose shit you got me off in?"

"I told you, I live by myself." Jayla giggled.

"Well, where you work at, 'cause this muthafucka is plushed-the-fuck-out?!" He continued to look around.

"Thanks; I work at Kroger's." She giggled again.

"Oh, I know I glottal bounce now because Kroger's ain't paid for all of this nice-ass-shit. Either you the CEO or you're lying like a muhfucka. Where's the nigga who paid fo' this shit?"

"I live by myself and my ex has been in prison for over two years."

"I knew you ain't pay for all this shit. Where's this nigga and when's the nigga gettin' out?" asked Joshua, looking around in a concerned manner. "I'm a workin' nigga. I don't be carryin' pistols and shit." He chuckled, although he was serious about everything he had asked and said.

Jayla pushed him back onto the sofa and straddled him. "Nigga, you trippin'. I wouldn't even play you like that." She kissed him. "Friends don't do that type of shit to friends." She looked at him seductively. "We are friends, right?"

Joshua chuckled. "What type of shit do friends do to each other?" He palmed her derriere.

"Hold on. Let me go change and I'll show you." Jayla pulled away from Joshua and walked off toward her bedroom.

"The drinks are in the cabinet of the breakfast bar."

Joshua walked to the kitchen and opened the door to the breakfast bar. *"Damn,"* he thought, *"this bitch is a slut and a lush."*

The entire shelf was filled with liquor. Cognac had to be her favorite drink because she had nearly every brand: Hennessey, Martell, Remy Martin XO, and one lonely bottle of Cuervo 1800 aligned the shelf. He grabbed the bottle of Remy Martin XO and two glasses. Getting back to the living room, Joshua poured large portions into each of the glasses and sat back. He modestly sipped from his glass, waiting on Jayla to return. He had already had a few at the bar, so he decided to cruise for the rest of the night.

Joshua heard music begin playing. It was R. Kelly's Wind. Jayla appeared at the entrance to the hallway. She began exotically rolling her hips to the melody. As Joshua looked on, she continued erotically dancing her way toward him. Once she reached him, she sensually removed her short silk robe.

Jayla's body was just as Joshua had remembered, caramel and thick. Her satin skin was covered with glitter. Joshua's penis began to swell as he stared at her freshly waxed vagina. He was eager to enter her. His manhood pulsated as Jayla ground and gyrated her buttocks against him. He cupped her tender breast with his hand and began sucking, nibbling, and kissing it.

Jayla knelt onto her knees and began removing Joshua's belt, pants, and briefs, looking into his eyes. She licked her lips salaciously after removing everything. Jayla lifted Joshua's legs and placed them onto her shoulders. She began gently sucking his scrotum and licking his rectum area. She used her tongue to massage the area between Joshua's sack and his anus, stroking his phallus.

Joshua moaned sounds of earthly pleasure as he reached a massive orgasm. "Ooh, shit!"

Jayla stood and reached for Joshua's hand. "Come on. Let's go to the bedroom."

Joshua stood and they walked to the bedroom hand-in-hand. As Joshua entered the bedroom, he was in awe. Jayla had a super king-size bed that sat beneath a ceiling full of mirrors. Jayla sat on the bed and pulled Joshua to her. She began giving him oral while he stood over her. She stroked his shank, gently sucking the crown of his penis, causing his huge erection to return. Jayla used her mouth to roll the condom onto his manhood before lying back onto the bed. She sprawled across it submissively and looked up to Joshua.

Joshua climbed onto the bed and mounted her. He pushed deep into Jayla, causing her to belt out loud, libidinous screams. As he plunged deeper into her, she moaned louder and her legs began stiffening. Jayla flipped Joshua onto his back and straddled him. She began slowly grinding and gyrating. She leaned over Joshua placing her mouth close to his ear.

"I want you to do something for me," she said, continuing her grind.

Joshua's body stiffened. "Like what?" he asked in a defensive tone.

After what she had just done to him in the living room, Joshua was cautious about okaying something without knowing what it was.

"I want you to squeeze my neck," she moaned, taking him deeper into her.

Joshua chuckled. "What?"

"Don't laugh at me," she whined. "I'm serious. I get off like that." She flipped back onto her back and placed Joshua's hands around her throat. "Choke me," she whispered erotically.

Joshua gently squeezed her neck, plunging into her.

"Squeeze harder," she moaned.

Joshua began squeezing her neck viciously while pouncing on top of her. He sweated and breathed heavily as he violently pushed into her. Jayla gasped wildly. Joshua had lost himself in the moment of savage passion. She gasped again, causing Joshua to come out of his seethe-filled haze. He released her throat and dismounted her. Joshua fearfully jumped from the bed.

As he stood over Jayla, he watched as she shook and panted erogenous and carnal sounds. He was shocked. Not by the sounds or the shakes; instead, he was amazed by her actions. Joshua was aware of the force he had used choking her, so it was surprising to him to see Jayla coddling her vaginal area instead of her neck.

Joshua had definitely had a rough night, so it was no surprise to hear the comment D'Vyne had made when he came into the salon. As Joshua exited the restroom, D'Vyne eyeballed him. She was impressed by the way he had quickly cleaned himself up, but she was still worried about him. D'Vyne questioned if Joshua's wild partying and drinking was becoming too excessive.

Joshua was known and loved for being the life of the party, but he was getting older and D'Vyne was concerned about him. She believed he needed structure in his life. Although Joshua was always bringing in new customers and he had filled up all the chairs on his side of the salon, D'Vyne could see the effects his lifestyle was having on him, physically and economically.

She and Joshua were supposed to come out with their own line of hair care products earlier in the year, but Joshua couldn't meet the financial obligations required of him. They had been in business for two years and their salon was growing rapidly. They had paid off all the debt to Demetric and they were up-to-date on the loans they had received from the bank. Therefore, they were both bringing in a fair amount of money. D'Vyne was disappointed in Joshua. She respected his hustle, but she also recognized the poor maintenance he did on his hustle.

D'Vyne continued staring at Joshua as she curled a wig. Joshua walked over to her and stared down at her but said nothing.

D'Vyne looked up to him. "What, Joshua?" She held her evil gaze on him.

"Why you mad at me? I got here on time. Ain't nobody even here yet?"

"So! I ain't worried about your work ethic. I'm worried about you drinking and partying so much. Boy!" D'Vyne shook her head empathetically. "You're running yourself ragged." She continued curling the wig.

"Let me do me. I been doin' this shit since I was yay big." He placed his hand by his knee.

D'Vyne smirked. "Nigga, you still that height." She began laughing loudly.

"I'm six-four when I stand on my bankroll." Joshua chuckled.

"More like, if you stand on your ego, because your bankroll ain't about shit. Humph!" she grunted sassily.

"Whatever," he replied, and waved her off. "I'm taller than Andre." Joshua paused briefly before continuing, "And Demetric."

"Yeah, but your bankroll can't match either one of theirs, nigga." D'Vyne childishly stuck her tongue out at Joshua. "Nah though, Joshua, I'm worried about you for real. Them hoes out there got that HIV."

"I always use protection, so you can save that bullshit."

D'Vyne threw her curlers onto the countertop of her workstation. "That's only 99%. Your dumb-ass can be the other 1%, stupid." She thumped him on his head and walked away.

D'Vyne was an only child, so she loved her friends deeply. She was emotional like that, especially with Joshua because he was so wild and carefree. They continued to talk for a while before their clients began coming into the salon. Although they had spoken about the situation, D'Vyne was still worried about him and planned to discuss it more when she had the opportunity.

As D'Vyne sewed a weave into a client's hair, she noticed Andre entering the salon. She smiled. Andre's presence demanded the attention of a king and he was receiving it from all the women in the salon.

The woman D'Vyne was attending to tapped her on the leg and asked, "Who is that?" nodding in Andre's direction.

"That's Andre. He grew up with me and Joshua," D'Vyne replied, continuing to sew the extensions into the woman's hair.

"That nigga looks like he's major. He's got his shit together, don't he?"

"Girl, shut up." D'Vyne snickered, although she knew the woman's assumption was correct.

"I'm serious. Does he?" The woman seemed persistent. "Ask him."

D'Vyne paused. "Andre," she called out to him, "come here for a minute."

Although Andre was engaged in a conversation with Joshua, he excused himself and walked over to D'Vyne.

"Hey, beautiful." Andre leaned over and hugged D'Vyne. "I called you Tuesday, but you didn't call me back. That's how you do a brotha, huh?" He smiled.

"I've been tired-as-hell lately. Things have been busy around here and I still haven't filled up any of my chairs." D'Vyne pouted playfully.

"I'm happy to hear that business is good, but why haven't you filled your chairs?" He looked around.

"Boy, you know I gotta hand pick the people I wanna work around every day. Pssh, I guess I just haven't gotten around to it yet."

"I feel you. I wouldn't want no riffraff off in my joint either."

"Right! You know." She giggled. "Andre, this is Debra," D'Vyne said, patting the woman's shoulder. "She wants to know if you have your shit together."

Andre looked at Debra and took a step back. He loosened his tie and posed, placing his fist on his waist, exposing a diamond bezel Jacobs watch snugly wrapped around his wrist. He smiled, showing his pristine white teeth.

"Do I look like it? Your honest opinion."

Debra briefly gave Andre a once-over and replied with a smile, "Yep; sure do."

"No disrespect intended, because I respect all women, even when they disrespect themselves. I'm sure that isn't the case with you." He smiled. "But if you can determine a person's worth by their appearance alone, the chances of you having your stuff together are slim. The measure of a man's success is by how he takes care of his family and his responsibilities, not his hygiene."

Andre touched Debra's hand, smiled at D'Vyne, and walked away. D'Vyne was pleased with Andre's response to Debra's question, but Debra was at a loss for words as she watched Andre strut away. She could tell Andre was confident in what he had told her, and she had confidence there was truth in his words.

Although Andre was successful by some people's standards, he was only a speck in his picture of a successful man. He knew D'Vyne wanted him to reproach Debra's statement, so he'd willingly played along. He was sure D'Vyne knew where his convictions lay because she knew him.

Andre's family was one of the less-fortunate families in their neighborhood. They didn't have much, and although they were poor financially, there were rich morally. Andre's father believed deeply in the cohesion of family and he instilled that in Andre. His father was also a man of integrity, accountability, and strength. He held Andre to the same standards.

As Andre thumbed the keys of his Blackberry, waiting for his turn in the barber's chair, Joshua called him. He walked to the chair and sat, still typing into the Blackberry. Joshua wrapped the cape around his neck and chuckled.

"Nigga, jump up off the Blackberry." He turned on the clippers.

"Whatever, bruh. Do your job and let me do mine," Andre replied as he continued punching keys.

"Nah, my nigga," Joshua chuckled. "You really wanna hear this shit." Joshua began trimming Andre's beard.

Andre placed the Blackberry in his pocket. "A'ight, dog. What's up?"

"Remember old girl I knocked at the Icon a while back?" Joshua asked.

Andre nodded. "Yeah. Why? Don't tell me you got some illegitimate kids runnin' around and shit!" He laughed.

"Nah. naw. Not the kid, but I did run into her last night."

Joshua started tapering Andre's hair, telling him about the late-night rendezvous he'd had with Jayla. He described the entire night in detail for Andre. Joshua could see the admiration his friend had for him as he told the story.

Andre's mouth was open in awe as Joshua gave intimate detail about his night. Although Andre had been through his share of females during high school, he had never been the player Joshua was. He was usually working. Andre's conquest with women was driven by the competition he and Joshua had had since becoming friends.

Over the years, Andre had become more attracted to the quality of women rather than the quantity, and most of the women with the qualities he liked were skeptical about casual sex, or they had certain timelines before they put out, so his sex life was dull. He vicariously lived through Joshua, which was why he was so attentive to his story. Andre burst into hysterical laughter. He tried to hold his tone down, but he couldn't. The barbers and clients stared at him, which consequently, brought attention to Joshua's story.

Andre looked up at Joshua. "Quit playing, man! You're exaggerating. She was shaking and shit?" He continued laughing.

"Man, listen! I'm dead serious. I thought I was on my way to the penitentiary for murder," Joshua replied, brushing loose hair from Andre's neck and taking the cape off him.

"So, what's up? You goin' back through there or what?" Andre chuckled.

"No!" Joshua defiantly shook his head. "Hell no! Shit! Next, the broad gonna be askin' me to give her a Dirty Sanchez." He chuckled.

Andre stood from the barber's chair. He was laughing, but Joshua's last statement had him puzzled. He turned to Joshua. "What-the-fuck is a Dirty Sanchez," he asked, brushing hair from his pants.

Rashaad, one of Joshua's employees who worked in the station next to Joshua, laughed. He looked over to Andre and cleared his throat.

"That's when you butt hump a broad, then take your piece and wipe it across her top lip, giving her what appears to be a brown, Mexican mustache."

Everyone in the area burst into a boisterous laughter. The women waiting in D'Vyne's area became uneasy w th that comment and got belligerent.

One of them yelled out, "THAT'S SOME WHITE PEOPLE SHIT!"

A woman sitting underneath a hair dryer yelled, "HELL NAH! NEGRO PLEASE! I'LL CUT A MUTHAFUCKA HE TRIES TO GIVE ME A SHITTY DEAL." The entire salon volcanoed into boisterous laughter.

After the feedback and the laughter settled, Andre waved goodbye to D'Vyne, gave Joshua a pound, and began walking toward the door. He stopped just as he reached the door and looked back.

"One question before I go." He looked over at Rashaad. "How did you know about that Dirty Sanchez shit?"

"Let's just say, I try to please the women I deal with," Rashaad replied and popped his collar.

The women went ballistic. "HOT GRITS, MOTHERFUCKER! DEAL WITH THAT!" the woman who was now sitting in D'Vyne's chair yelled.

Once again, the salon erupted in laughter. Andre curled over in laughter. He waved to everyone before disappearing into the midday Detroit street.

After leaving the salon, Andre went to the construction site of his new home. He was having a home built from the ground up in a neighboring suburb of Detroit. He'd kept the news about this home from his friends because he didn't want to seem like a braggart. Andre was that type of guy. He respected the boundaries of their coterie by keeping certain things to himself, so as not to show his friends up. However, he did need some help with furniture shopping, so he was sure he would have to reveal his secret to D'Vyne soon.

Andre needed to have the fashion sense of a woman and D'Vyne was his only candidate because Joi was ineligible. As Andre drove up to the site, he giggled to himself at the thought of having Joi decorate his home. He was sure she would do a horrible job, but she and D'Vyne were his only options because he wasn't familiar enough with any of the other women he knew to ask it of them.

Andre dated a few women occasionally, but he wasn't seeing anyone he believed worthy of investing the bulk of his time in. He was still apprehensive about jumping into a serious relationship because of his last one, which he'd rushed into without really knowing the woman as well as he believed he did.

ଓ•ଛ

During late 2006, Andre's business began to incline at a very rapid pace. He had signed several contracts with several large companies and solidified his name in the local business community. He felt as if he had everything he needed in life and it was time for him to work on obtaining his wants. He believed he needed an accomplished woman to complement him, so he began looking for her. Joshua persistently warned him about the situation he was trying to bring to himself, but Andre insisted he was ready to become a family man, so Joshua backed up and respected his friend's decision.

After months of premature failures, Andre was ready to stop his search and just play the field again, then he met Candice.

He and Joshua were at the Palace during a Piston's game, rushing to the bar, trying to beat the halftime traffic. They reached the bar in decent time, but the crowd had already become massive, so they had to wait in a slowly moving line. There was a large swarm of patrons scattered throughout the tight space. Women were everywhere, some of them nonverbally soliciting drinks from men, while others prowled around in search of the next man to pay their bills. Of course, there were some women sports fans, but they were in the minority of the crowd.

As Andre and Joshua reached the front of the line, someone reached over his shoulder and handed him a one-hundred-dollar bill. He turned to see who had given him the money and was pleased with what he saw. He stared into the eyes of a beautiful, auburn-haired woman.

"I think you mistook me for your man," Andre said, attempting to pass her the bill back.

"No," she said, refusing the money, "I don't have a man or a drink." She threw her empty hands into the air. "Cognac, any kind, and pay for yours, too." She smiled.

Andre was shocked by the woman's forwardness. He turned to the bar and ordered two triple Hennessy's and two shots of Cuervo 1800. He paid for the drinks and began walking toward the woman who had given him the money. As he approached her, he noticed Joshua lurking in the rear, shaking his head in disapproval.

Andre reached the woman and handed her a drink and a shot. "Here you go, baby girl," he said, smiling. "You owe me another hundred, too. I got us triple shots of XO."

The woman placed the drinks on the table and began opening her purse. As she reached into her purse, Andre casually touched her arm.

"I was joking, but it's nice to see a woman who is confident enough to by a man a drink . . . well, two drinks." He held up the triple and the shot. "My name is Andre," he continued, offering her his hand. As their hands clasped, Andre passed her the bill back she had given him.

"Thank you," she replied. "My name is Candice, and it's nice to see chivalry is still alive in Detroit." Candice popped the bill playfully and placed it back into her purse.

"You must not be from Detroit." He chuckled.

"Not from Detroit or America. I'm from Canada," Candice replied.

"Oh! Now I'm making the connection." He pointed to her Toronto Raptors jersey.

She smiled and snapped her finger, as a naïve gesture. She then grabbed her chest in a theatrical manner. *"Am I that obvious? I was trying to be inconspicuous. Dang!"* They both laughed.

"I bought the shots so we could toast to new friendship," Andre said as he pushed his glass towards hers. They toasted then drank the shots of tequila simultaneously.

Candice smiled suggestively. *"So, we're friends now?"* she asked and took a modest sip from her cognac.

"Exactly!" Andre laughed and reached into his blazer for a business card. *"I'm sure you don't come over the border often, but whenever you do, you have a friend now."* He passed her the card and smiled. *"Call me whenever you want to come kick it."*

"Thank you." Candice smiled. *"I guess I'll be calling you all the time because I live here now."* She smiled and nodded her head. *"Mmmm . . . Yep, Detroit is my new home."*

They spoke briefly before ending their conversation so they could get back to the game. As Candice walked away, Andre watched her sway, admiring her shapely body. As he watched, he could feel the heat from Joshua's stare. Andre knew Joshua was disapproving of the women who interested him, and as he approached Joshua, he could tell Candice was no exception. He reached Joshua and shook his head.

"What, nigga? Go ahead, because I know you've got something to say." He took a sip from his drink. "What, dog?"

Joshua lifted off the wall he had been leaning onto waiting on Andre. "She's gotchu, my nigga." He shook his head and they began to walk.

"How?" Andre asked, staring at Joshua, awaiting an answer.

Joshua smiled and chuckled insidiously. "Girl knew you were gonna pay for the drink from the jump." He shook his head and snickered lightly. "I hate to say it, but you're an easy target for a broad like that." Joshua shuffled some of the ice from his cup into his mouth and began crunching it.

"Whatever, dog," Andre replied, and shook his head. "I can't believe yo' hatin' ass. If girl would've chose you, you would've been smashin' that later on tonight!"

"You're right! I would've definitely been fuckin' tonight, but you can't." Joshua stopped and grabbed Andre's arm, causing him to stop as well. "I'm saying, look at me. I'm Timbo'ed up, baggy MEK jeans, and a Coogi hoody. A broad already knows three things about me from appearance alone. They know my morals and standards are low, and my sex drive is high." He chuckled. "Now you're a different story." He pointed to Andre's attire. "Slacks, a button-up, and Prada loafers. That's cool, but fo' a fuckin' basketball game? Come on, dog! That shit says high morals, high standards, and a high-paying career." Joshua crushed more ice and snickered as they began walking again.

Andre stopped Joshua as they neared their seats. "So what, nigga? That don't mean I can't crush that on the first night. I got game, too."

They sat and Joshua shook his head and chuckled lightly. He had empathy for his friend because of his naïve ways, but he refused to let Andre off the hook with this one.

"Crush?" Joshua said, and kicked his legs up onto the empty seat in front of him. He turned to Andre. "See! That's what I'm talkin' about. Crush! Pssh!" He waved Andre off. "What-the-fuck is that? That's the problem. Say fuck." Joshua paused briefly. "You can't, nigga. You know why? Because you're a gentleman. Me, I'm an animal! A dog! Woof-woof, nigga. I horse-mule-fuck bitches, but you . . ." He chuckled and rubbed his nose. "You do that candlelight shit. Broad wanna get her back blown-the-fuck out, she calls Joshua." He shrugged his shoulders and smirked. "Broad wanna get married, she calls Andre."

Andre didn't say another word. He was upset and disappointed in Joshua's perception of him for two reasons: He knew what Joshua had said was true and he wanted it not to be, and although Joshua had ruined what had started out as a good outing, Andre wasn't going to allow Joshua to impede on him getting to know Candice.

A few days after the game, Andre received a telephone call from Candice. Although he had some apprehension because of what Joshua had said to him about her, Andre pursued Candice as a personal challenge because he wanted to prove Joshua wrong. Shortly after the telephone call, he and Candice began dating casually. He was surprised they had so much in common because of the difference in their cultures. Things quickly began to get serious between them, but things took a subtle change just as fast.

Candice began putting pressure on Andre. She was demanding about nearly everything. She chose where they ate, what they ate, and how they ate. She even began choosing Andre's clothes.

Candice had become overbearing and almost impossible to be with, but Andre had fallen in love with her and began choosing the affection of a woman over his manly pride.

After a while, there were periodic sparks in their relationship, but they only lasted for a short period before the negative nature of their relationship returned. Andre's only refuge from Candice's constant bickering was his friends, and she even tried to destroy the bond he had with them.

One week, he and Candice had been getting along throughout the week, so they decided to join D'Vyne and Joshua at Captain's for drinks one evening. The night started off exceptionally. Everyone was drinking and having a nice time until Joshua went to the dance floor. Joshua began doing all the latest dance moves, while several young women surrounded him and cheered him on. They yelled and whistled as he did this thing. The other guys in the club looked on with grimaced faces as Joshua received all the attention from the women. This was a regular outing for D'Vyne and Andre. They were used to seeing Joshua's charming and lively personality attract crowds of females, so they cheered him on as well.

Candice abhorrently stared at Joshua as he partied with the ladies. "Can't take a Negro nowhere," she said lightly, turning her nose up at Joshua in a disapproving manner.

Although D'Vyne and Andre had faintly heard what Candice said, they ignored her and continued cheering Joshua on.

Candice held her vehement stare on Joshua. "He looks so stupid," she mumbled.

D'Vyne turned toward Candice with a contemptuous stare. "Look, bitch! We heard you the first time and didn't say shit, but I'm *not going to let you deep talkin' shit about my people. I don't know how y'all do it in Canada, but we'll whip a bitch and kill a snitch about ours in the D." D'Vyne held her hate-filled gaze on Candice.*

Candice pulled Andre's arm. "Let's go, babe. I don't want to have to smack your ghetto-ass-friend."

D'Vyne leapt across the table and punched Candice in the face. Andre tried to break them apart, but they were throwing smacks and kicks from everywhere, so he stood back and watched the rumble. Security rushed to them and broke the fight up. The security threw all of them out of the club, including Joshua. Once outside, they continued their rift, spitting and yelling profanities at one another. Joshua held D'Vyne as she continued her attempts to get at Candice. He had no idea what had transpired between the women, but he was pissed about them ruining his night.

"GET YOUR GIRL, ANDRE," Joshua yelled out, holding D'Vyne back.

"Nah, dog, fuck her! Put D'Vyne in your car and I'll meet y'all at your spot." Andre continued walking toward his car without acknowledging Candice.

Candice ran toward Andre screaming. "OH! SO, YOU'RE GOING TO LEAVE ME OUT HERE IN THE STREETS AFTER ALL I'VE DONE FOR YOU?"

"That's exactly why I'm leaving you out here." Andre unlocked his car door, reached into his pocket, pulled out a few bills, and tossed them to the ground. "Catch a cab back to Canada." He got into his vehicle and drove away.

Andre was furious about Candice's blatant disrespect for his friends. She had made comments to Andre about Joshua's behavior before, but he'd always brushed them off as simple insults. He never knew she had deeply-ill feelings for Joshua, at least, not to the extent she had showed this night. She'd called Joshua a "hoodlum with a job", but she had crossed a line at Captain's that couldn't be atoned for.

As Andre drove up in front of Joshua's home, he was reluctant to go inside. He knew Joshua would brutally ridicule him for not listening to him about Candice. After sitting in his car a few minutes, mentally preparing himself for the torture to come from Joshua, Andre went on in the house. He sat beside D'Vyne on the sofa. He noted a thick scar across her cheek where Candice had scratched her.

Andre touched D'Vyne's wound. "I'm sorry, D'Vyne. Candice was out of line for the way she acted."

"I bet you she's in line now! Old bitch! I still can't believe you left her out in the streets like that though." D'Vyne laughed. "You're cold-hearted, Andre."

Joshua appeared in the living room with a sandwich in his hands. "I can. Shit, let me tell it, he should have left her where he found her! That's how I do it." He took a bite from his sandwich. "Fuck 'em and leave 'em where I fucked 'em. I told you anyway, them Canadian broads are worse than a broad who's made it outta the ghetto." He chuckled.

"Fuck you, Joshua," Andre replied, and flashed his middle finger at Joshua.

"Whatchu mean anyway?" D'Vyne asked defensively. "I made it out of the ghetto and I'm still down to earth."

Joshua took another bite from his sandwich before replying to D'Vyne's question. "First of all, ain't nobody in this room grew up in the ghetto. Shit, Mack, the Herman Gardens, Dexter—now that's the ghetto." He giggled. "Second, y'all know what-the-hell I'm talkin' 'bout. I'm talkin' 'bout them broads who been slummin' all they life. Barely made it outta high school without getting pregnant. Then boom! Ford give 'em a job and a 401K, and they feel like they're high-maintenance and sophisticated."

They all burst into laughter because they knew Joshua had told a hilarious truth. Joshua had that type of personality. No matter how gloomy a situation was, he could change the atmosphere with a single statement. They all stayed the night at Joshua's place that night. D'Vyne and Joshua continued teasing Andre about what had happened. Andre made a promise to himself and his friends he would let life take its course and not settle for less than what he deserved again. And he had all intentions to keep his promise.

ઈ•ଓ

As Andre sat on top of the hood of his car, a very attractive young woman drove up and parked beside him. She got out of her car and waved at Andre.

"Hi," the woman said and smiled politely before walking toward the men who were working on Andre's house.

Andre looked on as the woman elegantly strutted toward the construction crew. Once she reached them, she opened her briefcase and passed an envelope to everyone. She then shook hands with the foreman and walked away. She stopped at Andre's car before she left.

"Hi, my name is Monica Payne," she said and formally extended her hand to Andre.

Andre accepted her hand. He had learned two things about her from the introduction: her name and she liked nice things. The 24K gold Aaron Basha charm bracelet with dozens of diamond charms that swung loosely from her wrist could not have come cheap.

"I'm Andre," he replied. "Pleased to meet you." He lifted himself off the hood.

"Okay!" She smiled. "A young, black homeowner—that's impressive." Monica had a subtle pride in her smile. She had known plenty of homeowners, but a young, black man building his home from the ground up was admirable.

"Thank you. You must work for Family First Construction? I saw you passing out payroll."

"Sort of." Monica smiled coyly. "I actually own the company— well, my brother and I."

"Now that's impressive. A young, black, successful career woman." Andre smiled brightly.

Monica blushed. She was successful, but her modesty caused her to become mildly uneasy with the compliment; however, Andre thought her humility added to her beauty.

"I saw a model of your home. Your wife must be happy," Monica said, trying to pry into his personal life without seeming too forward.

Andre chuckled and shook his head. "I get that a lot, but I'm not married." He knew Monica had purposely brought his marital status into the conversation, but he continued to play naïve.

"That's a lot of house to fill, so I hope you have a lot of friends and family." She flirtatiously combed her fingers through her hair.

"Yeah, I do, but I'm interested in meeting new people."

Monica stared at Andre in a prejudging manner before asking, "Any kids or crazy women stalking you?" She laughed, although she was dead-serious.

"Nope," Andre replied in an as a matter-of-fact tone, "no dependents. I file single, head of household on my taxes." He smiled.

"Okay then, man. We can be friends." She laughed. "Thing is," she said, and one of her eyebrows went up, "I don't lie to my friends, and I don't expect my friends to lie to me, so I hope you're being honest, *friend*."

"Great, but friendship not only has to be earned, but it has to be maintained as well, so let's continue our trend of honesty, *friend*," Andre mimicked her.

"You've earned my friendship by being honest, and you can maintain it by taking me to dinner." Monica handed Andre her business card.

"Are you Canadian, overly-bourgeois, or jealous?" Andre asked, intently staring into Monica's eyes.

"U.S.D.N.S. and *so* not jealous," she replied, stepped back, and sassily placed her hands on her hips. "Do I look like the insecure type?"

"No," Andre replied, with a chuckle. "And what-in-the-hell is U.S.D.N.S.?" He continued chuckling.

"The United States Department of Nigga-Shit. And you asked if I was snobbish . . ." She laughed.

They continued their banter briefly, but Monica soon left.

They went on their first date a week later. They had a lot in common, busy schedules especially. They enjoyed each other's company and began seeing more and more of one another as the weeks went on. As their dates propelled, Andre's life seemed to be a lot fuller, but he still held a degree of caution.

Chapter 3

After dressing, Joi sat on her sofa and sulked. She was still upset with herself for allowing Damon to make her cry. Although it had been a few weeks since the incident, she was still seething. Joi was sure she would never go back to Damon, but she couldn't figure out why she still thought of him so often. She wondered if her disdain for Damon was a camouflage for her love for him.

She went to the mirror and combed her fingers through her hair. "Hell nah, I don't love that scum bag," she said defiantly, but her words didn't match her thoughts.

She placed a fresh flower into her hair and left her apartment. She had plans to meet D'Vyne for dinner at the Bistro's and didn't want to be late. As Joi walked through the hallway of her building, she prayed she didn't stumble on Damon. Although she was a strong black woman, she knew Damon was her kryptonite.

Once she reached her vehicle, she let the convertible top down and smiled because she knew she had successfully dodged Damon; not to mention, she still had the BMW he'd bought her. In Joi's opinion, she had earned the car after all Damon had put her through, so she tried to enjoy it as much as possible.

After getting to the restaurant, Joi got a table and ordered her and D'Vyne's meals. She had spoken to D'Vyne while she was on the expressway. D'Vyne told Joi she would be a little late but assured her she would be there before their meals were served. D'Vyne was never known for her punctuality; therefore, Joi was sure she would be sitting alone for longer than D'Vyne had predicted.

As Joi awaited D'Vyne's arrival, the waiter who had been serving her came to the table with a bottle of champagne. He placed the bottle of Cristal on ice in the center of her table and smiled. Joi was puzzled. She looked from the waiter to the bottle, and back at him.

"Excuse me," she said. "I didn't order this." She smiled politely and pointed at the bottle of champagne.

The waiter returned a smile. "Oh, excuse me. The gentlemen who just left the restaurant pad for the champagne and the meals. He left a hefty tip in case you and your party wanted desert." He smiled once again before walking away.

Joi's mind began working a mile a minute. Her eyes roved the restaurant searching for someone she knew, but she came up empty. She prayed Damon hadn't followed her to the restaurant. She was sure he was capable of stalking her. She grabbed the wine menu and thumbed through it trying to find the price of the champagne. She gasped after seeing the ticket for the bottle. She was amazed someone would buy such an expensive bottle of champagne without wanting any acknowledgement. Joi reached in her purse and began rambling through things in search of her cellphone. As she rummaged through the purse, D'Vyne walked into the restaurant.

D'Vyne was looking beautiful. Her light bronzed satin skin shimmered. She was wearing a short cut, form-fitting Peter Hidalgo skirt. The material clung to her body, giving her 32-24-40 measurements a flattering enhancement. She sauntered across the dining room, commanding the attention of every man in the restaurant. Eyes gazed as she leaned over and kissed Joi's cheek.

"Hey, love one," D'Vyne said. "Sorry I'm late." She smiled and pulled out a chair. Afterwards, she sat and crossed her freshly-waxed legs.

"About time! You look nice." Joi pointed at D'Vyne's feet. "Are those Sergio Rossi sandals?"

"Yep," D'Vyne replied, pursing her lips and nodding her head sassily. "We ordered this Crist?" She grabbed the bottle and looked at it. "You'd betta have gotten a raise or a man if you're affordin' shit like this."

Joi leaned closer to D'Vyne. "You're not going to believe this shit."

"What? Spill it," D'Vyne said, and leaned closer to Joi as if they were trading deep, intimate secrets.

"One of these white guys paid for our food and bought that bottle of champagne." Joi grabbed the wine menu and showed D'Vyne the price of the bottle. "Look how much this shit costs."

"Three hundred bones! Where is the rat soup-eatin' cracker motherfucker?" D'Vyne looked around. "I'm telling him thanks, but no thanks, 'cause I ain't givin' him no pussy."

"That's the crazy part," Joi said in a whispered tone. "I don't even know who it was. The waiter said he paid and left."

"Then how do you know he's white?"

"Look around you, skeezer." Joi chuckled.

"Yeah? And? It could've been a successful brotha like Andre or something." D'Vyne shrugged her shoulders. "Hell, it could've been Damon."

"Fuck Damon!" Joi spat out vehemently. "I'd appreciate it if you wouldn't bring him into our conversation."

"Seriously, Joi, whatever he did to you, you need to let it go. Get over it or get it out." D'Vyne reached across the table and tenderly grabbed Joi's hand.

"It isn't that easy, D'Vyne. He really trashed a sistah."

Tears welled in her eyes. She looked hurt. She wanted to tell D'Vyne what Damon had done to her, but she was afraid D'Vyne would get upset with her because she had been placed in harm's way, too, and Joi hadn't told her.

"It is that easy, Joi," D'Vyne said softly. "Me and Demetric get into it all the time, but we talk about it, and at the end of the day, our shit is resolved. I may still be pissed at him, but we have an understanding."

"Nah, D'Vyne, it's deeper than that," Joi replied, and began telling her the story she had reluctantly been withholding from her.

Joi explained to D'Vyne she'd had no knowledge of Damon's plans to have them transport cocaine for him. Tears flowed from her eyes as she told the story. Joi's emotions had been suppressed for a long time because she'd had no one to talk to about what Damon had done to her. Telling D'Vyne about Damon's betrayal was relieving for her. She had finally lifted that heavy burden from herself.

D'Vyne slid her chair closer to Joi's. She wrapped her arm around her and rubbed Joi's back, consoling her. D'Vyne knew Joi was hurt and she wanted to help alleviate her pain. She placed her face closer to Joi's.

"Let it all out. It's gonna be all right," D'Vyne said, continuing to rub her friend's back in a consoling manner.

Joi looked to D'Vyne with tears rolling from her cheeks. "How, D'Vyne? I'm tired of men fucking over me!" Tears continued to flow down her drenched face as she profusely cried.

"We're gonna whip his ass! That's how. Shit! You remember what I did to Candice." They laughed.

Joi giggled, wiping tears from her nose. "D'Vyne please. That girl whipped your ass."

She used a table napkin to wipe tears from her eyes and they continued to laugh. The mood of their evening had changed. They began to talk and laugh. They ate their meals and drank some of the champagne that had mysteriously been sent to their table and enjoyed the little time they were able to spend together.

D'Vyne was happy she could be there for Joi during her time of need. She encouraged Joi to return the car to Damon, but Joi refused. Joi insisted the BMW was payment for all the things Damon had put her through. D'Vyne didn't agree with Joi, but she understood, so she didn't press the issue any further. She knew her friend was going through a lot, so she decided to keep the criticism to a minimum.

After they drank a few glasses of champagne, D'Vyne and Joi left the restaurant. Joi was relieved because she had lifted a burden that was becoming too heavy a load to carry, and D'Vyne was upset about how Damon had treated her friend. She planned to get some type of revenge for what he had done to Joi.

⋘•⋙

D'Vyne pulled her car into Demetric's driveway. She and Demetric had plans to go to CoCo's comedy club after she returned from dinner with Joi. She didn't want to ruin her man's evening, but after her dinner with Joi, she didn't want to go. She was still upset about what Damon had done to Joi. She hated him for treating her friend like that. She was also upset because Damon had placed her life and her freedom in jeopardy as well. She was a seasoned judge of character, but Damon had deceived her as well with his gentle and well-mannered facade.

After seeing Joi receive the BMW and the trip to the Super Bowl, D'Vyne had thought her friend was the luckiest woman in the world. She was even a pinch jealous of Joi because Demetric was unable to buy her expensive gifts like Damon had continuously lavished on Joi.

Although Demetric owned a clothing store and a few rental properties, his money had become limited once he'd stopped selling drugs, but he helped D'Vyne out whenever she needed help. He wanted to do more, but not at the expense of going to prison or losing his life, so he'd ended a good run while he still had the opportunity to do so. He assumed D'Vyne was content with their modest life style, so he, too, was content.

D'Vyne entered Demetric's home, kicked off her sandals, and pounced onto the couch. Joi had plagued D'Vyne with the burden of hate and it was surely bringing her day down. As she sulked on the sofa, Demetric walked into the living room and chuckled.

D'Vyne looked up to him and playfully rolled her eyes. "What's so funny?"

"You," Demetric replied, and continued chuckling. "You're the one in here poutin'. What's up? Joi piss you off or somethin'?" He sat snugly next to her on the sofa.

"Nothing." D'Vyne smiled weakly. "I hope they have someone funny on the stage tonight. I'm tired of seeing that one guy. What's his name?"

"Downtown Tony Brown; I like the nigga. He's still gutter with his shit." Demetric rubbed D'Vyne's thigh.

D'Vyne playfully pushed his hands away. "You'd betta keep them rusty-ass paws away from me." She smiled. "Pssh! Just because you're takin' me out to a little comedy joint doesn't mean you're gettin' any of this," D'Vyne said and seductively h ked her skirt up, revealing her naked vagina and began giggling.

Demetric stared at her Brazilian-waxed lovely and smiled. He scooted closer to her. "You'd betta quit playin'. You're gonna mess around and make us miss the show." He kissed her clavicle.

D'Vyne smiled. "I tasted some of that Cristal today." She grimaced. "It was nasty. I didn't like it, but Joi did."

"I ain't never tasted that shit and probably never will. Niggaz only drink that shit because Jigga says that's what's up. Fo' mines, a nigga can get bent off a bottle of White Label Wild Irish Rose and grape Kool-Aid. You feel me?" He playfully trounced D'Vyne and began tickling and muscling her.

D'Vyne laughed and pushed him away. "Stop, baby! Stop! You're gonna mess up my dress." She giggled. "I think you're perpin', too. Yo' ass ain't gonna drink no Rose."

Demetric rose from the sofa. "Bullshit!" he said in protest. "I got a bottle in the cabinet right now." He rushed to the kitchen and pulled the bottle from a cupboard. He raised the bottle. "See what I'm sayin'? I'm ghetto like that." He gaily walked back to the living room and sat next to D'Vyne.

D'Vyne laughed hysterically. "A'ight! A'ight! You got me, but I betchu won't order none of that shit at the club." She snickered.

"Seven years and you still sleep on a nigga. I ain't gotta impress none of them hoes at the club. I got a twelve already. Seven years trouble-free, and the love is still alive and kickin'. Shit! I'll leave that shit to them niggaz who're still lookin'." He grabbed his crotch and leaned into the sofa.

D'Vyne smiled. She knew she was attractive, but it was still rousing to hear it from the man she loved, and she was impressed with what he had said.

"If I'm a twelve, what is Lisa Raye?" D'Vyne asked, pursed her lips, folded her arms, and gave him a presuming look.

Demetric shrugged his shoulders and replied, "'Bout a seven, eight, somethin' like that."

D'Vyne shoved him playfully. "Boy, quit lying!"

"Stand up," he requested, standing and reaching for her hand. "Nah, momma, seriously, stand up." He held his hand out to her.

D'Vyne stood and smiled shyly. "What, Demetric?"

Demetric took her hands into his and stared at her deeply, caressing them. "I love you because when I look at you, I see everything I need to make this fucked-up-world worth being in." He held his stare.

Tears began welling in D'Vyne's eyes. She loved what she'd heard from Demetric, but her tears were for another reason. She desperately wished Joi could have a man as loving as hers. She felt terrible about her friend's misfortune and wished her life could be simpler.

"Don't say that, Demetric," D'Vyne said, and a single tear fell from her eye.

"Nah. This is real talk. I know you know I love you, but I don't think you know the extent of it. My moms and pops had one love: crack. I thought I loved my brothers and sisters, but I didn't. I used to get groceries from carrying bags at the supermarket and I would hide that shit from everybody. I was full every night, but sometimes them niggaz would starve. It was every nigga for them self around that muhfucka, but with you, it's different."

"How? And why are you telling me this now?"

"Because I understand shit now. I just got my GED, so it's no secret I ain't book smart; I'm hood smart. I learned through my experiences, and my experience tells me, when you're willin' to starve so someone else can eat, you love them. That's how I feel about you. That's why you're a twelve in my eyes. Well, that and all that ass." He slapped her behind.

D'Vyne was in tears. She rarely heard Demetric speak in the way he was speaking to her now. He had rescued her from the anger that had consumed her after dinner with Joi.

D'Vyne smiled and looked into her man's eyes. "What would you do to me off some of that Rose?" She giggled girlishly.

"Shit! You don't know?" Demetric wrapped his arms around her waist and kissed her tear-drenched cheek.

D'Vyne loved Demetric deeply. When they first started dating, her friends and family were against it because of Demetric's background. She'd considered their feelings concerning the situation, but there was a strong synergy between her and Demetric from the beginning. D'Vyne was in the principal's office for excessive tardiness when she met Demetric. As she sat in the waiting area of the office, Demetric walked in and sat next to her. She looked over at him and wasn't impressed. She thought he was cute, but he had a gritty, dingy-looking outfit on.

"Hey," D'Vyne spoke to him as not to be rude, then looked back into her book.

"What up, doe?" Demetric replied in his coolest tone.

"Whatchu in the office for?" D'Vyne looked over to him and asked nosily.

"Skippin', but they lied on me." He looked to the floor without making eye contact with D'Vyne.

D'Vyne chuckled. "I bet that's the story of your life, huh? People lyin' on you."

"What?" Demetric asked defensively. "Girl, you don't even know me!" D'Vyne closed her books and sassily pursed her lips.

"I know you lyin'!"

"You don't know shit! What I gotta lie to you fo'?"

"I don't know, but you did. I've got Chemistry with you second hour, and I only saw ya' lyin' ass in there one time. That was at the beginning of the semester." She rolled her eyes and reopened her book.

"So what? Why you checkin' up on me fo'?"

"I ain't checkin' up on you! I'm just callin' you on your bullshit."

Demetric stayed quiet for a while after D'Vyne's damning comment. He knew she was telling the truth, but he was offended because she was judging him without knowing his situation. He stared at her, nearly scorching her skin with his hateful gaze.

D'Vyne felt the energy of his stare. She placed a book marker in her book, closed the book, and returned his stare.

"Look, boy," D'Vyne spat out, "I know ya momma taught you better than to stare. You ain't scaring nobody with all that." She continued her stare down with him.

"My momma ain't teach me shit! That's why I'll smack a bitch. Humph!" he grunted angrily. "I don't know who you think you is! Shit, you in the office, too, actin' like you the shit, and my name is Demetric, not boy, slut!"

"I work in here, that's why I'm in here. Now what, hoe?"

D'Vyne waited for a reply from Demetric, but she received a tap on her shoulder instead. She turned to see who was tapping her shoulder and was shocked. It was the principal. She was sure he had heard her tell Demetric that lie and curse him.

The principal stared at her in a judging manner. "I was under the impression you were here for being excessively tardy to your third-hour class, but since you want a job in the office, that's what your detention will be. You can leave now." He gave her a hand motion to leave the office.

D'Vyne gathered her things. She was embarrassed about being caught telling lies in front of the principal, but it was more humiliating to be judged by Demetric. Demetric jumped at the chance to humiliate D'Vyne even further. As she passed him, Demetric began snickering.

"I'm gonna see if they'll give a nigga like me a job in this piece, too," he said to her as she reached the door.

D'Vyne threw her middle finger up and lip synched, "Fuck you," to Demetric as she left. She was embarrassed, but she still had to have the last word.

Demetric teased D'Vyne relentlessly after that incident. Whenever he saw her, he would make some type of reference about what had happened in the office between them, and she would fire back with a few jokes of her own. That became the nature of their friendship. Although neither one of them would admit it, they both secretly anticipated their hallway spats. After months of throwing insults back-and-forth to one another, they had become unconsciously connected to each other. But the truth of their feelings soon came out.

D'Vyne was approaching the entrance to the school one day, when she noticed an unusually large crowd gathering. She turned to see what the commotion was about and was taken aback. Her jaw nearly hit the ground as she saw Demetric running in her direction, being chased by the school police and some narcotics officers. She looked on, silently praying he outran them. She wanted him to get away desperately. As Demetric neared her, he made eye contact with her. He had a look of despair in his eyes. As he passed her, he dropped a crumbled-up box of Lemonhead candy near her feet. D'Vyne then understood what the look of despair meant. She stepped on the box and used her foot to slide it backward into the crowd. She then knelt, picked up the box, and hustled toward the entrance of the school.

Once D'Vyne reached the porch of the school, she looked back to see if Demetric had gotten away, but the police had tackled him onto the lawn of the school. They roughly handcuffed him and restrained him by placing their knees onto his back and legs. As she looked on, she saw the narcotics officer searching the area where Demetric had thrown the box, so she scurried off into the building and went to class. She was late once again, but this day she was more worried about Demetric than herself.

A few days later, during her walk home, D'Vyne saw Demetric sitting atop a wall near a local Coney Island restaurant. She noticed his bright smile as he saw her approaching. She returned his smile and walked over to him.

"You weren't doing all that smilin' when the police were behind your ass the other day." D'Vyne giggled.

"That shit wasn't funny," Demetric replied, staring down to her. *"They beat my ass."*

"So, that's why you haven't been at school in the last few days, huh?"

"Nah, nosy. They expelled me fo' good."

He had a look of disappointment in his eyes. He knew how valuable an education was, especially to himself. He wanted to make it out of the life of poverty and he knew how hard it would be without an education. He was already young and black, which were two strikes, and his third would be being uneducated. And in his juvenile mind, Demetric believed the third strike would be the signing of his death certificate.

It'll be all right," D'Vyne said in an empathy-filled tone. *"You can get a GED."* She was trying to remain positive, although she knew his chances of making it without an education would be slim.

"Need an education," he replied in frustration. *"Fuck a GED! That's just a piece of paper. I really need to learn some shit because I ain't got nothing or nobody out here!"* He leapt from the wall and began pacing, shaking his head despairingly.

"You've got me," D'Vyne replied sincerely.

"What? Girl, please. You probably got a moms and a pops, big crib, and the whole nine. Fuck is you gonna do with a friend like me?" He continued pacing.

"You're right! I do have all that, but I like you. Everybody ain't out to fuck-over-you, Demetric." D'Vyne began digging through her purse until she found the package Demetric had thrown by her foot

at the school. She pulled out the Lemonhead box and passed it to him. "Here; you dropped this."

Demetric was stunned. He looked from the box to D'Vyne and chuckled. "You picked this up?"

"Yeah," D'Vyne replied, nodding her head. "I thought you wanted me to the way you looked at me when you dropped it."

Demetric smiled intensely. "That look was fo' my man Noah." He chuckled. "He was supposed to pick it up, but his coward-ass said there were too many narcs around, so he couldn't get to it." Demetric smiled. "I didn't even see you that day."

"Oh, I thought—" D'Vyne began saying when she was interrupted by a passionate kiss from Demetric. Their lips unlocked and D'Vyne stared at him. She was intrigued by the kiss, but she had no idea why she had received it.

"What was that for?" D'Vyne asked.

Demetric shook his head and smiled. "D'Vyne, you're the first person who's ever done somethin' to help me." He held a look of deep appreciation in his eyes. He wrapped his arms around her waist and kissed her again.

"It's cool. I told you, you got me." She smiled.

After that day, D'Vyne and Demetric found a way to spend some type of time together each day. She soon told her friends about her relationship with Demetric, but she held off for nearly a year before she told her parents. She was afraid they would notice him as being one of the neighborhood drug peddlers and write him off as a bad person. After she'd told them, that's exactly what *happened, but they soon accepted him after getting to know him and his situation.*

Years had passed, judgments had passed, and their own inhibitions about their relationship had passed, but through it all, they were still together. They had become one another's rock.

As they lay across Demetric's bed, sweating and breathing heavily from an intense lovemaking session, Demetric reached for the half-emptied bottle of cheap wine and said, "That's what I'll do to you off some of that Rose." He playfully spanked her derriere and took a huge gulp of wine.

D'Vyne smiled. She had received relief from the anger she'd felt when she arrived, but the relief was only a temporary fix. There would be no resolve until she got revenge for what Damon had done to her and Joi.

Chapter 4

Although Joshua had sworn to himself and his friends, he wouldn't be seeing Jayla any more after she'd asked him to choke her, he did. He didn't plan to be around too long because he was sure the violent sex acts would eventually spill out into everyday life in a relationship. She was sexual and he was intrigued by her sexuality so, to Joshua, that was the perfect combination. As Joshua lay sprawled across Jayla's bed, he went into a reminiscent haze. He began thinking about the night he and Jayla had met.

Joshua met Jayla in the early fall of 2007. He and Andre were going to celebrate Andre's breakup with Candice. Andre was against the whole idea of celebrating a failure in his life, but Joshua assured him they would have a good time. Andre tried tooth-and-nail to dissuade Joshua from the outing, but in the end, he lost the battle.

As they entered Club Icon, all of Andre's inhibitions disappeared. Every table inside the lounge and the entire dance floor was filled with women. Diversity was Andre's atmosphere of choice, and that was the tone of Club Icon that night. There were women of all ethnicities, shapes, and sizes, and he appreciated the scene. After gazing through the nightclub, searching for his prey, Joshua separated himself from Andre and walked over to the bar.

"Hey, bruh," Joshua said to the bartender, getting his attention. "What's up wit' it? Is someone throwin' a party in here tonight?"

"Yeah; ol' girl," the bartender replied, and pointed over to an older, unattractive woman. "She works at Chrysler, so you know all

dem plant females gonna be through here tonight." He raised his eyebrow suggestively.

"Oh! Game on!" Joshua said to the bartender.

He looked to the group of women surrounding the birthday girl and began counting them, then turned back to the bar attendant and handed him three one-hundred-dollar bills. "Peep, let me get a bottle of Black Label Moet and twenty shots of 1800."

He turned and walked off in the direction of the birthday girl and her entourage. Joshua reached the women and put on his most-impressively-charming smile.

"Hey! How're you ladies doing? My name is Joshua," he said, turning to the older woman. "I'm not familiar with you all, but it was brought to my attention that this is your birthday party. I wouldn't feel right enjoying myself at your party without giving you the proper greeting. Happy Birthday." He extended his hand and formally shook with the older woman.

Joshua had no intention of becoming personally acquainted with the older woman; instead, he wanted to meet the younger, attractive females who surrounded her impressive entrance, however before he made his move he had to be respectful to the lady of the night. The older woman looked at Joshua. She was speechless. She couldn't believe a young, attractive, and seemingly-well-rounded man would flirt with her.

"Thank you," the birthday girl replied and smiled coyly.

"I'm Gayle." She snickered girlishly.

"Okay," Joshua said. "Now that we're acquainted, I'm sure you'll feel more comfortable accepting your gift. Ladies." He nodded to the women and gave them a hand gesture to lead him to the bar area.

Meanwhile, Andre had already purchased himself a drink and found a seat near the dance floor. He conspicuously watched from a distance as Joshua worked on the females who were with him. He didn't know exactly what Joshua's angle was, but he was sure his friend was planning something. He assumed Joshua was either trying to pick up new clientele for Perceptions or his standards had reached an all-time low, because the woman he seemed to be interested in was old enough to be his mother. Either way, Andre just sipped his drink and continued to watch Joshua work.

As Joshua approached the bar, he saw Andre watching him. He wanted Andre to show some self-initiative and come over to the bar and help him out, but Andre didn't. Joshua was sure Andre didn't know what he was up to, but Joshua had a plan and a contingency.

The bartender had decoratively placed the bottle of champagne in the center of the bar and surrounded it with the shots and a slew of lemon and lime slices. Joshua smiled at him, assuring him he had an extra tip coming.

"Okay, ladies," Joshua said, "it's six of us and twenty shots. That means three shots apiece."

He grabbed one shot and handed it to Gayle. The other women grabbed a shot apiece, smiling and snickering amongst each other. Joshua knew they were intrigued with his interest in Gayle, so he continued playing along.

"Gayle, this is your twenty-first birthday, right?" He smiled.

"No, but it feels like it," Gayle said and tapped glasses with one of the females standing next to her.

"There it is then. To Gayle's twenty-first birthday."

Joshua lifted his glass and downed the first shot. The women did as well.

"Okay! Okay!" Gayle said and giggled. "I've got one. To my girls and my new friend, Joshua." The group threw back another shot.

"Now, the last one is to Monday morning, because all our asses have to get back to work," Joshua said, and the entire group erupted into laughter.

Andre looked on in admiration, smiling because he knew Joshua had broken the barrier of the women's clique. Although he was impressed with what Joshua had done so far, he was still curious about his true intentions until he saw the women leaving. As the women rose from their seats at the bar, Joshua gently grabbed the hand of the woman closest to him.

He smiled at her and said, "The bottle and the last two shots are for us."

He was lying because he had actually purchased the last two shots for Andre, but he hadn't joined them.

"Oh, are they?" She smiled and took a seat next to Joshua.

"So, what's your name?" Joshua asked, popping the cork on the bottle of champagne.

"Jayla," she replied softly. *"Not Jay, and definitely not Jay-Jay."* She giggled.

"Good; good." Joshua nodded his head.

"What?" Jayla asked with a puzzled look. *"My name?"*

"That, too, but I was talkin' 'bout you seein' us becomin' close enough for me to give you a nickname." Joshua smiled and poured them a glass of champagne.

"I didn't say all that." Jayla blushed.

Joshua looked at her naughtily. *"You didn't have to say it with words. Your body language told me everything I needed to know."* He smiled. *"Besides, a name is a name, as long as it isn't Candice, Sharonda, or Tameka, I'm cool. Dem females are usually crazy."*

"Naw," Jayla replied, shaking her head. *"It's Jayla, but I've got issues, too."* She giggled.

"A'ight, boom! The last shot is to issues."

They drank the last shot, then sat at the bar and talked for a while. They drank a little of the champagne before Jayla excused herself and caught back up with her friends.

Andre was all teeth as Joshua walked over to him. He gave Joshua a pound and gave him his props. *"You're a cold piece, my nigga,"* said Andre and chuckled. *"Nah, seriously, that was nice. After all these years, you've still got it."*

"Sorry 'bout leavin' you hangin', but a nigga had to set the tone off in this joint. Feel me?" Joshua took a large gulp from the champagne bottle.

"Definitely, but you had me worried at first because I thought you were at the older broad." Andre chuckled.

"Nah, my nigga. That was the pump-fake." Joshua pretended to pump-fake a basketball. "Once they looked up, I crossed 'em over and scored because I'm fuckin' girl tonight!" He raised the bottle in Jayla's direction as she stood watching him from a distance with her girlfriends.

Andre knew Joshua was correct about his assumption. Joshua had a boisterous confidence and a persuasive quality woman absorbed willingly, and Jayla was no different because she left with Joshua that night.

CB•RO

That night was definitely a highlight in Joshua's player ways, but as he lay next to Jayla nearly a year later, he began to question himself. He wondered why he was there. Although he was impressed with her sexual prowess, he was still uneasy about what might proceed from their casual sexual encounters.

Jayla leaned upward onto her elbows and turned toward Joshua. She noticed he was in a daze so she shoved him.

"Joshua," Jayla called out to him with a look of concern on her face, "are you all right?"

"Yeah," Joshua replied. "Damn, my bad. I was just thinkin' 'bout the day we met." He smiled weakly.

"Damn, Joshua, that was a helluva look you just gave me. Usually a bitch would be happy about what you just said, but your face told the real story."

Joshua exhaled and looked over at her. "It ain't even like that." He scooted closer to her.

Jayla frowned and pushed him away. "You ain't gotta comfort me, nigga. I know you think I'm a slut. Go ahead and say what your face said. I ain't one of them females who wear their hearts on their sleeves." She rolled her eyes and pursed her lips agitatedly.

"No doubt," Joshua replied. "I got thoughts about you." He rubbed his nose. He wanted to be cautious about what he said to her as not to hurt her feelings. "You've got some strange sexual requests, but I wouldn't say slut. Tramp maybe, but slut might be a little harsh." He chuckled and tried to wrap his arms around her waist.

Jayla pushed his arms away. "Nah, nigga, that shit wasn't funny. I ain't no tramp or slut!"

"I was just bullshittin' with you. Quit trippin." Joshua placed his arms around her shoulders and pulled her naked body onto his lap.

"I bet you've been using your dick ever since you learned how to, so what's the difference between you and me, Joshua?"

"You can tell?" Joshua laughed. "Nah, but on some real shit, it ain't no double standard with me. It is what it is. We're both sluts." They both laughed at Joshua's last statement, but Jayla was still unpleased.

Jayla slapped the inside of Joshua's naked thigh. "See! You can't be serious at all." She smiled. "I think you're really feeling me. That's why you can't talk to me on a serious level. What, nigga, you scared you're gonna expose your hand?!"

"Nah, I just don't like to talk after sex." Joshua laughed.

Jayla pushed herself away from Joshua, leapt out the bed, and left the room. After she left the room, Joshua began thinking about what she'd said. He doubted he was becoming emotionally involved with Jayla, and he hoped he wasn't giving her the impression he was, because he had no interest in her other than sex. Joshua had been a player throughout his life and he planned to keep it that way, despite what Jayla or anyone else thought.

Chapter 5

Things had been going great for Andre. He and Monica had been seeing each other regularly and were getting along fine. He really appreciated her company and wanted to introduce her to his friends, but he was afraid.

Whenever he introduced one of his lady friends to his clique, something usually went wrong. He often joked about his friends being jinxes to his relationships. He knew he had to keep his female companionships personal until he was comfortable enough with his confidence in the woman because he knew bringing anyone around his coterie was putting his relationship into the hot seat.

As Andre sat at his table at Seldom Blues restaurant awaiting Monica's arrival, Joi walked in. She didn't notice him, but he definitely noticed her, and she was with a white man. Andre was instantly disturbed by that sight, but he didn't want to jump to any conclusions without proof, so he just looked on from his table. Andrew knew Joi had gone through a trying experience with Damon, but he was still uncomfortable with the idea of her dating a white man.

Andre did a lot of business with white men, so he knew how they treated their women. He had become friends with some and found out firsthand how they did things, and he refused to let Joi become part of their sordid lifestyles. Andre had met a white guy by the name of Bill Young at a technology showcase in Romeo Planks, Michigan, a few years back. He had just started his business and wanted to find himself a few gadgets that could help him out. Andre had been to a few tech shows before, so he knew how to get around. He walked up to a booth and smiled.

"Hi; are there any power-washing innovations on register today," he asked the man occupying the booth.

"Uh, I don't think so. This is a lawn and gardening tech show," the man said and walked from behind the booth. "I might have something you'd like to see though."

"Great," replied Andre as his eyes roved the area. "Where is it?"

"It isn't here; it's at my house. What type of business do you own?"

"I have a power-washing business," Andre quickly replied. "Excuse me for being rude, my name is Andre." He extended his hand to the white man.

The man accepted his hand and shook. "Great, Andre! I'm Bill Young and I have a newer model Silverado with some trinkets attached, including a power washer." He smiled.

"Oh, I'd definitely like to see that." Andre smiled.

He couldn't believe his good fortune. Bill Young gave Andre a business card and told him to call to set up a time to see the truck.

A few days later, Andre called Bill Young to set up a date to see the truck. They set a date for the following week and Andre went to Bill's home. He loved the truck, so he bought it. It was just what Andre needed to take his small company to another level. After buying the truck, Andre and Bill Young kept in touch. Bill gave Andre some contacts with some people he used to do work for when he was in the business. He even showed Andre some things he was unfamiliar with about the power washing industry.

Bill really became a friend to Andre, so when he invited Andre to dinner at his home, Andre was compelled to accept the invitation

Of course, Andre was nervous about having dinner with Bill and his wife, Rebecca because he had never been in such close company with any white people other than D'Vyne's father, but Andre's unease settled soon after he entered the Young's house. Andre, Bill, and Rebecca enjoyed a wonderful dinner together. They laughed and joked throughout the entire evening. Andre was surprised by how down-to-earth the Youngs were, especially with them being so successful financially. After dinner, Andre and Bill went to the den and began drinking.

While the men were drinking and enjoying one another's company, Rebecca waltzed into the den wearing a canary yellow, two-piece thong bathing suit. She looked over to Bill and smiled. "You boys want to join me in the hot tub," Rebecca asked, with a warm smile.

Andre gasped, nearly choking on the alcohol in his mouth. He was sure Bill was going to hit the roof about his wife's blatant disrespect, but Bill seemed delighted.

Bill jumped up and replied, "Sure! Let me get my trunks. I've got some for you, too, Andre." He rushed out the den, leaving Andre and his half-naked wife alone.

Andre thought that to be odd, especially since Bill didn't know him that well. He tried desperately not to stare at Rebecca, but her long, perky body was exceptional for a white woman. Rebecca's skin was a perfectly-even bronze tan and her sultry breasts bulged out the skimpy bikini tip she wore. Her nipples were erect and her clavicle line was beautiful. Andre wanted to compliment her, but he didn't know whether to say "nice breasts" or "nice breast job", so he remained silent and tried not to make eye contact with her.

Bill walked back into the room wearing his trunks, tossed Andre an odd-looking pair of Speedos, and began pouring everyone a round of drinks.

"Here you go, Andre," Bill said, and passed him a glass filled with scotch. "We're outside." He then turned, and he and Rebecca left Andre to change.

Andre wanted to call them and decline their invitation to the hot tub, but he didn't want to be rude, so he changed into the trunks Bill had selected for him and went to the patio. As he walked out onto the large concrete patio, he saw Rebecca sitting alongside the Jacuzzi. He looked around but Bill was nowhere in sight.

"Bill's getting drinks," said Rebecca, with a gay smile. "Come on in, the water's warm." She waved him over toward the hot tub.

Andre nervously entered the hot tub and smiled at Rebecca. He couldn't help noticing the animalistic stare he received from her as he entered the Jacuzzi.

"The water is warm," Andre said with a smile, although he was visibly uncomfortable.

Bill casually walked out of the sunroom that led to the patio. He was carrying a duffle bag over his shoulder and a couple of six packs in his hands. He raised the beers into the air as a greeting and laughed.

"PARTY TIME," Bill yelled out as he walked over to the Jacuzzi. He handed Rebecca and Andre a beer, then walked back to the patio and lay across a chaise longue.

Rebecca seductively touched Andre's chest. "Ooh, you're ripped," she said before erotically licking her lips.

Andre turned to Bill in a panic. He was sure Bill was on his way over to kill him, but instead, Bill raised his beer can in the air and winked at him.

"GIVE HER WHAT SHE WANTS," Bill yelled out. "SHE'S FEISTY! SHE'LL TAKE IT; I KNOW." He chuckled and pulled a camcorder from the duffle bag.

Rebecca reached beneath the water and cuffed Andre's penis. She gently began to message it, licking her lips and staring at him in a carnal manner.

"Ooh, it is true what they say," Rebecca whispered, continuing her salacious hand motion, causing Andre's penis to become erect.

Andre looked from Rebecca to Bill and back to Rebecca. He was speechless. He watched Bill taping as Rebecca went underneath the water and began giving him oral sex.

That night, Andre trashed Bill's wife. He even fulfilled his sexual fantasy of sodomizing a woman. But despite the excitement and fantasy fulfillment Andre had experienced, he knew he had crossed the line, and as he watched Joi with the white man, he prayed she didn't cross that line as well. Andre was sure Joi wasn't into the type of lifestyle that came along with being with a white man.

CR•BO

As Joi and her date sat awaiting their meals, she noticed Andre as he stood and gave a beautiful woman a kiss. Joi's face became flushed. She'd known she was going to be busted. She was sure Andre could keep his mouth shut, but she wasn't ready for anyone to know she was dating outside her race. She was sure Joshua would have a field day once he found out, not to mention what D'Vyne would say. Their whole group of friends relentlessly had teased D'Vyne about her mother marrying her father, so she was sure D'Vyne would have more than an earful for her.

Joi was so embarrassed to be seen with her date. She knew blacks had come a long way over the years, but there were still two things blacks didn't consider acceptable: Anal sex and a black woman dating a white man were still taboo in the African American community; therefore, Joi was breaking an unspoken rule and she knew it.

During their dinner, Joi continuously looked over her shoulder. She anticipated Andre creeping up behind her. She knew she was appearing to be nervous, so she occasionally smiled as to ease her date's apprehension. Joi wasn't a racist—at least she did not want to be—however, she knew she was indeed a hypocrite, because although she enjoyed the company her date provided her with, she really didn't want to be there with him.

She knew he treated her better than any of the black men she'd dated in the past, but she was afraid to go public with their courtship because of the response she would receive from her friends and her family. Therefore, Joi wanted to keep things between her and her date. Joi had felt a subtle comfort with him ever since they'd met. It was a mixture between the security of having someone around and her insecurity about being alone. Either way, she was happy to have met him. As the date continued, Joi drifted into a reminiscent haze of the day she met David.

She and a friend decided to leave their office and go to a local bar to have a drink. They had been stuck in their office for nearly thirteen hours, preparing a proposition for the purchase of a hotel resort in Costa Rica, so they felt deserving of a break.

As they entered the Bar & Grill, Joi was ready to turn and walk back out. The entire place was filled with whites. She was the sole black person in attendance. There were no black employees or any other black patrons. Joi was extremely nervous, but after a few shots of tequila, she loosened up. She went to the pool table and played a few lonely games before being interrupted by an extremely handsome white man. He stood next to the pool table and smiled politely.

"Hi," the man greeted her with a tilt of his head. "I'm David." He smiled and extended his hand to her.

Joi shook the man's hand and introduced herself. "I'm Joi. Nice to meet you, David." She smiled courteously. Although Joi thought David's approach was sub-par, she found herself mesmerized by his ocean blue eyes and his quaint confidence.

"May I?" asked David, pointing to an extra stick.

"Of course, but be careful because I'm nice with this." Joi chuckled.

The two of them small-talked while Joi beat him three games straight. Joi knew he was more interested in her than her pool game, and although she seemed to be uninterested, she played along. She had no intention of being David's token trophy.

"I thought you were the pool master, man?" Joi laughed and placed her stick back on the rack.

David threw his hands in the air and smiled. "Okay, you got me. I'm coming clean. Joi, I think you are the most beautiful woman in the room. I would say the world, but I'm not a well-traveled man." He chuckled.

"There are plenty of attractive women in here," said Joi, before pointing over his shoulder, although no one was there. "What about her?" She waited, assuring herself that David would look, giving her a chance to slip away, but he didn't budge.

"The only woman I need to see in here is you." David's blue eyes remained fixated on Joi.

Joi's face became flustered. David had a loud sincerity within his stare. She believed him, so despite her own prejudices and her own inhibitions about interracial dating, she exchanged telephone numbers with David; shortly after, they began dating. They had been on a few dates prior to the dinner they were currently having, but Joi wanted to slow things down. She explained to David about her self-esteem issues. She told him about what she had been through with Damon and asked him for his understanding. She was sure he understood her because he sent her a large arrangement of flowers to her office with a note of acknowledgment attached. After receiving the flowers and the letter, Joi decided to let her guard down and invited him to a late lunch. She wanted to thank him for the flowers, but now that she sat across from him, all Joi wanted to do was slip out the restaurant before Andre noticed her.

David stared at Joi, noticing a distant look on her face. He reached across the table and touched her hand.

"Are you all right, Joi? You look uncomfortable." David had a look of concern in his eyes.

"No, I'm fine," Joi lied and continued eating hastily.

"I'm sure you are." David released her hand and gave her a look of disbelief. He pointed over her shoulders.

Joi's body tensed as she felt someone touch her shoulder. She was sure it was Andre. She reluctantly turned and nearly gagged on her food. She used a napkin to cover her mouth.

"MAJOR," Joi belted, as her eyes bulged from her head. "Hi." She smiled unconvincingly.

Major stood behind her looking extremely debonair. He wore an off-white linen Dunhill suit and camel tan Prada loafers. He smiled brightly, taking in the look of shock that flashed across Joi's face.

"Hey, beautiful," Major said and held his smile.

"Uh um." David cleared his throat.

"Oh, I'm sorry," Joi said. "I'm so rude. Major, this is David. He's a business associate of mine," Joi lied without a blink.

Major smiled because he, too, knew Joi was lying.

"I hate to have interrupted, so call me when you're available," said Major, as he passed her his business card and walked off in a haughty manner.

Joi's embarrassment was evident as she patted her mouth with her napkin. She looked over to David and smiled weakly.

"So where were we," she asked shyly.

"In a business meeting, right?" David replied.

He slammed his napkin onto the table, rose from his seat, and stormed out the restaurant, leaving Joi alone, embarrassed, and ashamed she had been so disrespectful to a man who had treated her so special.

Chapter 6

D'Vyne carelessly fingered through a client's hair. She had been in a distant state for the entire time she had been at the salon. She was feeling horrible, physically and emotionally, and had been for the last few days, but today was especially trying. D'Vyne had awakened to an abnormal churning in her stomach which caused her to vomit violently. She had a keen idea of what the problem was because her body had given her a few warning signs, including a missed menstruation.

Although D'Vyne loved Demetric and wanted to have a family with him, she wasn't sure this was the right time. She was still young in her life and in her career, and she was sure a child would stagnate the rate of her success, which made her question her ability to go through with the pregnancy. She and Demetric planned to retire by the time they were forty-five, but she was sure that would be nearly impossible if she went through with the pregnancy.

Joshua watched as D'Vyne recklessly combed through her client's hair. He had noticed D'Vyne's sluggish and distant attitude from the time she entered the salon. He knew something personally had to be bothering D'Vyne; otherwise, she would be her normal joyous self. He wanted to ask her what was bothering her, but he didn't want to be too intrusive. He and D'Vyne were very close, so he was sure she would eventually discuss it with him. They shared a lot, and Joshua was ready to assist D'Vyne in whatever way she needed him and whenever she decided to talk about what was eating at her.

After briefly pondering over what was bothering D'Vyne, Joshua left his station to go to the restroom. As he passed D'Vyne, she swiftly grabbed his arm.

"Joshua," D'Vyne said softly, "I have to leave early. Please tell my evening clients they have to reschedule." She smiled weakly.

"A'ight," Joshua replied. "Is everything cool?" He had a look of concern on his face.

"Yeah; I'll let you know once I find out what's up." D'Vyne looked down, rubbed her stomach, and smiled at Joshua.

Joshua looked at D'Vyne. He was confused for a brief moment, so D'Vyne rubbed her stomach again. Joshua's eyes bulged.

"Aww shit! I got first crack at godfather status," Joshua blurted out.

"Don't start, Joshua, and don't tell anybody either, big mouth!" D'Vyne playfully slapped his cheek.

Joshua went on into the restroom. When he was inside, he smiled as images of D'Vyne experiencing motherhood passed through his mind. Thinking about the good news he'd heard from D'Vyne made Joshua take a look into the current state of his life.

Although Joshua was still in his twenties, he was becoming all-partied-out. He had been a player ever since he could remember, but the lifestyle was beginning to get old and played-out to him. He wanted to be with someone special and he liked

Jayla, but he was afraid to make a commitment to a woman with such weird sexual tendencies.

Joshua was confused about a lot of things in his life, but at this time, Jayla was his main concern. He appreciated her company, which was why he had spent night after night at her home. Jayla had even offered to give Joshua a key to her house since he was spending so much time there, but he'd declined her offer. He was sure she would expect him to make the same offer, and that was something Joshua wasn't willing to do. He had lived by himself since he'd left his parents' home and he intended to keep it that way—at least until he felt comfortable enough to change it.

It had been weeks since Jayla had accused Joshua of having feelings for her. Now after intensely denying her accusations, he sat in the bathroom of the salon sulking over the realization that he was emotionally involved with Jayla. After nearly a half an hour, Joshua left the bathroom. As he walked out, he noticed D'Vyne sitting at his station. She grabbed her purse, waved good-bye to him, and left the salon.

⋐•⋑

After leaving the salon, D'Vyne stopped by a local pharmacy and picked up a pregnancy test. On her way home, she tried calling Joi from her car, but she was unsuccessful in getting in touch with her. She wanted to have the comfort of her best friend once she got the results of the test, but unfortunately, Joi wasn't available.

Once D'Vyne reached her home, she administered the test. She paced the floor of her living room, praying for the desired outcome. She hoped the results of the pregnancy test were negative. After pacing for a few minutes longer, she snatched the test from the end table and was distraught by the results. She was pregnant!

D'Vyne's thoughts traveled everywhere. She wondered what Demetric would want to do. She knew a child was something he wanted, but for her, this wasn't the right time. She didn't have the confidence in her readiness to raise a child. Motherhood came with a lot of obligations, obligations D'Vyne knew she was unprepared to fulfill.

D'Vyne and Demetric had a spectacular relationship. They believed in each other. They inspired one another. The beauty of their relationship was they were whole without each other, so when they were together, the light of their love shined twice as bright. They each had their own lives that didn't depend on the other's. D'Vyne knew that and she loved their independence, but she was sure that would change with a child in their lives. D'Vyne knew a child would be the cohesion that would bind them as one, and ultimately, destroy their relationship as they knew it. She was sure she would have to render her body, her dreams, and aspirations.

D'Vyne threw the test to the floor. She was livid with herself for allowing this to happen. She fell onto the couch, curled into a fetal position, and began sobbing. She knew her life would be changed forever. Tears welled in her eyes, snot drained from her nose. She stood and wiped the tears from her cheeks.

D'Vyne was prepared to fight. She stared at the telephone. As she stared at the telephone, her mind began to race. She was confused. She knew she had to contact a doctor, but her intellect was in a conflict with her emotions. She didn't know whether to call a prenatal physician or an abortion clinic. She knew she had to make a choice, and she was sure whichever one she decided to go with would change her life forever.

ജ•൶

Joi sat in her car holding her cellphone, contemplating calling D'Vyne. Joi felt bad about dodging her friend's phone calls. She was sure Andre had told Joshua and D'Vyne about her dating a white man, and she wasn't up for hearing their criticism. She was already upset because David wasn't willing to see her any more. She really did like David, but had let her inhibitions affect her in a way that caused her to act childish. Now, she was ousted as a traitor to her race, and David refused to go out with her again.

After David stormed out of the restaurant, Joi had desperately tried to contact him. She'd called his cellphone and his home phone for days, but she never received an answer. Joi knew David was upset, but she didn't know the extent of his rage until she'd done the unthinkable. Joi knew calling a man's place of employment was a dating no-no. She understood calling a man's job was borderline stalking, but she'd done it anyway.

After David answered, Joi had squealed into the phone, "Hi, pool master!"

David held the telephone briefly before replying, "Hi, racist," in a mimicking tone.

"That was low, David. You know better than that." Joi was offended by David's accusation.

"Right! I know better than to date a woman who is ashamed of me, that's what I do know."

David had hung the telephone up without a good-bye. The line went dead. The buzzing sound of a disconnected call entered Joi's ear. She felt defeated and ashamed because she had become everything she hated in men. She had been selfish and insecure, and had blown a good courtship by not acknowledging David while in the presence of Major.

Major was old news in Joi's life, but she thought about him often. She had even attended a few church services with her parents, hoping to see him there, but it had never happened. When she saw him at the restaurant, she'd wanted to leap to her feet and kiss him. Joi had missed Major so much; he was her first love. Major had been everything Joi wanted in a man emotionally and mentally, but he'd lacked the self-motivation to excel financially. He couldn't offer Joi the financial security she felt she deserved, but after seeing him at the restaurant, she was sure he had accomplished a lot over the four years since they had seen one another.

Joi shook her head at the thought of the whole ordeal. She decided to just drive by D'Vyne's home and surprise her. She was sure she would be teased, but she knew she could not duck her friends forever. To avoid Joshua putting her on blast in front of everyone, Joi figured she would go by D'Vyne's home instead of the salon. She smiled at the thought of what Joshua would say. *'Hey, Joi; I mean, cracker lover.'* She laughed pulling into D'Vyne's driveway.

 C3•80

D'Vyne rushed to the front of her home and peeked between her window blinds after hearing a car pull into her driveway. She had just spoken to Demetric and was expecting him, but she was sure he hadn't arrived at her home so soon. D'Vyne saw Joi getting out her car and she rushed to the door to let her inside. She was so happy Joi had stopped by. This was a time D'Vyne needed the comfort of a friend. She closed the door behind Joi.

"Hey, friend," D'Vyne said, and hugged Joi. "I need you."

"What's up," Joi asked, walking into the living area. She sat on the Ostrich skin ottoman nestled beneath D'Vyne's wall aquarium and looked over at D'Vyne. She knew the billows of jungle fever jokes were coming.

D'Vyne rushed off to the bathroom and retrieved the pregnancy test from the waste canister. She returned to the living room and handed it to Joi.

Joi looked at the test and her eyes bulged from her head. She looked over to D'Vyne and smiled.

"QUIT PLAYING!" she yelled, and looked back to the test then to D'Vyne again. "QUIT PLAYING, D'VYNE!" She leapt to her feet and hugged D'Vyne. "I'm so happy for you!"

D'Vyne looked at Joi with a look of desperation in her eyes. She had to confide in Joi, although she was unsure how she would accept what she intended to do.

"I don't know if I'm going to keep it."

"What?" Joi asked, staring at D'Vyne in a judging manner. "What are you talking about?"

"I'm not ready, Joi. I don't even know if Demetric is ready." D'Vyne fell onto the couch.

Joi sat on the couch and began combing her fingers through D'Vyne's hair. She knew her friend needed comfort.

"Skeezer, you and Demetric have the type of relationship people envy. Shit! *I* envy your relationship." She laughed. "Have you told him yet?"

"Nope, but he's on his way here now." D'Vyne sighed and slouched deeper into the sofa.

Joi knew she had to let D'Vyne in on her secret. If not for anything else, she was sure it would give D'Vyne a good laugh. She smiled and closed her eyes.

"I've been dating a white man," Joi said coyly.

D'Vyne leaned forward and looked over to Joi. She couldn't believe what Joi had just said. She was sure she was just kidding.

"Aww, hell naw! You're bullshittin' me!" D'Vyne's mouth hung open in disbelief.

"I was, but I'm not anymore." Joi smiled shyly and abruptly looked away.

D'Vyne knew Joi was holding something back.

"Spill it!" D'Vyne demanded. "It is true?" She held up her pinky finger, inquiring about the size of his penis, and they burst into laughter.

Joi went into the story about how she'd met David. She told D'Vyne about Major showing up at the restaurant while she was on a date with David. As Joi told the story, D'Vyne held on to every detail, her mouth hung open in disbelief. She refused to believe what she was hearing.

"Hold up," D'Vyne said, as she wildly threw her hands into the air, stopping the conversation. "Hold-the-hell-up! You said Andre kissed who and Major looked what?" She giggled.

"I ain't lying." Joi nodded her head, assuring D'Vyne she was serious about what she had said. "Andre had a dime piece and Major . . . Whew!" She fanned herself playfully. "I'm telling you D'Vyne, he was looking good."

D'Vyne sassily curled her lips and raised her eyebrows.

"So, Demetric said I was a twelve." D'Vyne giggled girlishly. "Did you call Major? You owe him that much, Joi."

Joi snapped her neck back and stared at D'Vyne. She did not feel like she owed anyone.

"I don't owe Major shit! If anything, he owes me."

"Excuse-the-fuck outta me then!" D'Vyne said and teasingly stuck her tongue out at Joi.

Demetric walked into the house and startled the women as they talked.

"What's up with' it, MIA?" asked Demetric as he walked past Joi. He leaned over and kissed D'Vyne once he reached the sofa she was sitting on.

"Fuck you, Demetric!" Joi said toyingly and gave him the middle finger.

"Nah, ma. I had to getchu; plus, we miss you around here. Where've you been anyway?" Demetric touched Joi's shoulder.

"I've been around." Joi giggled.

"Yeah," D'Vyne blurted out, "around the block a few times." She burst out laughing. She was sure Joi knew where she was coming from.

Joi rose from her seat and kicked D'Vyne's foot. She snickered.

"Oops! That's for sticking your tongue out at me, skeezer."

Joi turned to Demetric. "Demetric, you should teach your girl some hospitality." She turned and playfully rolled her eyes at D'Vyne.

"Hospitality is fo' strangers," Demetric replied. "You know, niggaz who don't know we ghetto like that." All three of them burst into laughter.

"See," Joi said and winked at D'Vyne. "Blessed. I'm out of here. Call me, Vee." She waved as she walked out her friend's home.

Joi left D'Vyne's home feeling lousy about the current state of her love life. She often wished she could have the same good fortune D'Vyne had in her relationship with Demetric. Joi was actually serious when she'd told D'Vyne about her quiet envy. She wasn't all-out jealous of her friend, but she did wonder why she couldn't find someone as special as D'Vyne had.

When she got home, Joi decided to take D'Vyne's advice and call Major. She was lonely and wanted to see him; furthermore, she was curious about what Major had been in to since she'd last seen him. She knew she and Major had unresolved issues; she wanted closure and was sure he did as well.

"Hello," she greeted after receiving an answer. "May I speak with Major, please?" Although she recognized his voice, she pretended she hadn't.

"Hey, Joi," Major replied, acknowledging her voice immediately. "How are you?"

"I'm fine. Do you want to talk?" Joi jumped straight to the point.

"Yeah; of course."

Joi gave Major directions to her apartment and hung up the phone. Although she was sure she and Major would never get back together, Joi wanted to make amends in their relationship. She was surprised Major was so strongly willing to see her after their long detachment from each other. She'd expected a much different reception, especially after the way their relationship ended.

During the entire length of their courtship, Joi was the primary bread winner. For months, she footed the bill on nearly everything without complaint, but she'd soon gotten fed up. She'd realized Major had a serious lack of ambition. He would lounge around their apartment day in and day out. He had no job, no hustle, no ambition, nor any drive to achieve anything.

One afternoon after working a ten-hour shift at a local dry cleaner, Joi decided she was through. She was tired of coming home to a tiny, under-furnished, one-bedroom apartment, especially with a grown man lying around being unresourceful. When Joi walked into the apartment that day, she became livid at the sight of Major sprawled across their filthy futon bed playing a video game. Joi dropped her purse and stood in front of the television, blocking his view. She folded her arms and gave Major a vehement stare.

"YOU WERE PLAYING THIS SHIT WHEN I LEFT THIS MORNING!" Joi yelled.

"And I'm trying to play it now, if you get outta the way," Major replied with a stare of his own.

"Nah, motherfucker! I thought you were going to look for a job."

Joi placed her hands on her hips. She needed them to be somewhere; otherwise, she was sure they would be on Major. She was pissed, and the evil glare in her eyes told it all.

"I ain't say that shit. You did. I told you, I ain't getting' no job until this fall . . . I'm chillin'." Major leaned back into the futon.

"Not around here, you ain't! I ain't your mamma, nigga!" Joi stormed off and went into the bedroom of the apartment.

After Joi rushed off, Major continued to play his video game. He heard screams and rants coming from the bedroom, but he ignored them. He was sure they would end soon or Joi would become hoarse; either way, he wouldn't have to hear it much longer.

Joi rushed back into the front of the apartment carrying two plastic grocery bags filled with Major's clothes. She threw the bags to the floor and gave him a vile stare.

"Brotha," she said coldly, "you have to bounce. I'm trying to better myself and I can't do it with a lazy-ass-nigga lying around playing video games all day! My life ain't no game, no jukebox, or no joke. I need dollars, not cents. Nigga, bounce!" Joi opened the door and kicked the bags into the foyer of the apartment.

Major was shocked. He held a look of disbelief in his eyes as he rose from the futon and left the apartment without protest. As he walked out, Joi forcefully slammed the door behind him. Joi dropped to her knees and prayed she never saw Major again, but as time passed and relationships came and went, she yearned for him to return.

Now, after years, Joi was preparing her apartment for Major's arrival. As she lit a scented candle, she heard a knock on the door. She rushed to the door and opened it, without seeing who it was, because she was sure it was Major.

"Hi," Joi greeted him after opening the door. She stepped aside, allowing Major to enter her apartment.

"This is nice," said Major, nervously standing by the entrance.

"Come on in and sit."

Joi took Major's hand and led him to the sofa. After Major sat, Joi walked into the kitchen and grabbed two glasses and a bottle of Chardonnay. She then returned to the living area, handed Major a glass, and poured them a drink.

"This is a long way from the place we had on Chalmers," said Major as his eyes roved throughout the open space in the apartment.

"Yeah, it is." Joi smiled modestly. "Major, I'm sorry about the way I acted. I was wrong."

Major looked over to Joi. He had a look of puzzlement on his face. He was sure Joi was talking about the way she'd broken things off between them, but he had no idea why she believed she was wrong.

"Yeah, right," Major said, with a subtle chuckle. "You were right about everything you said to me. My mom should've told me the same thing a few years prior to you saying it."

"No! I shouldn't have said it like I did. It could've been done better."

"Bullshit! If you hadn't embarrassed me and exposed me for the bum I was, I'd still be that bum today." Major chuckled. "It's cool. I should be thanking you." He took a sip from his glass.

"So . . . what are you doing with yourself these days anyway?" Joi crossed her legs, purposely exposing her beautifully-thick chocolate thigh.

Major noticed the crossing of Joi's legs. He knew her body all too well and craved to touch what had once belonged to him, but he remained reserved, although it was extremely hard.

"Actually, I'm still playing video games." Major chuckled. "I'm co-owner of a video surveillance company."

"Oh, all right!" Joi smiled. "That's good. How long?"

"About three years, but I've only been spying on you for about a month." Major smiled.

Joi nearly gagged on her drink. She wondered what Major was implying by what he'd said.

"What?" Joi asked.

"I sent the bottle of champagne at Bistro's. I was there closing a deal and I was at Seldom Blues making one." He laughed. "I ain't really stalking, so don't trip. I just figured . . . damn, two times in two months I run into the only woman I've ever loved." He shrugged his shoulders.

Joi snickered. "Yeah, that's crazy, ain't it?"

"Nah, Joi, that's fate." Major smiled and raised his eyebrows.

Joi stared at Major in awe. She was impressed by his whole package. His appearance was impeccable, his presentation was thorough, and his appeal was desirable. Joi's vagina pulsated. Her body recalled remembrance of his touch. She had not had sex since her break-up with Damon. She was horny and tempted to jump on top of Major. She envisioned herself straddling him and making love to him, but she used restraint. She didn't want to seem too forward, not to mention she didn't know if he was already involved with someone.

They continued talking into the late hours of the night. Joi offered Major the sofa for the night since they had been drinking, but he declined. He gave her the impression that neither she nor the sofa looked attractive enough to keep him there overnight. Joi convinced herself that what she'd perceived weren't Major's true feelings. She wanted to believe he still felt something for her, just as she felt for him. Despite what Major appeared to feel, Joi was certain he would return and she would see to it he felt welcome to do so.

Chapter 7

D'Vyne weaved through traffic in a zombified state as she drove to work. She had been stressed for the last couple of weeks. After telling Demetric she was pregnant, everything had been almost unbearable.

Demetric was ecstatic about the pregnancy. He instantly went into a breathless rant about being the best father ever. Although D'Vyne didn't want to dampen Demetric's parade, she felt compelled to tell him about her doubts. She explained to him she was unsure about her readiness to be a mother and that she still held abortion as an option, but Demetric was adamant about her keeping the baby. He was unwilling to listen to her insecurities.

As D'Vyne drove up to the front of Perceptions, she smiled for the first time that morning. Joshua was inside. He had been consistently opening the salon daily since she'd told him about the pregnancy. She noticed he had been well-rested as well. She hoped it was due to her talk with him about partying so often, but either way, D'Vyne was proud of Joshua for making an attempt to getting his life together.

After parking, D'Vyne entered the salon from the rear and overheard Joshua talking to someone on the telephone. She had no idea who he was speaking to, nor what they were talking about, but she did hear sincerity in his tone. She smilec at the thought of Joshua being nice to a woman because that wasn't a usual occurrence for him. As she passed him, Joshua playfully kicked her in the behind. D'Vyne turned and gave him the middle finger.

"I'm gonna fuck you up, wit yo ugly ass."

Joshua ended his telephone conversation shortly after D'Vyne entered the salon. He walked over to where D'Vyne sat and stood in front of her.

"Where're the donuts?" Joshua asked rudely. "Coffee, fruit cake, somethin'?"

D'Vyne rolled her eyes at Joshua and threw her hands into the air wildly.

"Tim Horton's, Dunkin Donuts, wherever they make 'em."

"Niggaz ain't got no type of manners. That's why I'm getting' me some white friends." Joshua laughed.

D'Vyne laughed devilishly. Joshua had given her an opportunity to clown him and she was fully prepared to take advantage of it.

"You have manners," D'Vyne teased. She pretended to hold a telephone to her ear. "I heard you sweet talkin' to whoever you were on the phone with!" She laughed and continued to mock him.

"Psssh . . . You got me fucked-up! Ain't shit sweet about me."

"Negro, please!" D'Vyne laughed. "Baby, I'll be back as soon as D'Vyne gets here." She mimicked what Joshua had said while on the telephone. "You thought I didn't hear that part, huh, homey?"

Joshua dropped his head playfully. He knew he'd been busted and there was no way he could deny it.

"Yeah, Vee, you're right. A broad done caught a player sleepin'. She got me, Vee." They both burst into laughter after Joshua's gut-wrenching admission.

"Not the Mack!" D'Vyne blurted out, laughing. "Nigga, Pimpin' Ken's gonna be disappointed in you." D'Vyne clasped her palms together, laughing hysterically. "Is she nice?"

"Yeah," Joshua replied. "She's cool people."

He then began explaining the dynamics of his and Jayla's odd chemistry. He was sure D'Vyne would bring some clarity into the situation, so he told her what he thought of Jayla in complete detail. As he told the story, Joshua was surprised because D'Vyne didn't intervene. She would have usually interrupted with a glib comment or two, but this time she listened with complete attention.

D'Vyne and Joshua had that type of friendship. They'd shared a lot of intimate secrets over the years, so it wasn't surprising to him or D'Vyne they were having this conversation. As Joshua continued the story, D'Vyne finally interrupted him. She raised her hand in the air in protest of something he'd said.

"Hold up," D'Vyne said. "Hold up, Joshua. So, she's a hoe because she sucked yo' dick? Is that what you're tellin' me?"

"Damn straight," Joshua replied confidently.

"Is that what you think about me? Because I suck dick well and often." D'Vyne drew her head back sassily and waited to hear Joshua's reply.

"Nah, Vee! And I didn't need that picture in my head either."

"So what makes me and her so different?"

"She asked me to choke her. Now, if you're into that type of shit, my answer might change."

"Did you?" D'Vyne asked, looking steadily into his eyes.

"Yep," Joshua replied candidly.

"So what makes you so different? Shit, you participated, so you're a slut, too." Dyne teased.

"DAMN!" Joshua belted out. "That's the same thing I said, and she got mad at me."

"Boy, bye! You didn't!" D'Vyne chuckled. "You are too much for me." She sighed weakly.

Joshua stared at D'Vyne. He had heard the despair in her sigh. He moved closer toward her and touched her shoulder.

"What's up, Vee?" Joshua rubbed her back in a comforting manner. "I noticed you've been down lately. What's going on?" Joshua continued comforting her with his touch.

Tears appeared in D'Vyne's eyes as she stared at Joshua. All the emotions she had been feeling throughout the past weeks had come to a head.

"I don't wanna do it, Joshua," D'Vyne cried.

Joshua was confused. He was sure she was talking about something other than having the baby. He knew D'Vyne had a lot of resentment toward her parents for pushing her out of their lives so early, but he hoped she wasn't affected by it to the point she was considering aborting her own child.

"Don't wanna do what, D'Vyne?"

"Have the baby," D'Vyne replied quickly. "I don't want to, Joshua." The tears that had risen in her eyes began falling. D'Vyne's cheek and became billows of emotion as her feelings erupted.

"Vee," Joshua said in a solemn tone, "that's regicide. Think about what you're talking about doing." Joshua began pacing the floor. He was really disturbed by what D'Vyne was considering. He knew raising a child was hard, but he was sure she could rise to the challenge. That was the type of person she was.

"I'm scared, Joshua." D'Vyne sniffled back sobs.

"Why, D'Vyne? Shit! You've been like a mother to me, and we're the same age. Scared of what D'Vyne? You're the bravest person I know—dead or alive." Joshua paused his pace.

"I'm scared Demetric is going to love the baby." D'Vyne sniffled.

"What? He'd better love the baby!" Joshua was puzzled by what D'Vyne had just said, but he dismissed it as a misquote due to her hormones.

"I'm scared he's going to love the baby more than he loves me." D'Vyne placed her face in her hands. She was embarrassed about what she had just told Joshua; however, she knew it was the truth.

Joshua was devastated by D'Vyne's revelation. He didn't know what to say to her. He would usually make a joke to ease the tension, but this was a time like no other. He walked over to her and began rubbing her back again. He knew she needed comforting, so he tried his best to ease her affliction. He wanted to console his friend, but he knew he was unable to do it verbally.

"It's gonna be cool, Vee. Demetric is a good dude."

"I know he is." D'Vyne replied between sobs. "I love him more than I love myself, Joshua. He ain't never loved nobody, but me. I like it like that, but a baby, Joshua?! A baby is gonna change everything between us."

"How yo' family feel about abortions?"

"*Family?!*" D'Vyne replied, and looked up, exposing her tear-drenched and swollen face. "Family?! You, Joi, and Andre, y'all are my family! My parents bounced on me the minute I hit eighteen. Nigga, y'all are my family."

Just as Joshua was fixed to reply to what D'Vyne had said, Demetric began banging on the window of the salon. Joshua walked to the door and let Demetric inside. As Demetric came into the salon, he grimaced at Joshua. He had a death-charging look in his eyes.

"NIGGA," Demetric yelled in an abhorrent tone, "WHAT-THE-FUCK YOU DO TO MY GIRL?!" He held his vehement stare on Joshua.

Joshua instantly became offended by Demetric's question. He had been friends with D'Vyne since they were children and would never do anything to hurt her intentionally; therefore,

Demetric's question was not called for and out of line in Joshua's eyes.

"Nigga, don't be comin' off in here like you crazy!" Joshua spat out at Demetric.

"WHAT, NIGGA? I PAID FO' THIS MUTHAFUCKA! WHAT-THE-FUCK'S SHE CRYIN' FO'?" Saliva flew from the corners of Demetric's mouth as he yelled into Joshua's face.

"STOP IT, DEMETRIC!" D'Vyne yelled frantically as she rushed over to them. She stood between them and tried to separate the men with her arms. She looked into Demetric's eyes. "We need to talk Demetric."

Joshua turned to walk away to give D'Vyne and Demetric some room. He knew Demetric was amped up and he didn't want to trouble him any further. As he walked away, Demetric pulled a pistol from the waistline of his pants.

"Y'ALL FUCKIN'?" Demetric yelled and a single tear fell from his eyes.

Yells came from D'Vyne. "NO!"

The gun fired a thunderous shot and Demetric hastily ran from the salon, leaving Joshua's seemingly-lifeless body lying on the floor with D'Vyne sprawled out next to him.

Cʒ•ꙅᴼ

Andre pulled into the circular driveway of Monica's home. He chuckled and shook his head in empathy for himself.

"I am a grown-ass single man sneaking around like a child."

He still hadn't told any of his friends about he and Monica's courtship. Actually, Andre had become good at keeping secrets because he hadn't mentioned the finishing of his new home either. He knew he would never hear the end of it from Joshua about the house, but he was more concerned about what they would think about Monica.

 Andre's feelings for Monica were becoming serious. It had been over a month since they met and they had been on several dates. Although they had become familiar with one another, they had yet to be intimate, other than a few passion-filled kisses. Andre was sure Monica was ready, but he remained cautious. He didn't want to leap into a commitment that would cost him in the end.

Earlier in the month, Monica had offered Andre a chance to spend the night at her home, but he'd turned the opportunity down. He was feeling her, but he didn't want to make a physical connection so early into their relationship. After all the emotional troubles he'd been through with Candice, Andre had become apprehensive about all women, especially ones he hadn't introduced to his friends.

After shutting the car door, Andre pulled down the sun visor mirror and checked his teeth. He then reached into the glove compartment, pulled out a bottle of cologne, and sprayed it into the air letting it fall onto his clothing. He was always conscious about his appearance, but even more so around Monica. He left the car and approached Monica's porch.

As Andre reached the porch, Monica was opening the door. She smiled as he walked up.

"Hi, Andre." Monica greeted him with a hug. "Ooh, you smell good." She gave him a teasing smile, assuring him she had seen his performance.

"Oh, you saw that, huh?"

Andre kissed her lips softly and walked into the house. He heard the faint sound of jazz coming from one of the rooms inside the home. As he looked around, he noticed the flicker and the scent of candles. He smiled because he knew Monica was sending him a subliminal message. He knew Monica was ready to take their relationship to an intimate level, and by the looks of the tone she had set, he was sure right then wouldn't be too soon for her.

Monica sat next to Andre and gently touched the collar of his shirt. She moved her hand down to his chest and smiled.

"You look nice. And what is that cologne?" Monica moved her face close to his and took in his scent.

"Thank you," Andre replied. "It's Valentino Rain, and you look beautiful, too."

"Thank you." Monica smiled shyly. She looked away from Andre, the back to him. "Baby . . ." She went silent.

"What's up?" Andre asked.

Monica snuggled up closer to Andre and placed her hands on his thigh.

"I like you a lot and you treat me nice, but I don't know how you really feel about us." Monica grabbed Andre's hands, clasping them into hers.

"I'm definitely into what we're building, but it's too early for me to be making any kind of commitment or something like that. You feel me?"

"Yeah," Monica replied. "But do you feel me? Are you interested in me intimately?"

"Yeah, no doubt, but I was just trying to respect your space. You deserve that type of space. I'm not trying to apply any pressure."

"Right!" Monica seemed to become agitated. "You're not trying to apply any pressure. Andre, please apply some pressure!" She giggled and softened her expression. "I get respect at work, I get respect from my nieces and nephews, but I want some dick from you, Andre." She giggled. "What, you're not going to have respect for me in the morning?"

At first, Andre seemed speechless. He was a little off-balance because Monica had started off so aggressive, but as she eased her demeanor, Andre eased his apprehension.

"That's that Department of Nigga Shit coming out, huh?" They burst into laughter.

"Stop teasing me," Monica cried out playfully, and shoved Andre.

"Is that why all of the candles are lit?" Andre smiled.

"See! I'm embarrassed now." Monica pouted in an affected manner. "Quit teasing me." She shoved him again.

Andre laughed as Monica put on a theatrical rendition of a sad woman. They continued their playful banter before Andre's cellphone interrupted them. Andre grabbed the phone from his pocket and noticed Joi's telephone number on the caller I.D.

"Hello," Andre answered the call.

"JOSHUA'S BEEN SHOT!" Joi's panic-filled voice came blaring into Andre's ear. "We're at St. John's Hospital!"

Andre's body went numb. He dropped the phone; he was in shock. His friend had been shot! For what?!

Monica shook him. She didn't have any idea what had happened, but she could tell it was serious.

"ANDRE," Monica yelled out to him. "ANDRE!" She shook him frantically. She heard a voice coming through the speaker of Andre's phone, so she grabbed it. "Hello?"

"HAS ANDRE LEFT?" Joi asked. "HIS BEST FRIEND IS IN INTENSIVE CARE!" Her tone was still earsplitting.

"Okay," Monica said in an alarmed tone. "What hospital is he in?"

"St. John's," Joi replied.

"We're on our way." Monica hung up the phone and placed it in her pocket. She touched Andre's face in a comforting manner.

"Andre, please don't shut down on me. Baby, I'm scared." Andre took Monica into his arms, assuring her he was fine. It was a nonverbal confirmation of his strength. After feeling the warmth of Monica's body pressed against his, Andre knew he was ready to face the inevitable. He took her by the hand and they left for the hospital together.

ଔ•ଈ

Joi sat outside Joshua's hospital room, crying and shaking and rocking frantically. She held herself because there was no one around to hold her. She was confused and wondered why such bad things happened to such good people. Joi wanted to go back to D'Vyne's room. She had been bouncing back and forth from Joshua's bedside to D'Vyne's ever since she'd reached the hospital. She was glad the police had called her, but the whole ordeal was still unusual to her.

The detectives told Joi Joshua was awake when they'd found him. They said he wouldn't cooperate with them, which surprised Joi. She knew how much Joshua loved D'Vyne, therefore, she was puzzled by the revelation he was unwilling to come forth with information concerning the shooter. Joi found that suspicious and upsetting because the police had limited information and no serious leads. They only knew what the courier who found Joshua and D'Vyne had told them.

The courier had stumbled across the scene delivering a package to the salon. She told the authorities Joshua was lying in a pool of his own blood, pleading for help. D'Vyne lay unconscious a short distance away from Joshua. The courier believed D'Vyne was dead. She called the police, alerting them of a murder and an attempted murder, but D'Vyne was actually still alive. The police described the scene as suspicious because nothing appeared to be missing. Joi agreed with the policeman's observation. She found it strange as well, which led her to an assumption of her own. She had a suspect, but she was unable to think of a motive.

Earlier, when Joi first reached the hospital and realized she was the only person there, she'd immediately called Demetric. He didn't answer her call so she left a message. She continued calling his home, his boutique, and his cellphone, but she never received an answer. She had left him several messages, but Demetric never showed up to the hospital. Hours later, Joi concluded Demetric was the culprit who'd committed the crime, or he did not care about the woman he professed to love or his unborn child. Either way, Joi wrote him off as a scumbag.

Joi was becoming restless awaiting Andre's arrival, so she decided to go back to check on D'Vyne. As she rose from her chair, she noticed Andre rushing down the hall. He was being trailed by the woman Joi had seen him kissing at the restaurant. Once Andre reached Joi, he embraced her.

"Is it bad?" Andre asked. He clenched his fist, preparing to hear the news. "Please tell me he's gonna be alright?"

"He's out of surgery, so he should be okay . . . Andre, I didn't tell you everything." Joi dropped her head. She hadn't told Andre about D'Vyne being involved. She wanted to wait until he arrived at the hospital so she could tell him face to face.

"Don't tell me that broad he's been chokin' did this shit?!" Andre grimaced and clenched his fists tighter.

"What," Joi asked in confusion. She had no idea about Joshua and Jayla's sordid sexual adventures. "D'Vyne is here, too. Something happened at their salon this morning, Andre."

A tear fell from Andre's eye. He was devastated at the thought of someone hurting Joshua, but learning D'Vyne had been hurt as well was tormenting for him.

"She got shot, too?" Andre asked and tears began flowing from his eyes.

Monica could see Andre needed some time alone to talk to his friend so she casually slipped away. She felt empathy for Andre and his friends because she too had been through a trying incident of the bloodshed of someone she loved.

Joi grabbed Andre's hand. She knew he was ready to take things hard, so she quickly consoled him.

"No, Andre," Joi said softly. "She's fine. She just fainted. Her and the baby are fine." Joi used her thumb to wipe the tears from Andre's cheeks.

"Baby? Whose baby?" Andre was puzzled. He had been spending so much time between preparing his new home and maintaining his new relationship that he hadn't heard about D'Vyne's pregnancy.

"She didn't tell you?" Joi asked with a look of surprise. "D'Vyne is pregnant, Andre."

"Nah. Hell nah! I haven't talked to her in a while. I've been busy."

"I can see." Joi smiled and nodded toward Monica as she walked into their direction carrying a cafeteria tray.

"Cut it out," Andre said, and chuckled softly. "You know damn-well I saw you, too."

"I knew it!" Joi smiled.

Monica reached them with the tray. She had gone to the cafeteria and gotten them some coffee and cakes.

"Here you guys go," Monica said. She sat the tray between them and used a napkin to wipe the remaining tears from Andre's face.

"Thank you, baby. Monica, this is Joi, one of my closest friends. Joi, this is Monica, my woman."

Monica and Joi cordially shook hands. They were equally as shocked by Andre's comment. Joi had no inclination that Andre was in a serious relationship, and Monica had no idea she belonged to anyone. Monica was insulted by the title she unknowingly carried. Earlier, Andre had assured her he wasn't ready nor willing to be in committed relationship. Now that they were in front of his friend, they were suddenly an item. Monica wanted to address the issue, but she knew now wasn't the time to do so.

A doctor appeared in the hallway a short distance from them, walking in their direction. Andre's heart fell. He was sure the physician was the bearer of bad news. As the doctor reached them, he looked to Joi.

"Ms. Valentine, your sister is awake and I'm sure she'd like to see you."

Joi smiled. "Thank you."

She, Andre, and Monica rushed off toward D'Vyne's room. They were all relieved to know D'Vyne was awake; however, they still had the burden of Joshua's condition lurking around them.

CR•RO

D'Vyne lay in her hospital bed in a dazed state. She was still shocked by what had taken place. She didn't know what to do or what to think. She was sure her friendship with Joshua was over, just as she had thought the child growing inside her had changed her life forever.

D'Vyne loved Demetric and would have never considered cheating on him. She and Joshua were childhood friends. She loved Joshua like a brother, and Demetric was aware of that, which made his crazed actions even more puzzling. D'Vyne had had no warning Demetric was capable of doing what he'd done. He had questioned her fidelity and tried to kill one of her closest friends without cause.

D'Vyne wished she'd been able to prevent the shooting, but it had happened so suddenly. Her only reaction had been to faint from disbelief. Now, she was sprawled across her hospital bed lonely. None of her friends were there to support her. She was sure Joi and Andre had heard the story and hated her for what had happened to Joshua. The more she thought about the incident, she began to hate herself.

Tears wailed in D'Vyne's eyes and she cried violently. She was distraught at the thought of losing her friends. As she cried, the door of her room opened, startling her. Joi and Andre entered, followed by Monica. D'Vyne was sure Monica was the beautiful woman Joi had saw Andre kissing. D'Vyne's emotions overflowed. At the sight of her friends, she began crying harder. She thought she had lost them, but they were still there, waiting to comfort and console her.

Andre rushed to her bed side. He knew she needed him. He sat next to her and clasped her hands into his.

"Joshua is gonna be alright," Andre assured her.

"Yeah, Joshua is going to be fine." Joi reiterated, as she began rubbing D'Vyne's shoulders.

Monica developed warmth in her body as she looked on. She was amazed with the harmony of their camaraderie. She smiled as she watched Andre console D'Vyne with words and Joi comfort her with touch. She had never been with a man who possessed such passion. She loved Andre's convictions and his confidence within himself. The ill feelings she had developed after Andre called her his woman had disappeared. In that moment, Monica realized it would be an honor to be a part of Andre's life. She could see Andre was a man of integrity and honor from the bond with his friends. That scene made her question her own chances of rising to the challenge to keep him.

Monica's feelings were genuine, but she doubted herself. She didn't know if she could love Andre in the capacity he was worthy of being loved. Monica had grown up in an industrious family setting. Their way of showing love to one another was by creating a sound economic structure. They lacked the emotional chemistry a family needed. She'd tried to dodge the trend of emotional ruin which had been set by toil, but she had failed.

Although Monica appeared to be the total package, she lacked the emotion and spontaneity required to sustain a long-term relationship. Throughout Monica's life, she'd been accused by friends and lovers of being emotionless and calculating, but she wanted things to be different with Andre. She was willing to learn new things with him. She believed she was ready. Her level of commitment to her newfound relationship was high because she desired to love him and wanted him to love her in return.

As Monica watched the synergy between Andre, Joi, and D'Vyne, a doctor walked in the room. He was smiling, which gave everyone the impression he was bringing good news in with him.

"Everyone," the doctor said, interrupting the room. After realizing he had everyone's attention, he smiled brighter. "Joshua is fine. No paralysis, but he is a whiner." He chuckled lightly and turned to Joi. "Are you Jayla?"

"Jayla?" Joi asked. "No. Who is Jayla?" Joi looked to D'Vyne. She was confused. Everything was being kept from her. She wondered if Jayla was the woman Joshua had been choking.

"She got 'em, Joi," D'Vyne said, and chuckled lightly.

Andre and Joi fell into laughter with D'Vyne.

"Not the player!" Joi covered her mouth in shock. She wasn't willing to believe what D'Vyne had said.

The doctor turned to D'Vyne and smiled.

"He said he wanted to see you before anyone else came in. I spoke to your doctor and he said it was fine for you to leave your bed. We just need to keep a twenty-four-hour watch on you as a precaution." He smiled and waved to everyone before leaving them.

D'Vyne nibbled her bottom lip. She was nervous. She was sure Joshua was going to end their friendship, but she had to face the situation.

CB•BO

When Joshua woke, he had a vague remembrance of the shooting. He could vividly recall the thoughts that had shot through his mind as Demetric pulled the gun from his waist.

As Demetric screamed, Joshua had looked over his shoulder and saw him pulling the pistol. Surprisingly, his thoughts went to Jayla. He knew he was in love with her, and after he heard the thunderous gunshot, he was sure he was going to his grave without telling her how he really felt. Now, as Joshua lay in his hospital bed, severely wounded by the bullet that had pierced his back, he yearned to see her. He looked toward the ceiling and thanked God for His mercy, and made a promise to God to get his life in order. And, he planned to start with his relationship with Jayla.

As Joshua thought about the path of his and Jayla's relationship, D'Vyne entered his room. She smiled at him and he smiled back.

"After you get off that IV, you owe me some pussy," Joshua said, chuckling softly. He could see the despair in D'Vyne's eyes, so he wanted to confirm to her their friendship still existed

D'Vyne hung her IV bag on Joshua's rack and crawled into the hospital bed with him. She gently rubbed his head and tears appeared in her eyes.

"I'm so sorry, Joshua," D'Vyne said in a sincerely apologetic tone.

"Why," Joshua asked. "You ain't shoot me." He looked around playfully. "Where's that-nigga Demetric anyway? He owes up! I got some bullshit insurance and this shit ain't cheap." He pointed at the television hanging from the wall. "You see I got a twenty-five-inch off in this joint." He snickered.

"Stop, Joshua!" D'Vyne became agitated. "Stop it! Ain't shit funny about what he did!"

Tears fell profusely from her eyes. Joshua heard the seriousness in D'Vyne's tone and saw the hurt within her eyes. He knew she loved him. He also knew how much she loved Demetric. Knowing those two things and the seriousness of what had happened, Joshua didn't want to complicate the situation any further by making her choose between her friend and her lover. Joshua took D'Vyne's hand into his.

"Vee," Joshua said softly, "I love you. We're business partners and best friends." He paused and wiped the tears that fell from D'Vyne's face. "This is the worst-case scenario of our friendship. Ain't shit me and you gonna experience together throughout our lives gonna match this. I understand that and I can accept it."

"How, Joshua?" D'Vyne blew her nose on her hospital gown. "In fact, why?"

"Because I know how much you love Demetric," he replied solemnly. "Don't get it twisted, I'm serious about him owin' up, but we gonna work it out." Joshua placed his hand beneath her chin and lifted her head. He looked into D'Vyne's eyes. "We gonna work it out as a family." He gave her a reassuring smile. He wanted D'Vyne to know she didn't have to choose because he was a bigger man than that and they had a bigger friendship.

"Thank you, Joshua."

D'Vyne hugged him. She needed to hear what Joshua had said. She was pleased to know she and Joshua would remain friends; however, she was unsure about her relationship with Demetric being worked out.

"Vee," Joshua said. "We gotta keep it real with our people, but when the law talks to you . . ." He pretended to zip his lips. "Stick to the G-code."

"Aww, please," D'Vyne said between sniffles. "What the hell you know about a G-code?" They laughed together for the first time since Joshua had awakened.

"Shit! I just got shot! Fuck-you-mean . . . I'm a gangsta now!" They talked for a while longer and laughed together some more.

Andre and Joi heard their laughter, so they knew it was okay for them to enter the room. As they walked in, Andre looked to D'Vyne and Joshua with a stern gaze.

"This is a hospital," Andre said in a seemingly stern tone. "Cry, weep, or look sympathetic, but no laughing." He smiled and everyone inside the room broke into laughter. They were elated to know Joshua was going to be fine.

"Aww, nigga please," Joshua said. "Shut up wit' that bullshit! D'Vyne told me how you were rubbin' her hand and all that emotional shit. Hell, we're friends!" Joshua teasingly held out his hand. "Come do me!" Everyone laughed.

Andre smiled at the good nature of his friend, although he was sure there was something deeper. He knew Joshua; therefore, he wasn't fooled by the façade Joshua was putting on. He knew Joshua was afraid to out his true feelings. Joshua had always given people the impression he was content but, as his best friend, Andre knew Joshua's truths. Although Andre knew Joshua was really afraid and shaken, he laughed along with the rest of the room. He had even prepared a gag of his own.

Andre had saved Jayla's telephone number after receiving a call from Joshua from there a few weeks back. After learning Joshua would be fine, he used the number to call Jayla. Andre had made the situation sound gravely. He then sent Monica to pick Jayla up from her home and bring her to the hospital.

Andre lay back and listened as Joshua told the story about the shooting. He was shocked by what Demetric had done, although it didn't surprise him as much as it surprised everyone else. Andre had never trusted Demetric. He had warned D'Vyne about being with a man who lived in the street life, but she was adamant about her relationship, so Andre had stood back. Now, as Andre sat in a hospital room with his friends hearing about Demetric's crazed behavior, he wished he had done more to intervene in D'Vyne's relationship.

ଓ•ଛ

Jayla dashed out her home and jumped in the car with Monica. She was pained after hearing about Joshua's shooting. She was as sure as the tears running down her face that she loved Joshua. As Monica drove to the hospital, Jayla prayed for forgiveness. She had been so selfish.

After speaking to Joshua earlier, Jayla had cursed him and wished bad things would happen to him. She was upset because he had promised to return to her after D'Vyne arrived at the salon. She waited hours for him, but he'd never showed. She'd believed he was with another woman, so she'd cursed him. Now, as she rode to the hospital in horror of what had happened, she felt ashamed—ashamed for being so hateful and selfish—but she had grown attached to him.

Although they were only casually dating, Jayla had developed a deeper commitment to Joshua. She remained monogamous to him, although she was sure he slept with other women. Jayla's loyalty defined her. It was hard for her to detach herself from men, which was why she couldn't reveal her true feelings to Joshua. She was caught between what she wanted and deserved, and what she had and was used to.

Although Jayla had been dating Joshua for months, she still had a feeling of obligation to Dwight. She and Dwight had been a serious couple for five years. She was fearfully in love with him before he was arrested a couple of years ago for complicity to murder. Dwight was sentenced to eighteen years to life, and Jayla had been taking good care of him ever since, despite the torment he had put her through. Dwight use to beat Jayla relentlessly. He was even brutal to her during sex. She'd loved him initially, but that love had become fear after years of mental and physical abuse. That abuse had remained well after Dwight's incarceration and so had the fear.

After arriving at the hospital, Jayla followed Monica as she rushed through the hallways. As they reached Joshua's room, they heard laughter seeping through the door. Jayla entered the room followed by Monica. She became nervous and uneasy by the sight of D'Vyne and Joi lying in the hospital bed with Joshua. As Jayla shyly approached the bed, the hospital room went silent.

"Hi, Joshua," said Jayla in a coy tone and smiled weakly.

Joshua smiled. He was elated to see Jayla. Although his entire coterie was in the room, he was fixated on her.

"Hey, baby," Joshua said and pulled her closer to him. "Come here."

D'Vyne and Joi rose from Joshua's bed. Andre grabbed Monica by the hand and began walking toward the door, followed by D'Vyne and Joi. As Joi reached the door, she looked back and smiled at Jayla.

"WORK, GIRLFRIEND," Joi yelled out to Jayla and chuckled on her way out. She was congratulatory to Jayla because any woman able to take Joshua knew her craft.

Jayla got into the bed with Joshua and gently laid her head onto his shoulder.

"How're you feelin'?" Jayla asked softly. She had genuine concern in her stare as she rubbed his face.

"Shit," Joshua blurted out gaily, "like a rapper! You tryin' to be a nigga's groupie?" He playfully slapped her behind.

"Shut up, boy! I'm serious. Are you gonna be all right?"

"You're here, so I guess I should be cool." Joshua tenderly kissed Jayla's lips.

"Oh, hell nah! I would've been shot you myself if I'd known you'd be this sweet afterwards." She smiled and rubbed the top of his chest.

"Whatever," Joshua said and waved Jayla's statement off. "On some real shit though," he chuckled, "they say I woke up callin' fo' you." He nodded his head, assuring Jayla his statement was true.

"What?" Jayla's eyes bulged. She was shocked. She wasn't shocked it had happened; instead, she was shocked Joshua had actually admitted it.

"Straight up, when this shit happened . . . I was like, damn, I ain't gonna never get to tell my baby how I feel."

"I'm your baby?" Jayla smiled and kissed Joshua's neck.

"I should've been real with you before, but I am now."

Joshua looked into Jayla's eyes. "I love you, Jayla."

A tear fell from Jayla's eye. She had wanted to hear those words so desperately, but now she was afraid of them. She knew she had unresolved issues in her life and she wanted to end them before she moved on with Joshua.

"Why, Joshua?" Jayla asked as she quietly wept.

"Whatchu mean, why?" And I hope those tears are tears of joy." Joshua combed his fingers through her hair.

"They are," Jayla replied, sniffling back tears. "Joshua, this is the happiest I've ever been in my life, but I don't know if I'm ready for this, and I know you ain't ready for my shit either." She wiped tears from her cheeks and chuckled. "I told you I had issues when we first met."

"Shit," Joshua said, "you don't even wanna go that route, baby girl." He sighed because he was sure Jayla's issues couldn't surmount the issues that had landed him in his hospital bed.

"Yes, I do," Jayla replied and began telling Joshua the story about her and Dwight.

She'd wanted to put the story off until she felt comfortable talking about it, but the time seemed right. Jayla expected Joshua to have a bitter reaction to her story, but he was compassionate and he assured her he was all in despite her situation with Dwight.

Joshua rubbed Jayla's back and pulled her closer to him. He loved her and was ready to commit to her regardless of the weight she carried. He was sure he could overlook her baggage because he had problems of his own to work out.

Chapter 8

As Major finished his daily workout, he smiled at the thought of his life finally stabilizing. He was back in his hometown trying to establish a Detroit location for his business. Although Major was drawing in some great clientele, he had been unsuccessful in finding a building to work from. He knew it would be hard to get potential customers to do business with him if he didn't have a tangible location; therefore, it was imperative he stayed in good graces with Joi.

Major knew Joi worked for one of the largest real estate firms in Michigan, and he was sure she had some major connections that could help him out. Originally, Major had planned to humiliate Joi at their first run-in, but after learning about her status in the Regal Management Group, he decided to play things out until he had what he needed from her.

Although Major seemed to be content with the way he and Joi's split had happened, he still had a deep resentment toward her for belittling him throughout their teenage relationship. He'd been honest about her being the reason he had become so successful; however, he hadn't been fully forthcoming about reacquainting with her. He wanted to chastise her. Throughout the time he was in North Carolina trying to get his life in order, he'd dreamed of the day he would be able to reprove Joi for how she had treated him. He wanted to destroy her, and now that he had the opportunity to accomplish his treachery, he wasn't turning back.

Major rummaged through his closet for nearly an hour searching for the right outfit. After mixing and matching different sets of clothing, he settled on a pair of Red Monkey jeans, an artsy Son J Couture T-shirt, and Mauri loafers. After he showered and dressed, he completed his look with a Burberry blazer and Cartier shades before leaving his apartment. He was impressed with himself and he was sure Joi would be swayed by his appearance as well. Major had history with Joi, so he knew what struck her as golden. His style was what had initially attracted Joi to him in high school. He knew Joi only respected men who resembled dollar signs. He knew this because she had said as much to him when she kicked him out of her apartment four years ago.

"My life ain't no game, no jukebox, or no joke! I need dollars, not cents. Nigga, bounce!" The sound of Joi's voice blared through his mind. He chuckled at the thought because he knew he had passed the most embarrassing episode of his life; furthermore, he was sure Joi's humiliation would be catastrophic in comparison to his own after he was finished toying with her.

After arriving at Joi's apartment complex, Major gaily strolled through the parking lot. His conceit was evident in his appearance and his demeanor. He received looks of endearment from nearly every woman he passed. He smiled brightly as he entered the building. He was sure Joi would give him the same reception he'd received from woman after woman since he'd left his car.

Before knocking on Joi's door, Major put on an authentic-looking smile. He knocked and casually leaned on the wall, awaiting her answer. After Joi opened the door, Major's affected smile became genuine. She looked beautiful and he admired her beauty with a lust-filled look. He grabbed her by the hand and pulled her into the hallway.

"Damn," Major said in amazement. He spun her around and gawked at her. Her short-cut Cavalli slip dress exposed her thick, silky, chocolate thighs.

Joi smiled. She was flattered by Major's reaction to her and subtly embarrassed by her own beauty. She was sure his surprise was due to her newfound style, but either way, she was accepting of his praise.

"Stop, Major," Joi said shyly and continued smiling.

She noticed Major's libidinous stare as he eyed the bare skin of her legs. Joi knew her dress was unusually short so she'd tried to retain her dignity be wearing a summer blazer to cover her cleavage. Although she had worn the dress to entice Major, she did not want to appear whorish to the public.

Major continued to stare at Joi. He had thirst in his eyes. He had tried to maintain his swagger, but somehow, he'd failed. His attraction was unmistakably evident to him, and he was sure it was equally as revealing to Joi. He grabbed her hand.

"You ready, ma?" Major asked.

"Hold on," Joi replied.

She leaned back into her apartment and grabbed a fresh flower from a vase on the table near the entrance. She placed the flower in her hair, grabbed her handbag, and closed the door to her apartment. She smiled at Major and grabbed his hand. "I'm ready now."

As they walked down the hallway of Joi's building, she was suddenly startled. She saw Damon standing near the elevator. Her unease became evident after she tightly squeezed Major's hand and pulled him closer to her. She cursed because she was sure Damon would act a fool if she and Major got onto the elevator with him. As they approached the elevator, Joi stopped in mid-step, causing Major to stop as well. She smiled weakly.

"Let's take the stairs," Joi requested.

"I've got a job and a little bread, but I'm still lazy," said Major with a chuckle. "Girl, come on; let's get on this elevator." He placed his arm around Joi's waist and they began walking in the direction of the elevator.

As they got closer to the elevator, the door opened and Joi was relieved. She'd hoped Damon would get on the elevator and go down without them. When Damon got on the elevator, Joi sighed. She had beaten him. She believed Damon hadn't seen her and Major, or he was being spiteful, but either way, he had done her a favor. Just as her stomach began settling, Damon held the doors to the elevator, leaned out, looked at her and Major, and smiled.

"Goin' down," Damon asked, an insidious smile spreading across his face. A smile that assured Joi she wouldn't be getting a pass.

Major released Joi's waist and grabbed her hand. He pulled her into the direction of the elevator. After they comfortably got onto the elevator, Major turned to Joi and smiled.

"I gotta surprise for you," Major said and kissed her cheek.

Joi smiled and remained silent. She did not question Major's surprise or make a move. She did not want to give Damon any reasons to get started on her so she just smiled.

Major had an idea Joi was uncomfortable with Damon being in their presence. He knew when she'd asked to take the stairs. Now that they were in the elevator with Damon, the tension got thicker. Major was curious, so he decided to play deeper into the situation. He wrapped his arms around Joi's waist and smiled.

"What's up ma," Major asked. "You look like you uncomfortable or somethin'. Tell Major about it." He smiled.

Damon tried to retain his laughter, but he burst after Major's statement. As Damon laughed, Joi dropped her head. She was seething with humiliation. She was near tears, but she held them back. She had promised herself she would never allow Damon to make her cry again. Major looked from Joi to Damon and back to Joi. He knew there was something between the two of them, but he couldn't figure out exactly what it was.

"Joi, are you all right?" Major asked in a seemingly-concerned tone.

"Nope," Damon replied in Joi's place and snickered.

Joi kept her face to the floor. She had passed embarrassment, instead she was mortified. As she listened to Damon's devilish laugh, she wondered why the elevator ride she took daily seemed so much longer than it usually did. Major turned to Damon and stared at him in a challenging manner. He felt disrespected because Damon had answered him after he had asked Joi a question.

"Do you know me, playa?" Major asked Damon, vehemently staring at him.

"Nah," Damon replied, "not really. I only know what Joi told me."

He chuckled again. He was trying to take full advantage of the opportunity to humiliate Joi because he didn't think he would have another moment like this. He was sure he was upsetting Major in the process, but that wasn't going to stop him.

"If you don't know me, don't address me, pimpin'." Major continued his challenging stare.

"You're right, my nigga," replied Damon. "I shouldn't be addressin' people I don't know. My bad, dawg." Damon snickered and turned to Joi. "Eh, Joi, shit, since you're givin' out second chances . . ." He paused and rubbed his nose, chuckling. "Let a nigga like me get another crack at that pussy." He laughed a sinister laugh and the elevator door opened.

Joi immediately rushed from the elevator. Tears flowed from her eyes as she ran. She faintly heard Damon's demonic laugh echoing throughout the lobby. She couldn't believe Damon had succeeded in causing her to cry again. She darted from the building and leaned over the wheelchair ramp weeping. As Major walked out the elevator, he turned and smirked at Damon. He was no longer upset with Damon. They were now allies and Major was satisfied with the ugly ridicule Damon had placed on Joi.

As Major walked out of the building, he saw Joi leaning on the wheelchair ramp crying profusely. He walked over to her and rubbed her back in a comforting manner. Although he loved seeing her broken, he still had to play his role. He grabbed her and pulled her into his embrace.

"I hollered at dude," Major lied. "He won't be bothering you anymore."

Joi continued crying for a short period longer. Although she was completely ashamed, she agreed to go through with her date with Major. She had experienced the torment of ten women, but her comfort and solace came from believing she was on the path to reconcile with her first love.

C3•80

The clientele at Perceptions had declined rapid y since Joshua had been shot. Joshua's humor and supreme people skills were what brought customers into the salon week after week. With him in the hospital, D'Vyne was sure their business would remain substandard.

It had been three weeks since the shooting had taken place, and D'Vyne could see the significant difference in the salon without Joshua's presence. She and Joshua spoke about the incident every time she went to see him. Joshua assured her they could work things out. D'Vyne was still uncomfortable with the thought of him being shot by Demetric on her account, especially knowing it had happened without reason. Closing the salon, D'Vyne became teary eyed as the morning of the shooting replayed itself through her mind.

She hadn't heard from Demetric since the morning of the shooting as well, and it bothered her. D'Vyne had thought about tracking him down, but that thought quickly disappeared. She loved Demetric and desperately wanted him back in her life, but she refused to chase him down. She believed reaching out to Demetric would send the wrong message. She assumed Demetric would get the impression she and Joshua were guilty of what he had accused them of doing. She and Joshua were the victims, therefore, she expected Demetric to acknowledge that and make it right by them.

After shutting off the lights, a sense of apprehension suddenly overcame D'Vyne. For the first time since the shooting, D'Vyne gave thought to Demetric trying to harm her. After seeing his rage when he shot Joshua, D'Vyne was sure he was capable of anything. As she thought about it further, she dismissed the idea. She settled on the belief that Demetric loved her too much; furthermore, she was sure he would have harmed her when he shot Joshua, but he ran from the building without attempting to do any physical harm to her.

As D'Vyne left the salon and approached her car, she became livid. There was what appeared to be a parking ticket under her windshield wiper. She angrily snatched the paper from her wiper and opened it. It wasn't a ticket; it was a note from Demetric. She looked around her immediate environment in panic. She didn't know what to think. He had shot her friend, so there was still a possibility he would harm her. She opened the paper.

If you want to talk, turn on your headlights and wait, the note read.

D'Vyne was filled with mixed emotions. She wanted to talk to him, but her intuition warned her against it. After a moment of thought, D'Vyne got in her car and turned her headlights on. She awaited Demetric's arrival, but instead, she was startled by the ringing of a telephone. She searched around the car and found a cellphone on her back seat. She reached into the back and grabbed the phone.

"Hello," D'Vyne answered the telephone.

"Hey, baby," Demetric said in a solemn tone.

"*Baby*?" D'Vyne mocked him angrily. "*Baby*?! That's all you have to say is baby?" She was appalled by Demetric's seemingly-casual demeanor.

"I'm at your house waitin' on you. We gonna talk when you get home. Go ahead and pull off."

"At my house?" D'Vyne questioned. "You ain't been waitin' there! Why you waitin' there now?" D'Vyne drove off.

"You're right," Demetric said. "I was wrong fo' leavin' you hangin'. Now throw your cellphone outta the window while we're talkin'."

"What? What-the-fuck you mean? I ain't throwing shit of D'Vyne's out the window!"

"D'Vyne, if you want me to be here when you get home, throw the phone out the window."

Although D'Vyne was uncomfortable with Demetric's request, she threw her cellphone out the window, against her better judgment. She was sure Demetric was having her followed, so she continued driving. She didn't want him to think she was up to something tricky.

"It's out, Demetric," D'Vyne said nastily. "Now, what-the-fuck you want me to do?"

"Throw the one you're talkin' on out the window and I'll see you when you get here."

D'Vyne obeyed Demetric's request and threw the cellphone that had been placed in her car out into the busy Detroit traffic and continued driving. She knew Demetric was trying to keep her from calling the police to alert them that he was at her house. She didn't know why because she could never betray him in the manner he had betrayed her. Although everything in her told her not to go see Demetric, she wanted answers and she planned to get them once she arrived home.

CR•&O

Although the ride to the restaurant was long and silent, Joi was pleased as they pulled up to the valet of The Lark. She had never eaten there, but by the location and the looks of the restaurant, she was sure she would enjoy her meal. The company Joi worked for owned property in the West Bloomfield area, so she was familiar with the prestige of their community. Joi continued smiling as they entered the restaurant and she took in the breathtaking ambiance. Intimacy filled the air of the small dining room.

Immediately after they were seated, the upscale and personal service began. A waiter appeared with a six-appetizer hors d'oeuvres trolley that had the appearance of a personal buffet. Joi was speechless. She wondered how Major knew about such a haughty place. She grabbed her chest and exhaled. She then combed through her hair and turned to Major.

"Major," Joi said, "I'm sorry about what happened at my apartment."

"It's cool," Major replied. "Don't even trip. Besides, we've both experienced our most-embarrassing moments together. Only, I didn't cause yours." He chuckled.

"Shut up." Joi laughed. "I can't even believe that shit happened." She shook her head.

"What's up with you and dude anyway?"

"Nothing! He's just a jealous-hearted stalker." Joi eyes wandered after her statement.

"I'd respect it more if you just said, 'Hey, man, let's not talk about him.'" Major chuckled lightly.

"That isn't the case, Major. It's just deep and incredibly embarrassing." Joi shook her head at the thought of Major finding out what had happened between her and Damon.

Major looked into Joi's eyes. He reached across the table, took her hands into his, and leaned toward her.

"Joi," Major gently called her name, "I knew you before the Cavalli dresses, before the plushed-out downtown apartments . . . and before dude." He smiled. "I loved you then and I'm learning to love you now, but there're certain things I wanna know before we can keep it movin'." Major continued to stare at her. He was sure she would divulge everything to him about the relationship between her and Damon after that line.

Joi sighed. It was a sign of mental exhaustion. She wanted to confide in Major. She wanted so badly to tell him every detail, but she was afraid. She did not want to bring a rift into what she and Major were building by bringing the troubles of past relationships into the picture. She knew bringing Damon into their realm would be suicide to their relationship.

Major stared into Joi's vague face and knew she wasn't there with him. Instead, she was drowning in the pain the man on the elevator had caused. Major rubbed her hand.

"Joi," Major called out to her in a soft voice.

"He hurt me, Major," Joi said and tears abruptly fell from her eyes.

As the tears continued to flow from Joi's eyes, she began telling Major the story behind her and Damon's animosity. She detailed the ordeal, omitting the trip to Miami for the Super Bowl weekend. She was sure she would have to disclose everything eventually if she wanted their relationship to work; however, for the time being, she wanted to use some discretion. As she told Major her story, she noticed his attentiveness. He held a deep look of concern in his eyes. He seemed to be empathetic to her ordeal, but Joi wasn't sure.

"Major, are you okay?" Joi asked curiously. She was worried and wondered what he thought.

Major shook his head, staring down at the table. He looked up at her. In his eyes, he still held a look of concern.

"Yeah," Major finally replied, "I'm good, but homeboy's a fucked-up-type of nigga. It's cool though." Major slid his chair closer to Joi's, creating a more intimate atmosphere between them. "You're gonna get through it, and dawg . . . he's gonna get what he's got comin' to him, too. That's how the law of the land works." He placed his arm around Joi and rubbed her back comfortingly.

"I wish we could have stayed together," Joi said. "I'm so sorry about the way I acted." She snickered shyly. "I used to go to the church with my parents hoping I'd run into you."

"Cut it out!" Major laughed. "Are you serious? I thought you knew I was in Carolina."

"Nope," Joi replied with a smirk. "I thought you were in prison." She giggled.

"What? The joint?" Major laughed. He was amazed to think Joi had believed he was in prison.

"Yep, umm hmm." Joi pursed her lips and giggled. She smiled and nodded her head, looking at Major. "You know how we do it." She rubbed the dark skin of her arm. "Oh, he's down south! Everyone knows that's nigga code for, he's in prison but mind your own business."

They burst into a quiet laughter. Joi was having the best time of her life. Her love for Major was alive and well, and she hoped he still retained some feelings for her.

Jim and Mary Lark, the owners of the restaurant, came to their table and introduced themselves to Major and Joi that evening. Joi and Major reminisced about old friends and made new ones as they enjoyed one another's company. Joi hoped her love life was on the path of mending itself, but she knew this was still the beginning.

03•80

As D'Vyne drove into the driveway of her home, the apprehension that had overcome her at the salon returned. The entire house was dark. She wanted to back out the driveway and drive off. She felt cold and nervous about seeing Demetric after what he'd done, but she wanted answers. She wanted answers for herself and for Joshua. That was an obligation, therefore, she decided to go through with it.

D'Vyne approached the dark house filled with fear. She opened the door and gasped. Her entire house was filled with all types of flower arrangements. Rose petals were spread throughout the floor leading to the dining room. She followed the petals and found a note requesting her to follow the trail to the bathroom. She followed them to the bathroom where a note was attached to the door. *Please undress*, the note read.

D'Vyne undressed by the bathroom door, exposing her nakedness. She walked into the bathroom, leaving her clothes outside the door. The bathtub was filled with warmed water and lavender. Candles flickered and soft jazz played, giving the intimate space a warm ambiance.

Demetric stood from the chair he sat in and helped D'Vyne into the bath water. He wanted to show his deep regret for his actions. Demetric loved D'Vyne and was distraught after seeing the pain he'd caused her by violating the sanctity of her friendship with Joshua.

D'Vyne's eyes filled with tears. She felt guilty being in Demetric's presence after what he had done to Joshua. She sat and wept profusely.

"Why, Demetric?" D'Vyne asked between sobs.

Demetric pulled a bucket from beneath the chair he sat in. He grabbed a lathering sponge from inside and began washing D'Vyne's back in silence. He felt his guilt, knew his guilt, and understood his guilt. He wanted to wash the pain away from the woman he loved, but he knew her heart was too soiled with grief behind what he'd done.

"WHY, DEMETRIC?!" D'Vyne yelled angrily.

The pain of what he had caused began building inside her. She wanted answers. Why would he do such a thing? Why would he cause harm to her friend?

"You know me, Demetric! Why?" she cried. She demanded answers.

He continued washing her back in silence. He knew there were no words that could soothe the affliction in D'Vyne. The distress he had caused had depth. He looked to the floor, searching for words.

"I comfort you," Demetric said in a solemn tone. He too hurt from what he had done. It was evident in his actions and prevalent in his tone. "I love you." He got choked up. "When I saw Joshua rubbin' your back, I just lost it." He cleared his throat and continued washing D'Vyne's body.

"Joshua?! He loves you, Demetric. That's why he didn't press charges, because he loves you!"

"I didn't wanna shoot him. The pistol just went off, so I dipped." Demetric lied without hesitation.

D'Vyne turned wildly, causing water to splash everywhere, and viciously smacked Demetric's face.

"IT JUST WENT OFF?" D'Vyne screamed. "WHO LOOKS STUPID IN HERE, DEMETRIC?"

"I'm sorry. I just lost it. I was fucked-up by the thought of you lovin' some other nigga."

"That's the reason I was crying, Demetric! I was tellin' Joshua, damn, I wanna have an abortion because I'm scared Demetric is gonna love the baby more than he loves me. And Joshua's like, nah, Vee; Demetric's a good nigga. Then you come in and blast the nigga. What-the-fuck kinda-shit is that?" She stared at Demetric, noticing that he, too, had tears in his eyes. D'Vyne had never witnessed him cry. She knew her man was passionate, but she had never seen him so poignant. D'Vyne rose from the water and began unbuttoning Demetric's shirt.

As D'Vyne undressed him, Demetric looked to her with sincerity. His eyes were glazed with tears.

"I'm sorry, baby," Demetric apologized, although he was sure it would take a lot more than what he had done to mend things.

D'Vyne finished undressing Demetric. She welcomed him into the bath with her, washed and scrubbed him. She, too, wished she could cleanse the sorrow the entire incident had caused, but that was only a wish. She knew, just as one night couldn't mend their relationship, neither could one night alleviate the complexity of what had taken place.

Chapter 9

Jayla sat in the visitation room of the Michigan Reformatory prison awaiting Dwight's arrival. Although Dwight had brainwashed Jayla into believing she was nothing without him, she had learned different. She had found a man who loved her and respected her. Her love for Joshua had given her the strength she needed to leave Dwight for good.

As Jayla sat, nervously planning her words, Dwight entered the visitors' area. Jayla's nervousness became fright. She was suddenly uncertain about her plans. She obediently stood as Dwight approached her.

"Hey, boo," Jayla said, as she embraced Dwight.

"Hey, beautiful," Dwight replied, and passionately kissed her. "You look nice today."

Jayla was taken aback by Dwight's compliment. He had never been so affectionate to her throughout the five years they were together, and he had never given Jayla a compliment. Dwight had consistently abused her throughout their relationship. He had called Jayla bitch so often she had started answering to it. Abuse was the norm in their relationship, so she wondered why he had decided to be so tender now.

After sitting, Dwight reached across the table and took Jayla's hands into his. He rubbed them and smiled at her. It was a sorrow-filled smile.

"Jayla, I love you and I'm sorry," Dwight said gently as he rubbed her forearm in a soothing manner.

Jayla stared at him. She had seen that look in Dwight's eyes many times before. It was the look he would give her during an apology, after she had taken a beaten by his hands. She wondered what he was up to and considered the possibility he would do her the favor of breaking things off.

"Why?" Jayla asked in an apprehensive tone. She was confused about his motives for apologizing and hopeful he would end her torment. "What're you apologizing for?"

"For everything," Dwight replied. "Jayla, I'm here doin' a life sentence for some-shit I didn't even have shit to do with. The last two years, I've been like, damn, did I do the right thing by stayin' solid, or would it have mattered?" He stared at her with an authentic look of shame on his brow. "Would it have mattered if I'd stuck to the code?" He sighed. "Nah, 'cause tragedy would've kicked my door in regardless 'cause of the way I treated you."

As Dwight spoke, she was pulled into his sincerity. She could see something had brought change into Dwight's life, but she had no idea what or why. Had he turned to Jesus? Had Allah given him a glimpse of hell? Although Jayla was there to tell Dwight it was over, a small piece of her wanted to stay—if only to hear the words he spoke, which were foreign to her ears. Compassion was never a part of their relationship, so she felt deserving of hearing it from him. After all the abuse, she was finally getting something from Dwight she had desired for years. After listening to Dwight for minutes that seemed like hours, she smiled a weak and desolate smile.

"I accept your apology," Jayla said in a reserved tone. "It was heartfelt, but it's over, boo boo."

She chuckled as she rose from her seat and sashayed toward the exit of the visiting area. Although she had heard the sincerity in Dwight's voice, and despite her compassion for his situation, Jayla was finished with him.

After leaving the prison, Jayla decided to give Joshua a surprise visit. He had been home from the hospital for two days. She had begged him to stay at her home until he was fully recovered, but Joshua had declined. Joshua insisted he was ready to return to his salon for work. She'd spent the first night with him at his home, but knowing she was going to visit Dwight the next day, she'd decided to stay at her own place last night.

Jayla and Joshua had spoken on the telephone earlier in the day, but she missed him and desired to see him, especially since she had freed herself from the tyranny of old love. She wanted to assure him she was his completely. She felt compelled to tell Joshua about her bravery. She knew it was the strength she had gotten from him that had helped her end things with Dwight. Jayla loved Joshua and she knew he would love her the way she had never been loved in return.

CS•ಏ

As Joshua walked into Perceptions, he was greeted with a warm welcome. He knew he was well-liked, but he was amazed by the large group of friends and clients who had gathered to welcome him back to the salon. He looked into D'Vyne's direction and lip synched a "thank you". He was sure she had orchestrated the gathering and he was thankful. After receiving dozens of hugs and handshakes from the crowd, Joshua took his shirt off and threw it into his work area.

"LOOK, Y'ALL!" Joshua yelled. He pointed to the healing gunshot wound in his back and to the hideous railroad scars that led from his sternum to his naval. "I'm like Tupac!" He laughed.

"UGH, BOY!" Joi yelled. "YOU'RE NASTY!"

As Joi covered her eyes as not to see the wounds, others surrounded Joshua and eyeballed the repulsive scars. Joshua twirled, proudly modeling the ghastly-looking physical aftermath of his gunshot wounds. He suddenly ceased his twirl.

"Listen up, everybody," Joshua said in a bold tone. "I'm an honorary gangsta now, so some things are 'bout to change around here." He paused and looked around, making eye contact with everyone in the salon. "First change! No mo' R&B. Gangsta rap only!" He gave Rashaad a high-five.

Everyone in the salon burst into laughter. D'Vyne nearly dropped her curling iron after hearing what Joshua had said. She shot him a harsh look.

"NEGRO, PLEASE," D'Vyne yelled out. "Ya mouth is probably what gotcha-ass shot in the first place." The laughter in the salon got louder.

Joi looked over to D'Vyne. She was confused at first, but she quickly remembered no one knew the truth about the shooting besides them. She turned toward Joshua.

"Shit, Joshua," Joi spat out. "No more R&B! I guess we won't be listening to no Ja-Rule, no 50 Cent, and definitely none of that Chingalinga nigga."

"Whatever," Joshua replied quickly. "We listenin' to 50! He's a gangsta! Shit, he got shot mo' times than me and Pac!"

Rashaad looked over to Joshua and chuckled. "Shit, Josh," Rashaad said, "I'm wit' Jigga. I respect the shooter."

Everyone erupted again. All eyes were on Joshua. They were awaiting a comeback from him, but he wasn't quick enough. D'Vyne looked over to Rashaad with a sinister grin.

"Well-spoken for a nigga who ain't gonna shoot shit," D'Vyne said to Rashaad and laughed along with everyone else. "Check this out, y'all. When Joshua was in the hospital, I was like, Rashaad, we should get a gun in case someone else comes back in here trippin'." She laughed harder because she knew the punchline was going to be hilarious. "This scary-ass-fool, he was like, no, D'Vyne. Un-un! Kids be in here." She did her best to imitate what Rashaad had said when the incident had taken place.

Laughter echoed throughout the salon. Rashaad waved D'Vyne's rendition of what had happened off, although, in truth, he knew it had happened exactly like she'd said.

Joshua put his shirt back on, grabbed a cape and popped it, and smiled. "Who's first?" he asked and looked around.

No one threw their hands in the air; no one nodded. Everyone just casually looked around trying to see who was going to be Joshua's guinea pig. Joshua had only been out of the hospital for two days and it had only been three weeks since the shooting had taken place. His clients were skeptical about getting into his chair so soon after what had happened. They questioned his readiness. As everyone stood around staring at one another, Andre entered the salon. He smiled at Joshua.

"What's goin' on?" Andre asked.

Everyone scrambled to find them a place to sit and giggled amongst themselves. They had found their guinea pig. They were sure Andre would take the position, so they just waited.

"Come on, Dre," Joshua said. He pointed toward the customers. "They trippin'."

Andre loosened his tie and looked over at the clients who had been there before he arrived. He wondered why they doubted Joshua's skills, but he wasn't going to let a good opportunity pass.

"Are y'all sure?" Andre asked.

Everyone gave him the go-ahead, so he got into the chair. He looked up to Joshua and laughed.

"You remember what Joi did to you in junior high, right? If you jack me up, I'm gonna put her on you, son."

Everyone in the salon, except Joi, burst into laughter. Joi shot Andre a dirty look.

"I ain't a dog," Joi said. "Put me on someone? Who-in-the-fuck do you think you are?" She rolled her eyes evilly.

"Joi," Joshua called out to her, and snickered. "Yo' check-hand is impeccable, fo' real." He looked down at Andre and laughed.

Andre knew Joi and Joshua had gotten him with their double team, but he was sure he would receive a heroic laughter after his comeback. He turned to Joi and smiled devilishly.

"Joi," Andre said in a casual tone, "I thought you and Major were kickin' it again."

"And?" Joi replied, with a sassy roll of her eyes at Andre.

"Is y'all?" Andre asked and smiled sinisterly. "Ya know," he made a sexual gesture toward Joi and chuckled, "'cause I'm sayin', ma, you got a lot of sexual tension you need to get off."

Joi smiled. She was sure Andre would come back hard, so she'd kept something in her holster for him.

"Vee," Joi said, tapping D'Vyne's shoulder. "Isn't this the same cat who came floating through the hospital with a Stepford wife? Girl just dropped out of nowhere with tea and crumpets, like bam!"

Joi burst into a boisterous laughter along with everyone else.

"Andre, didn't she know we were ghetto like that?"

The entire room was in hysterics. Even Andre laughed uncontrollably. He knew Joi's observation of Monica was spot on, but he had to defend himself. He quickly diverted the attention to Joshua.

"Agh, agh," Andre gasped, pretending to choke himself.

"I got the clippers," Joshua said in defense. "You niggaz betta quit trippin'," he teased, waving the clippers.

D'Vyne placed her flat iron into its stove and walked away from her work station. She knew the direction of the jokes were coming her way, so she decided to leave before they came. No one knew about her crazed boyfriend being the shooter and she wanted to keep it that way. She knew the conflict between having a lunatic boyfriend and a great clientele. D'Vyne was sure people would stop coming to Perceptions if they knew Demetric was the person running around blasting people. That was a potential reality D'Vyne did not want to fathom.

It seemed as if no one noticed D'Vyne's quick getaway. Everyone continued throwing insults back-and-forth to one another and laughing. Perceptions was back on track now that Joshua had returned. He felt great because he was home and doing what he loved—entertaining.

ം•ഔ

During Jayla's drive back to Detroit from the prison, she stopped at a gift shop and bought some balloons and cards for Joshua. Although she had already welcomed him home, she wanted to show her continued support of him.

Jayla was nervous when she walked into Perceptions. Although she had dropped Joshua off at work a few times, she had never been inside. Once inside, she noticed everyone's attention shift to her. That gave Jayla an awkward feeling, but that feeling dissipated when Joshua rushed over and kissed her. Jayla blushed shyly. Although she was a sexual person, she wasn't comfortable with public displays. She passed Joshua the balloons.

"Here, baby," Jayla said and smiled.

D'Vyne dried her hands with a paper towel as she walked out the restroom. She smiled at the sight of Joshua standing in front of Jayla holding a handful of welcome home novelties.

"Aww," D'Vyne said, holding her chest. "Ain't that sweet?" She waved at Jayla and walked back over to her workstation.

"SEE!" Joshua shouted. "Y'ALL SEE THIS? This is how you treat a nigga comin' home from the gunshot ward." He wrapped his arms around Jayla's waist and kissed her again. "Thanks, baby."

"*Straaaangers in the niiiight*," Andre sang, and the salon erupted again. "I'm just sayin'; all they needed was some music." He laughed.

"Shut up, boy!" D'Vyne said. She threw a piece of wet paper towel at Andre and laughed. "You're stupid."

"I'm doing them a favor," Andre said between laughs.

"You ain't do shit but piss me off," Joshua said. "I'm a gangsta and I said, no mo' R&B!" Everyone joined in with him as he made his demands.

Jayla silently stood by the entrance. She marveled at the harmony of the salon. She observed the camaraderie of the customers and the employees, and she was amazed. It was something she had never experienced in a beauty salon. Jayla believed all beauty salons were filled with catty, insecure women underneath blow dryers, but Perceptions had proven her beliefs wrong.

Joshua wrapped his arm around Jayla's waist and walked her over to his workstation. Everyone else continued engaging in petty insults and meaningless chitchat. After briefly talking to Jayla, Joshua returned to finish Andre's haircut.

Jayla continued watching, enjoying the atmosphere. She now understood why Joshua was in a haste to return to work. She realized at that moment that cutting hair wasn't only an occupation for Joshua; it was his lifestyle.

After Joshua had finished up the last of his clients and proved his barbering skills were still official, he and Jayla left the salon. Once they were in Jayla's car, she turned to Joshua and smiled.

"I did it," said Jayla in an upbeat tone. She was so proud of herself for finally cutting all ties to Dwight.

"Did what?" Joshua asked in reply.

He was puzzled as to what Jayla had done. He knew he'd been teasing her relentlessly about working at a grocery store, so he hoped he hadn't mistakenly convinced her to quit her job.

"I told my ex I was moving on."

Jayla was visibly excited about what she'd done. He knew it was time because she wanted to be exclusive with Joshua, especially since he'd given her the strength to love again.

"You tryin' to get a nigga shot again already?" Joshua replied with a chuckle. "Damn, baby girl! Even Tupac waited a few years before he caught another one." He continued laughing.

"Shut up, Joshua. You're silly."

Jayla continued telling Joshua the story about what had happened at the prison. She was still stunned by the unforeseen kindness Dwight had displayed to her. She knew something was suspicious about the way Dwight was acting, so she asked Joshua for his male opinion about what had happened.

Joshua rubbed his nose and nodded his head. He knew Dwight was an animal because Jayla had told him as much during the course of their relationship. Joshua was usually the type of person who looked for the best in someone, but after what he'd been told about Dwight, he was sure Dwight didn't have any good in him.

"Shit, baby," Joshua finally began to answer. "It's either one or two things. Either the nigga's celly is bringin' the softer, more sensitive side out of him by treatin' him the way he treated you, or he finally realized he's doin' a life bit and will eventually need you."

"You think so?" she asked, referring to the latter of the scenarios.

"Definitely!" Joshua chuckled.

Jayla pulled away from the curb with an awkward expression on her face. Although she was through with Dwight and his abuse, she was still uncomfortable with the thought of him being raped or turned out by a homosexual. She knew it was a possibility because she'd heard countless rumors about the lifestyles prison inmates led, but she couldn't imagine a calloused and cold-hearted man like Dwight becoming someone's boy toy.

Throughout the rest of their ride to Jayla's home, there was little conversation between the two of them. Jayla was sick with the idea of Dwight being a man-gina, and Joshua was sure he had placed his foot in his mouth by putting that image into Jayla's head.

ભ•ર

D'Vyne closed up Perceptions and left the salon shortly after Joshua left with Jayla. She was happy to see Joshua with a woman who loved him. D'Vyne loved Joshua and wanted him to have the luxury of experiencing an adult relationship. D'Vyne wanted the best for her friend in every way; therefore, she was planning to work something out where Joshua and Demetric could talk about what had happened. She knew Joshua deserved some clarification and an apology amongst other things.

After arriving home to a house full of fresh roses and the smell of lavender and scented candles, D'Vyne undressed and rushed to the bathroom. Demetric had been faithfully awaiting D'Vyne's arrival ever since he had returned. He had bath water with lavender waiting for her to enter. This was an apology and a promise that had become a ritual in their healing process. D'Vyne smiled and stepped into the tub. The bubbles from the bath gave her beautiful skin an instant shimmer. She lay back and turned to Demetric.

"Thank you," D'Vyne said in a soft, pleasant tone. She hadn't fully forgiven Demetric for the treachery he had brought into their lives, but she was healing. "Joshua is doing good. He cut about nine heads today. His girlfriend came by today, too."

Demetric continued washing D'Vyne's back. He gently wiped the lathered sponge across her breasts, letting soap slide between her cleavage.

"D'Vyne," Demetric softly spoke, "you have to get Joshua away from Jayla."

"What?!" D'Vyne shot out at Demetric. "How do you know her name, Demetric?" She was instantly apprehensive because she knew she hadn't told him Jayla's name, therefore, she wanted to know where he had gotten it from.

"D'Vyne, I didn't even wanna say, so I lied to you."

D'Vyne jumped out the tub and flipped the light switch on. She had fire in her eyes. Her slippery body glistened and her normally soft contours hardened from the tension that had suddenly filled the bathroom.

"What-the-fuck are you talking about, Demetric?" D'Vyne stood near the entrance of the bathroom, staring at him in a crazed manner. She wanted answers and she intended on getting them immediately.

 Demetric dropped the soapy sponge into the tub and walked over to D'Vyne with a contrite glare in his eyes.

"Baby, I'm in a situation," Demetric said before dropping his face toward the floor.

Bubbles evaporated from D'Vyne's body as she wildly swung out, hitting, slapping, and kicking Demetric. Her breasts swung freely and her eyes became flushed with tears.

"YOU WERE FUCKIN' HER, DEMETRIC?"

Tears fell from D'Vyne's eyes as she screamed and assaulted Demetric. She felt as if she were in a nightmare that was never ending. One ordeal had propelled into another. Demetric forcefully grabbed her hands and pulled her into his embrace. He held her tightly and stared down to her.

"D'Vyne," Demetric said to her softly. "Stop it. The bitch's man is doing a life bit fo' a murder I did three years ago." He had a serious and regretful look in his eyes as he stared down into D'Vyne's. It was as if he were searching for her soul in hopes of retrieving redemption for what he was causing her.

D'Vyne kicked and wiggled, trying to get loose from his firm grip, but he was too strong. She shook her head in disbelief. She didn't want to believe what Demetric was telling her.

"NO, DEMETRIC!" D'Vyne screamed.

She continued to cry. Demetric released D'Vyne from his powerful hold. He wrapped his arm around her neck and pulled her into his chest, allowing her to rest her tear-drenched face. He was sure what he would tell her would be crushing, but Demetric knew all that healed required a wound.

"The nigga gave me an ultimatum. He said kill Joshua or get told on. I was in a helluva position, D'Vyne! I wasn't expecting you to be there that morning, but you were. I saw Joshua rubbing your back and got upset." He released his embrace and sat in the chair.

D'Vyne followed him and sat in his lap. She sat nervously, shaking and crying profusely. The billow of events in her life had ascended to a place where her imagination wasn't able to go. She was in self-loathing disbelief at what her life had become.

"I'm glad you were there though," Demetric said in a humbled tone. "I would have killed him if you weren't, D'Vyne."

He wrapped his arms around her waist and pulled her closer to him. "You have to get Joshua away from her, D'Vyne."

D'Vyne remained silent. She quietly sat in Demetric's lap. Although she received comfort from his embrace, she shook from nervousness and the cold fall air that flowed in through the window. Demetric wrapped D'Vyne's shaking body in a bath towel and continued to hold her. He was hurt from the pain he had caused. Regret was a stranger to his door prior to this point in his life, but it had finally made its rounds. His regret was deep and unyielding because his love for his woman was so strong.

D'Vyne knew her life would never be the same. She was comatose from what Demetric had just revealed to her. She continued to rock and cry until she fell asleep in Demetric's arms.

Chapter 10

Joshua woke in a cold sweat. His eyes roved throughout the room as he wiped sweat from his forehead. He had heard a noise that startled him while he slept. As his eyes searched the room, his apprehension settled. He noticed his cellphone vibrating on the dresser top and reached for it. Joshua noticed Jayla had left him several messages while he slept. He slid out of bed and peeked at his watch. It was three o'clock in the afternoon. He hadn't realized he had slept until so late in the day.

As Joshua walked toward the bathroom to take care of his daily hygiene, he tried desperately to remember the nightmare he'd had while sleeping. He knew it was eerie because of the apprehension he felt upon waking, but he didn't have the slightest idea what it had been about. The details were missing. All that remained was the feeling of fear.

When Joshua stepped into his bath water, he was still uneasy because he couldn't remember what had appeared to him in his dream. It had been a month since the shooting, so Joshua shook his head and tried to pass his feeling of caution off as posttraumatic stress. He knew his own strength, therefore, he was sure he would be all right.

After bathing and dressing, Joshua called Jayla. He smiled as Jayla answered the telephone.

"Hey, baby," Joshua spilled into the phone. "What's goin' on? I just got your messages."

"I let you sleep this morning," Jayla replied. "You looked so peaceful I didn't wanna bother you." She giggled girlishly.

"Oh yeah?" Joshua replied with a chuckle. "Since when did yo' horny-ass become so considerate?"

"Forget you, punk." Jayla laughed. "I need to see you after I get off work, but right now, I have to get back to it."

"A'ight! That's cool. I'll come *getchu* from work. You can leave your car there and I'll drop you off tomorrow."

"Okay! I love you, Joshua."

"A'ight. I'll be there when you get off."

Joshua hung up. He was sure Jayla wanted to hear him tell her he loved her, but he hadn't. Joshua knew for certain he loved Jayla, that wasn't a question to him, but he preferred to display his feelings actively rather than vocally. He believed words were just keys to open doors and he was already in; therefore, he chose to leave the emotionally-driven banter to a minimum in his relationship.

Joshua left his home. He was sure D'Vyne would be upset with him for being late to the salon. He had noticed her unhappiness throughout the week. Although they worked together daily, he and D'Vyne weren't communicating the way they usually did. Joshua was sure the distance between he and D'Vyne had been caused by the shooting.

Earlier in the week, Joshua had tried to discuss what had taken place between him and Demetric, but D'Vyne had casually changed the subject. After she had blatantly dismissed the topic, he'd made a mental note not to bring it back up.

Joshua loved D'Vyne. She was his best friend and he understood what she was faced with on a daily basis knowing the man she loved had shot her friend without cause. What he didn't understand was why D'Vyne felt guilty about the incident Joshua knew she'd played no part in what had happened and he'd assured her he held no resentment of her, but for some reason, unbeknownst to Joshua, D'Vyne carried the burden of a guilty woman.

Joshua was greeted by smiles and sighs as he entered the salon. A few of the clients who had been waiting for a while looked at their watches, assuring Joshua he was entirely too late. Joshua dropped his bag onto the floor near his workstation. He looked around at everyone with an affected grimace. As his eyes traveled throughout the salon, he suddenly settled on D'Vyne and held his fake mean-mug.

D'Vyne's eyes bulged and flinched toward Joshua. She placed her curlers in the oven and casually walked over to him, staring directly in his face in a challenging manner.

"What, chump?" D'Vyne playfully barked at Joshua. "Why are you staring at me like you're crazy or something?"

Clients and the other employees stared and instigated. "Ooooo." They all snickered, awaiting the show to begin.

Joshua grimaced and clenched his fist. "I thought I said, no mo' R&B?"

"AWW, NIGGA, PLEASE!" Rashaad shouted. "SHUT YOUR ASS UP!"

D'Vyne playfully slapped Joshua's chin and walked away. She returned to her workstation and continued styling her client's hair.

Joshua smiled. He was surprised by D'Vyne's sudden change in attitude. He preferred their chemistry to be upbeat, rather than the humdrum atmosphere that had loomed throughout the salon during the past week. As he prepared his station for work, Lucky Luciano's Chronicles of a D-Boy came blaring through the Bose stereo system. Joshua nodded his head approvingly. He began to lean and rock rhythmically.

"That's what I'm talkin' 'bout!" Joshua said before turning the clippers on. "Who's first?"

He smiled and continued to dance. The day strolled on. Joshua and D'Vyne continuously threw insults across the room, but Joshua could tell D'Vyne was still holding back. For the first time all week, Joshua began to consider the possibility he had said or done something to offend her, therefore, causing the rift between them.

After Joshua's last customer left the saloon, he walked over to D'Vyne's workstation and sat in her chair. He looked up at D'Vyne with an inquisitive stare.

"What's up, Vee? You've been lookin' evil all week."

"For real?" D'Vyne questioned with an unconvincing cheer in her tone. "One of my clients said something like that to me. I'm cool though. What's up? It's Saturday. You wanna go to the bar?"

She was trying to change the subject. Of course, D'Vyne knew she'd been down all week, but she wasn't ready to tell

Joshua about what she had learned from Demetric. Instead, she planned to plant a seed of doubt in Joshua's head about Jayla.

"Yeah," Joshua replied. "Hell yeah, but I can't. Me and Jayla have plans. I'm s'pose to go pick her up in a minute." He glanced at his watch to be sure he wasn't running late.

"Pssh," D'Vyne sighed. "You're changin', Joshua. That girl must have some gorilla pussy because she's changin' you."

She stared down at her hands and began fidgeting with her fingernails. She was sure Joshua would pick up on what she was implying, however, she had no idea if he would run with it.

"Nah, not really. The pussy's mediocre . . ." Joshua replied then chuckled. "Aww, fuck it! I ain't gonna lie. She's got a nigga."

Joshua rose from the chair and gave D'Vyne a hug. As he walked toward the exit of the salon, he noticed through the reflection in the store-front window D'Vyne was watching him closely. He saw her saddened face and had deep empathy for her. He wished he could help her or give his friend some type of refuge from her torture, but he knew D'Vyne had to figure this one out on her own.

As Joshua pulled away from the salon, he started having vivid, almost lifelike flashes of the dream he'd had earlier. He heard a gunshot and saw someone falling to the pavement, but he was unable to see who had fallen. Joshua pulled into the gas station a few blocks away from Perceptions. A cold sweat beaded on his forehead. He nervously looked around as apprehension consumed him. His intuition was telling him something, but he had no idea what that something was. He calmed himself slightly and tried to remember the face he had seen in the premonition, but it was useless because he couldn't remember. He banged his hand on the steering wheel.

"DAMN!" Joshua shouted.

He drove off, a faint fear surrounding him. He had lived his entire life carefree. Now, weeks after the shooting that had nearly taken his life, eerie dreams were haunting him, causing him to worry. For the first time in Joshua's life, he was concerned about his well-being, mentally and physically.

೧•ಬಿ

Jayla impatiently waited inside the alcove of her job. She was waiting Joshua's arrival to pick her up. Although she had spent the night with him, there was an urgency in her needing to speak to him. After leaving Joshua's home that morning, Jayla had stopped by her own house before going to work. She had been at Joshua's house ever since he was released from the hospital, so she wanted to check her mail and her answering machine.

Before entering her home, Jayla pulled the mail from the mailbox, walked inside, and went straight to the answering machine. She pressed play and pounced onto the sofa. While listening to her messages, she thumbed through the accumulation of mail that had come throughout the month. She was surprised by what she saw, and it wasn't the usual bombardment from bill collectors. It was a letter from Dwight.

Jayla had never expected to hear from Dwight again. She had made it clear to him, and everyone else in the visitation room that afternoon, that their relationship was over. Jayla laughed and tossed the letter onto the cocktail table. She was sure it was filled with poetic apologies, begging, and pleading, but she had no interest in hearing them or reading them.

"Nigga, please," Jayla said to herself before rising and walking to the kitchen.

Jayla opened the refrigerator and grabbed an open jar of orange juice from inside. The answering machine continued to spew messages into the air.

"Beep . . . message 16. Bitch! You spendin' nights wit' this nigga now? I guess you think that nigga gettin' blasted was a coincidence, huh?"

Jayla dropped the orange juice container to the floor and rushed to the answering machine. As her hand hovered over the replay button, another message began playing.

"Dollar signs, bitch!" Dwight's evil voice blared from the answering machine speaker. "Dollar signs make niggaz do shit and blame it on love! Don't come up here by Sunday and I'ma make it rain dollaz on yo' head, stank-ass trifflin' bitch!"

Jayla was contorted. Her heart beat erratically. Her thoughts returned to the letter she had dismissed and thrown onto the table. She rushed into the living room and retrieved it. She tore the letter open in panic. The letter read:

Dear Dirty Slut Bitch,

I'm writing because yo stupid ass won't return my calls. I guess pretty-boy Joshua is the reason you think you can leave me, BUT IT'S NOT GONNA HAPPEN! The chances of you leavin me are slimmer than the chances of him livin. He's gonna die and if yo simple ass ain't here by Sunday, you gonna die. I told you, I got dollars on yo head, beyotch! Now test me!

After reading the threatening letter, Jayla fell onto the sofa. The fright Dwight had caused in her returned. She was petrified. She feared that her and Joshua's lives were in jeopardy. Jayla knew the depth of malice in Dwight's heart, so she was sure he was capable of what he had threatened to do. After sulking briefly, she called Joshua but the telephone just rang. She tried again and again there was no answer, so she left for work.

After getting to work and clocking in, Jayla had tried several more times to contact Joshua, still without contact. Eventually, she began to worry. She wondered if something had happened to him. She had even considered punching back out and going to his house, but Joshua had eventually called her. After speaking to him, Jayla was relieved. She told him she needed to talk and he'd decided to pick her up from work that evening. Now, as Jayla peered into the parking lot, searching for Joshua's car, the worry that had consumed her earlier in the day was returning.

"Fuck it," Jayla said to herself as she snatched her belongings from the bench and walked out the supermarket. As she approached her car, a smile spread across her face. Joshua was parked on the side of where she had parked. Jayla scurried to the passenger's side of Joshua's vehicle, got in, and slapped his arm.

"How long have you been out here?" Jayla asked. "I've been waiting in the store."

"Shit, about twenty minutes," Joshua replied and drove off.

During the drive to Joshua's home, he and Jayla shared sporadic, meaningless conversation. Jayla didn't want to talk about what she had experienced earlier in the day while they were driving. She was sure Joshua would be upset and she wanted him to have room to vent. She didn't want to create a situation where he judged her and she could not sit down and defend herself without the fear of being driven off a cliff, so she remained composed.

C3•80

After D'Vyne left the salon, she went to meet with an attorney. She wanted to be sure about her next move. D'Vyne wanted to out everything she knew about what was going on, but she didn't want any backlash for being an accomplice in the cover-up.

As D'Vyne waited, her conscience pecked at her. She felt horrible about keeping secrets from Joshua, especially since the secrets were life threatening. She was desperate for a solution to Joshua's situation. She wanted to tell him about Dwight's blackmailing Demetric into killing him, but she was afraid Joshua would question her sincerity.

After the ordeal went down, D'Vyne had given Joshua the initial excuse Demetric had given her. Although love-crazed-jealousy was no justification for Demetric's actions, it was the explanation he had used. Now that she had learned the truth about the shooting, she questioned whether she should tell Joshua. She was sure Joshua would question the authenticity of the ultimatum Dwight had proposed. She knew Joshua was in love with Jayla, furthermore, she loved seeing Joshua with Jayla, so she wanted to find an alternative to breaking them up.

D'Vyne gently rubbed her stomach. She had become attached to her unborn child. She and Demetric had discussed their options and settled on going through with the pregnancy. She knew Demetric could be on his way to prison, but she'd still chosen to keep the baby because she loved him and their child.

 D'Vyne became irritable, tired of waiting. She glanced at her watch. She had already been waiting half an hour. She sighed and continued rubbing her stomach. As she continued her wait, her thoughts drifted to the night Demetric had committed the murder Dwight held over his head.

It was during the summer of 2005. During that time, Demetric and D'Vyne were going through financial hardships. They had just opened Perceptions and Demetric's clothing boutique. Perceptions was an instant moneymaker, but the boutique was slow in its progression. They were both strapped for cash. D'Vyne was paying excessive bills and loans, including her debt to Demetric, and Demetric was experiencing the devastation of a failed business venture.

Demetric had stopped hustling and had little money and large liabilities. He started pressuring D'Vyne and Joshua to pay their debt to him sooner, but they were unable. D'Vyne was a lot more intelligent and business savvy than Demetric. She tried to explain that she and Joshua couldn't hastily repay their debt to him without the possibility of Perceptions folding. At first, Demetric seemed to be understanding, but as his money shortened, so did his patience.

D'Vyne was sure Demetric would turn back to the dope game. She knew Demetric was a proud man and unwilling to become poverty stricken again, especially with the success of his woman looming around him. D'Vyne became distraught. She didn't want her man to destroy his life. They had come so far together and she was torn by the possibility of Demetric jeopardizing his freedom.

On the night of the incident, D'Vyne was at Demetric's home. She was waiting on him to arrive from the boutique. She knew he had been stressed out, so she wanted to take him out to dinner. D'Vyne believed an outing would be good for them because they had been so consumed with their businesses they hadn't been spending any time together. She thought an outing would give them needed quality time they had been missing. She also wanted to throw some ideas at Demetric about boosting the image of his boutique.

As Demetric entered his home, he noticed D'Vyne sprawled across the sofa. He was shocked to see her there, especially with her busy schedule. He had some things to do, but from the look in her eyes, he was sure she wanted to spend some time with him. He knew they hadn't spent much time together lately, and he wanted to devote some time to her, but he had already committed himself to another engagement.

As Demetric approached D'Vyne, she smiled and rushed to her feet. She was so happy to see him.

"Hey baby!" D'Vyne squealed and wrapped her arms around his shoulders. She kissed him and giggled in a girlish manner.

"What's up, baby girl?" Demetric said to her in a nonchalant manner. He spanked the side of her behind and brushed past her on the way to his bedroom.

"I WANT TO GO OUT TONIGHT," D'Vyne shouted into the hallway of the bedroom. "I know you're probably tired, but I'm hungry and I

want to spend some time with you." It sounded as if she was begging, and she was.

Demetric reappeared from the bedroom, carrying a large duffle bag. He walked to the door and sat the bag down. Then he walked back over to where D'Vyne stood.

"Baby," Demetric started, in an almost apologetic tone, "I know we haven't spent any time together, but niggaz is on the grind." He shook his head. "I can't do it tonight, Vee."

"Work hours are over, Demetric." D'Vyne frowned and placed her hands on her hips. She was becoming upset because she knew what type of mischief Demetric was probably up to.

"Fo' you maybe, but my situation is different. This shit is twenty-four/seven wit' me. It ain't enough hours in a day fo' my grind, ma!" Demetric laughed as he tried to make light of what he had planned for that night.

D'Vyne didn't laugh. Her face remained frozen stiff. She wasn't persuaded by Demetric's theatrics because she loved him and wanted to see him doing the right thing.

"Whatchu fixin' to do, Demetric?" D'Vyne asked in an accusing tone. "What? You fixin' to go sell some drugs?" Tears began to fill D'Vyne's eyes. A nightmare she believed had passed was returning. "You might not give a fuck about your life, but I do! Shit ain't that fucked-up, Demetric! We gonna make it." She was nervous and desperate to change Demetric's mind that night.

Demetric wrapped his arms around D'Vyne's thin waist. He kissed her forehead and stooped to be eye level with her. He did that when he was reassuring her.

"You're right. We're gonna make it, but you're wrong too 'cause I ain't fuckin' wit that work no mo.'." He kissed her cheek and walked away.

D'Vyne watched as Demetric grabbed the duffle bag and walked out the door.

That day had been devastating for her. She had been sure Demetric had lied to her and was selling drugs again. Now, as she sat in an attorney's lobby, sulking over the truth of what had happened that night, D'Vyne wished he had lied to her because drug charges were a lot lighter than the murder charges Demetric could face if Dwight snitched on him.

D'Vyne was brought out of her daze by the calling of her name. She saw a tall, elderly man inviting her into his office. Although D'Vyne knew what she was considering doing would be considered deplorable in her community, she reluctantly went inside and talked to counsel about her situation.

ᏣᎾᎾ•ᎡᎾ

After arriving home, Jayla and Joshua spoke about Dwight's threatening letter and voice messages. Jayla expected Joshua to be upset, but he was the exact opposite. His compassion took Jayla by surprise. She was amazed by the consideration and empathy Joshua showed her.

Joshua seemed to be more concerned with Jayla's well-being and safety than his own, even though Dwight had threatened both of their lives. Joshua asked Jayla to stay at his home with him until everything blew over. Although Jayla really wanted to, she refused because she believed Joshua was asking her to stay out of obligation and force, rather than his own free will.

As Joshua lounged in the living room area of his home, sprawled across the couch, Jayla came into the room and lay between his legs. He placed his arms around her waist and tenderly kissed the side of her cheek.

"I really want you to stay, Jayla," Joshua said in a soft whisper.

Although Jayla had refused to stay with him earlier when they spoke about it, Joshua was determined to change her mind. He knew persistence was one of his stronger qualities and he planned to use it because he wanted to protect his woman.

"I know," Jayla replied with a subtle whine and touched his knee. She hated to tell Joshua she wasn't staying, especially knowing she wanted to, but her drama was her drama and she wanted to keep it that away.

"So, are you gonna stay?" Joshua's tone perked up.

Jayla rolled over, wrapped her arms around Joshua's waist, and laid her face into his stomach.

"I want to," Jayla replied, "but I feel like I'm bad luck to you."

"What? That's crazy, Jayla. Dude . . . he's bluffin'. He either heard about that shit on the news or one of his niggaz saw me over yo' house while I was still fucked-up."

"You think so?" Jayla asked. She didn't think so herself, but she hoped Joshua would say something to convince her.

"Definitely! He's a hoe. Any nigga who would beat up a female like that nigga did you is a broad. That's why the nigga's in the joint fo' some shit he didn't even do! He's scared to tell on the nigga who did it!"

"You got a point because . . .Whew!" She fanned herself. "Life is a long time." She smiled and kissed Joshua's stomach before looking up at him. "It wouldn't be long enough if I could spend it with you though."

"Don't fuck-the-moment-up," Joshua teased.

"Nah, I ain't talkin' about getting married or nothin'. I just—" She suddenly went silent as if she had experienced a loss for words.

"What?" Joshua questioned. "You just what?"

"I love you, Joshua." Jayla sat up. "I feel safe with you. I've never felt safe with any man before."

Joshua peered into Jayla's eyes. He was searching for doubt or contradiction but found none. What she'd said to him was authentic, and the window to her soul assured Joshua of that.

"What about your pops?" Joshua asked, holding his questioning stare. "He's a man."

Suddenly, Jayla went silent again. She lay back onto his lap. She wanted to hide her face because she knew Joshua was searching for something, something she wasn't ready to give him. There were some things she preferred to keep private, and her relationship with her parents was one of them.

Joshua rubbed Jayla's arm. It was a symbol of understanding. He was sure there was something there, something that had depth, but Jayla's silence closed that topic of conversation.

Although eager to know, Joshua didn't want to pressure her. Jayla's silence assured Joshua there was a dark past with her family, so he just held her snugly. He wanted to shield her from every horror of her past with the luxury of knowing he was her present and her future.

As they lay across the sofa in a tender silence, Jayla's thoughts traveled to Dwight. She wondered if he would harm her. "Joshua," Jayla called in a hushed tone, "do you think I should go see Dwight tomorrow?"

"No, but that's your decision. If you go, then he wins."

"How?" Jayla asked, and sat back upright.

"Shit! If you go, that means he got what he wanted. But if you don't, you win because you get the satisfaction of hurtin' him worse than he ever hurt you."

"I guess you're right, but I wasn't going anyway." Jayla smiled although she was still fearful inside. "You wanna go to the bar?"

"Nah; I told you that's over for me. I'm tryin to put some bread together so I can shoot this movie. You can go though; it's cool."

Jayla shook her head defiantly. "No. I ain't goin' out any more unless you take me." She giggled. "I'm a housewife now," Jayla teased.

"Yeah, right," Joshua said before bursting into laughter. "Your ass will burn a bagel, talkin' 'bout you're a housewife." He continued laughing.

Jayla giggled and lay back in Joshua's lap. She was curious about the movie Joshua was intending to shoot. She wondered if he was going to disappear because of Dwight. Most of all, she wondered if she was included. Jayla loved Joshua and would travel to the end of the earth as long as she was with him.

They lay on the sofa of his living room throughout the night, Joshua holding Jayla close until they fell asleep. They desired to be together in the manner they were, but unknown to them, there were a lot of people who did not.

Chapter 11

Andre left his office feeling optimistic about the rest of his day. He was meeting Monica at the furniture store to pick out the furniture for his home. A lot of things were going on in Andre's life. His best friend had been shot by another friend's boyfriend, his home was finished being built, and he was dating a woman who intimidated him. Amongst all the things that were going on, he still had the everyday responsibility of running his company. With all of that on his plate, Andre hoped his day with Monica went smoothly.

Andre knew it was time for a vacation. He planned to go alone, but Monica insisted she go as well. Although he had vaguely planned the trip, Monica had forcefully included herself. After including herself, she'd detailed and paid for the vacation as well. Andre was offended by Monica's presumptuousness. He'd begun to notice her compulsive generosity toward him about a month ago when she started picking up the checks for their dinners. Andre was flattered initially, but after she picked up the bill for their vacation, he realized her generosity was excessive.

Andre worked hard for his money and he spent it with integrity. Although at first, he did not want her to come along with him, after the decision was made, he would have loved to pay for the trip, but Monica had leapt at the chance. He knew Monica came from a wealthy background and he respected that, but he wasn't sure she appreciated his humbled and impoverish beginnings. He was feeling like the victim of parvenu. With that thought, Andre planned to show Monica the strength of his current financial stability during their evening of furniture shopping.

After leaving his home, Andre made a quick stop by Joshua's house. He wanted to have a drink and kill some time before meeting Monica. As he approached Joshua's front door, he heard loud music. As he edged closer, he recognized the music of Tito Puente, a salsa musician. It was blasting. Andre peeked in the porch window and smiled. Joshua and Jayla were inside salsa dancing in their underwear. Andre wanted to knock, but he didn't want to interrupt their moment for the sake of a joke, so he walked back to his vehicle and drove off to meet Monica.

on his way to the furniture store, Andre burst into laughter. The picture of Joshua's and Jayla's salsa dancing invaded his mind. He didn't know much about Jayla, but what he'd seen confirmed she made his friend happy, therefore, she was good in Andre's book. He had also noticed a quiet change in Joshua since he and Jayla had become a couple. Joshua had been partying less and was being more responsible with his spending habits. He was also a lot more conservative with his views and opinions about women. He was sure he could attribute the change to Jayla and the love she and Joshua shared.

Andre wished he and Monica's relationship had the spontaneity Joshua and Jayla's did. Although he enjoyed the time he spent with Monica, he noticed their outings were always on a schedule. Andre was a businessman and lived by a schedule daily in his line of work; therefore, a planned social life was unattractive to him. He desired some things to happen unrehearsed, especially sex.

Not to be mistaken, Andre loved his and Monica's first sexual experience together, but only in the sense of pleasure. Otherwise, he felt like he had taken part in a high-scale pornography movie. Monica had invited him over for dinner a few days after Joshua's shooting. When he entered her home, he'd nearly tripped over the welcoming mat because the entire house was dark.

"Damn, baby, the lights got shut off?" He chuckled as Monica led him through her lightless home.

"Nope," Monica replied with a light giggle.

She smiled as she walked Andre into her four-season sunroom. The room was lit by candles and the glow of the moon. Colorful pillows surrounded a cocktail table decorated like a dining room table with Tiffany china place settings. Andre was impressed.

"This looks nice," said Andre. He chuckled. *"It's real nice, but where's the food?"*

"Shut up, man," Monica replied with a giggle.

After Monica brought the food, they both sat and shared some banter as they enjoyed their meals. Andre was pleased with Monica's assertiveness and hospitality. After they ate, Monica excused herself from the sunroom. Andre assumed she was using the rest room and would be returning shortly. After fifteen or twenty minutes Andre became uneasy. He believed Monica was being rude and dismissive for leaving him alone for so long during their date. As he set impatiently awaiting Monica's return, he pondered over things to say to her. His legs were becoming restless from sitting so low to the floor and his patience was shortening.

Suddenly, Andre heard footsteps from a short distance. He turned to see where they were coming from, and his unease settled at the sight of Monica as she swayed across the threshold of the sunroom. Monica looked amazing. Her cocoa dark skin had the appearance of satin. She wore a tan lace lingerie set with French-

cut bottoms. She grabbed Andre's hand and led him through her home. Her four-inch stilettos echoed across the mahogany wood flooring the home. She walked Andre into her bedroom.

Andre looked around the spacious bedroom in awe. It was immaculately decorated. A king-size cherry oak contemporary bed sat in the center of the room atop a huge multi-earth-tone-colored rug. The cherry wood baseboards aligning the room accentuated the rest of the oak furnishings. Andre sat on the bed and started removing his shoes.

Monica used a remote to ignite the fireplace. She sat next to Andre, wrapped her arms around his neck, and passionately kissed him. She continued kissing him, removing his shirt. After removing his shirt, she trailed his chest and stomach with kisses as she knelt and began stripping him of his pants.

Andre's penis was fully erect. His blood circulated rapidly causing an inhuman beat to his heart and a visible pulsation of his manhood. Monica had completely unclothed him, exposing his innate masculinity. She kissed his lips and smiled.

"You have to bathe first, Andre." She smiled and pointed to the bathroom. "I've already run you a bath."

Andre's face cringed. He was taken aback. Monica had purposely teased him into believing they were about to have sex, only to insult him. Although Andre wanted to protest, he wanted to get laid also, so he went to the bathroom. He wondered if Monica had smelled something he hadn't. After entering the bathroom, he sniffed himself. He smelled fine to himself. He had always thought of himself as a cleanly person, but it was evident to him Monica did not share the same sentiment.

After bathing, Andre walked back into the bedroom. Monica was sprawled across the bed. Her body glistened as she lay in a sexy pose. Andre smiled for the first time since he was asked to bathe. He was eased by the light flickering from the fireplace giving Monica's body an opulent glow. As Andre reached the bed, Monica rose into an upright position. Andre sat and Monica slid behind him and kissed his back.

"Lie on your back," Monica instructed Andre.

Andre lay across the bed and Monica began oiling his body. He wanted to short circuit her prolonged foreplay because he was ready to enter her, but the deep-tissue massage became soothing. After the massage, Monica introduced him into the world of Tantric sex.

As Andre reminisced about he and Monica's intimate experience, he frowned. He realized the power he had given her over him. He felt emasculated because he had no power in his relationship. Monica controlled everything. He didn't even have free reign in their sex life. He felt defeated.

"Damn!" Andre whispered to himself, rubbing his goatee. "She's even pickin' my furniture out."

He knew his relationship would make a change for the worst after he introduced Monica to his friends. She had seen him at his most-vulnerable moment when they were visiting Joshua and D'Vyne in the hospital; therefore, he was sure she was trying to exploit that. Finally, he shook his head and chuckled. He tried to denounce the negative thoughts invading his thoughts. He wanted to have a good outing and he knew it would be impossible if he continued to have phantom relationship drama.

‹з•во

As Monica pulled into the parking lot of the furniture store, she used her cellphone to contact Andre. Andre was already inside the store. He instructed her to come inside and he would meet her at the entrance. After parking, Monica entered the store. As she crossed the entrance, Andre awaited her with a smile.

"Hey, baby."

Monica wrapped her arms around his broad shoulders. Andre kissed her and pulled her close. Although he still had thoughts about the issues of control, he had settled himself some.

"Hey, babe," Andre said after their kiss. He took her hand in his and began walking.

Monica's eyes roved throughout the vicinity of the entrance. She hoped no one had seen their kiss. Monica wasn't a woman who endorsed public affection. She believed in discretion in her personal life, especially her sex life. She believed sex was a private engagement of two souls. A secret, of sorts, that should not be shared with voyeuristic eyes. As they walked the aisles of the store hand-in-hand, admiring the furniture displays, she felt restricted and uncomfortable with the hand holding. She believed men and women who found comfort in holding hands in public suffered from possessive ways. In essence, Monica wasn't fond of the restraint of relationships, but she loved Andre, therefore, she tried her best to adapt to his passionate habits.

As they strolled through the bedroom displays, Andre suddenly released Monica's hand and jumped onto an ultra-king-size bed. He smiled and stretched his arms out toward Monica.

"Come on," Andre called out to her with his arms still outstretched.

"No," Monica replied, shaking her head defiantly. "Get off that bed, Andre." She spoke in a muffled tone, her eyes roving the room in search of employees. Monica was sure potential customers weren't allowed to touch the displays. She walked closer to Andre. "Get off!" she demanded.

"All right; help me up." Andre reached for her.

Monica stepped closer and took Andre's hand. As she went to pull him up, he pulled her onto the bed with him. Monica tried to leap from the bed, but Andre forcefully pulled her into his lap. He started kissing and tickling her playfully, causing her to laugh hysterically. Although she wasn't into the type of intimate displays they were having, she found herself enjoying their camaraderie.

"I'm buying this," Andre said.

He kissed Monica's neck as she lay between his legs. Andre knew Monica was initially uncomfortable, but he felt her tension settle as their bodies molded into each other's.

"Can I help you break it in?" Monica asked seductively, rubbing her foot on his inner thigh. She'd nearly forgotten where they were because she felt loose lying with Andre.

As they lay across the bed, they suddenly heard someone clearing their throat. They turned to see an older, attractive white woman towering over them. Monica's eyes bulged from her head. Her dark skin became flush. Although the woman was greeting them with a pristine smile, Monica was severely embarrassed.

She jumped from the bed, looking as if she were ready to sprint away.

"We're sorry," Monica apologized to the woman. "I know we shouldn't have." She looked over to the bed, noticing Andre still casually lay across it as if he was unfazed by the woman's presence.

The sales woman continued smiling. "No," she said with a wave of her hand, "you're fine. I'm just a commission hound. I wanted to assist you, that's all." She reached for Monica's hand. "I'm Anna."

They shook during their brief introduction, then Monica introduced her to Andre. Andre smiled and waved from the bed display, but he still hadn't moved.

"Okay," Anna said, "you all continue. You can have me paged if you need my assistance." She smiled and waved as she walked away.

Monica fell back onto the bed with Andre. She was relieved. She was sure Anna would try to humiliate them for the way she and Andre were carrying on in the store, but she hadn't. Instead, Anna was polite and offered her assistance rather than her judgment. Andre and Monica strolled throughout the furniture store for the next couple of hours before they concluded their shopping.

Monica was tempted to pay for Andre's furniture, but she thought against it. She was sure Andre had noticed her generosity, therefore, she kept her money in her pocket this time. Although Monica was successful and financially stable, her life wasn't as polished a few years prior to meeting Andre. She had developed a habit of spending money on her men. It all started with her last relationship. The last man that Monica was with, Akil, mesmerized her with his wittiness and charm.

Monica was a frequent guest at The Club House, a poetry lounge, and a member of the National African American Poet Society, or NAAPS. She attended almost every event and was accepted with the same warmth each time, so it wasn't surprising to her when Akil pursued her after her gift of lyric.

Monica had just finished her rendition of Damon Purvey's Rhapsody of a Madman *at NAAPS' recognition of his contributions to the urban community. As she left the stage, the crowd roared and snapped excessively, approving her deliverance of the poems. Monica was in a state of euphoria. She smiled and waved, rushing to the restroom. After leaving the restroom, Monica was approached by Akil. She smiled politely and tried to brush past him, but he stepped directly into her path. Monica stopped abruptly.*

"Excuse me," Monica said. She held a smile on her face although she was steaming eternally because she knew what would come next.

"Monica," Akil said with a smile and reached for her hand.

Monica was apprehensive because Akil's face wasn't a familiar one to her, but she allowed him her hand because she wanted to be polite. Akil firmly held her hand and placed his other hand atop hers. He wanted to make consuming eye contact with Monica.

"My raison d'être *is life, love, and community. The reception of the tongue is the acknowledgment and understanding of emotion. Your rendition of the rhapsody was angelic and spoken in a passion that only a kindred soul could comprehend."*

Monica smiled and politely pulled her hand away from Akil. She was flattered by his attempt, but unmoved by his game. Monica had seen it all before, so she let Akil know as much.

"So," Monica began, "I'm an angel and we're kindred souls . . . So, I guess that makes you an angel, too, huh?" She giggled, trying to appear shy and schoolgirlish. She was sure Akil, like any man, would accept her bait and she would use it to slaughter him.

"No," Akil replied, "of course not." He smiled and reached for her hand again. "That makes me Akil by name, but that alone doesn't define me."

"Man, please!" Monica burst into a boisterous laughter. She was amused by Akil's choice of wordplay. "Good try, wrong girl, playboy." She continued laughing.

"Try what?" Akil asked. He seemed to be puzzled by Monica's reaction.

"You're trying to consume me with words." Monica laughed. "It's not going to work with me, but look, you can saddle up and roll with me. I'll be your wing woman." She snickered and patted his shoulder in a patronizing manner. "I'll turn you on to some sistahs who'll love to have some of that 'Venus is the woman' bullshit."

"What?" asked Akil. "Nah, ma, you've got me mistaken. I was giving you the gift of poetry, flirtin' and tryin' to get to know you, to show you I'm not a misogynist." He shook his head in disappointment and walked away.

Monica shook her head and walked away as well. She was used to guys like Akil. Within the poetry community in Detroit, there were several young attractive wordsmiths who wooed women at *the bookstores and clubs, but Monica refused to be one of those women. Not that night and definitely not with Akil. As she reached her table, she heard the announcer call Akil to the stage. Monica smiled and shook her head again because she was sure she had exposed him. Akil came onto the stage to a flattering welcome. One that far surpassed Monica's as he took the microphone from its stand.*

"Hey," Akil greeted the audience. "How is everyone doing? For those who don't know me, I'm Akil, a Bronx native and a visiting poet. As I came, so shall I leave. I'd like to take something with me and leave you with this." Akil smiled and began his spoken word.

As Akil spoke, Monica looked on in awe. She was impressed with his delivery. He spoke elegantly, pulling the crowd into the depth of his words. Akil's tongue was rhythmic and passionate. Although Monica had been repulsed by Akil's forwardness earlier, she lost herself in his verse. She became vulnerable and powerless. After the completion of his piece, the crowd erupted. Akil had captivated everyone, including Monica. It was now her who sought Akil out. As Akil left the stage, Monica approached him with a reconsidering smile.

"Okay," Monica began, "okay, that was nice." She casually touched his chest.

"Even though you believe I'm a womanizer?" Akil smiled.

"Oh, so you're a poet and a mind reader?" Monica giggled.

"So you do believe I'm a womanizer?" Akil rubbed his chin, briefly staring at Monica. He pointed at her. "Yeah, that's what you thought because you offered me the naïve sistahs on a platter."

"Man, please! I was seeing if you'd bite." Monica laughed and waved Akil's observation off as nonsense.

"Did I?"

"No, and my thoughts of you have changed."

"To what?" Akil looked apprehensive about hearing Monica's answer.

"I think you're arrogant! Too arrogant actually." Monica smiled.

"Why?" Akil asked with a slight chuckle. "Is it because I'm sarcastic?" He smiled and raised his eyebrows.

"Bam! You are a psychic." Monica chuckled.

"So your sarcastic, presumptive, and judging comments are what?"

"Humor!"

"I see what it is." Akil chuckled. "You're one of those types who judge but aren't prepared to be judged." He nodded his head, reassuring himself that his assessment of Monica was right.

"Are we going to play word games or are you going to ask me out?"

"I'm going home tomorrow, but we can keep in touch."

"How about you touch me tonight?"

Monica batted her eyelashes and giggled as Akil took her hand. She and Akil slept together that night. She was overwhelmed by his confidence. They kept in touch and created a long-distance sexual friendship. After months of traveling, it became too monotonous, so Monica offered to help Akil relocate to Detroit. Akil was against the move originally, but he eventually succumbed to her persuasion.

After moving to Detroit, Akil tried to find work. He was uncomfortable with being taken care of by Monica, but the job market was rough at that time. After months of failed interviews, Monica offered to pay for Akil's schooling; Akil accepted. He attended Wayne State for the first semester, but his grades weren't impressive. Akil soon found out his savvy wordplay wasn't going to carry him through college. After dropping out, he fell into a deep depression. He began blaming his failures on everyone and everything.

Day in and day out, Monica had to hear the accusations of the typical black man. "The white man's tryin' to hold a brotha back." She was tired, so she did the unthinkable. She offered Akil a high-paying position at her company. She was sure Akil would be bruised, and her assumption was right. Akil's ego was crushed. He rejected Monica's offer. He knew the feeling of working for his woman was too overwhelming, so therefore, the actual deed was unfathomable. He refused to stoop that low, so he made the choices of a broken man.

Akil hooked up with some of his friends from his home town. They started a heroin pipeline from Harlem to Detroit. Even though Monica knew something was suspicious about Akil's newfound wealth, she played naïve. She knew he was desperate, so she allowed him to settle.

Things were going great between Monica and Akil after his hustle took off, but shortly into the good times, the tragedy *occurred. Akil was robbed and killed by some guys he was doing business with. voice Monica loved Andre and knew he was structured, she'd done things for him to assure him she was always available for his needs. She lived daily with the guilt of allowing Akil to settle for a life that was beneath him, but she would never make that mistake again.*

Cヌ•ヌ>

Joi high-stepped out of her office building. She was elated. Her life was ameliorating. She had just received a promotion to regional manager. Joi knew her capabilities; on the other hand, she also knew about the negative connotation of women excelling in their workplaces. Therefore, she didn't expect to propel through the ranks of management so fast. Joi was unwilling to prostitute herself for a better position. With that compounded by the heavy competition of white men, Joi's rise to the top was everything but a walk in the park. She had earned her position by merit and she was proud of herself.

As Joi entered her vehicle, she exhaled loudly and smiled. She had weathered a storm in her personal life because she had accomplishments to gain in her career. She had retained her composure throughout her climb to the top. She'd survived the heartache of Damon's betrayal and deception. She had weathered the storm of her own prejudices concerning David. And her reunion with Major was looking promising.

Joi loved Major and she attributed her emotional recovery to him. He showered her with the love she felt worthy of having. He had given her everything she desired from a man, especially understanding. Joi had become so watchful of men after Damon's treachery, but that caution had dissipated under the loving ways of Major. He had broken through Joi's barricade and she was ecstatic she could finally let her guard down and love again.

After getting home, Joi lit a candle, put on some music, and called Major. The thought of hearing his voice caused her to smile as she awaited his answer.

"Hey, baby," Joi sang into the telephone after receiving an answer.

"Oh, hey, ma," Major replied in a bland tone.

"Is this a good time?" Joi sensed Major was under the microscope of another woman.

"Not really. I was on my way out, but I can call you once I'm stationary. I ain't tryin' to be talkin' and drivin'."

"Is that what it is?" Joi grunted after her response. She was sure that there was more to what held Major distant from her.

"Yeah." Major chuckled, signaling he had heard her angst, but refused to address it. "So I'll be calling."

"Okay," Joi replied in a snide manner. "I guess I'll be waiting."

She disconnected the call. She held her cellphone in her hand and stared at it as if it had betrayed her in some way. She smiled weakly and let out a depressing sigh. She was sure Major was with a woman when she had called and that bothered her.

Joi wanted to share her good news with Major. She believed they had that type of relationship, but her assumption became disappointment after the call. Although she and Major hadn't consummated their relationship sexually or verbally, Joi was given the impression she and Major were together. He'd made a commitment to Joi with his actions that didn't need confirmation with words.

Now Joi lay across her couch lonely and confused. She couldn't understand the complexity of her and Major's relationship. What was it? Were they dating? Were they a couple? Or was she just fooling herself? In her confused state, she picked up the phone. Her first thought was to call Joshua, but she didn't feel up to the ridicule he would surely give her, so she settled on calling Andre. She had questions and doubts she wanted to discuss and she was sure Andre would have answers.

"Hi, Andre," Joi sang into the telephone. The smile she had earlier reappeared. Andre was her best friend and she was sure he would give her the real.

"Joi," Andre responded, "how're you doing? I was just talking to Monica about you."

Joi paused before answering. She was jealous. She and Andre shared their loneliness, but now he had Monica and she was in a romantic dilemma.

"I hope it was something good, lil fella," Joi replied with a snicker.

"Nope!" Andre chuckled. "Nah, I wish I could say yeah, but I don't lie to my peoples." He continued laughing.

"Fuck you then, punk." Joi laughed. "Guess what?" Joi smiled brightly.

"What's up?"

"I got a raise and a promotion! I'm the regional manager now!"

"All right then! That's good news. I thought you were about to say you're pregnant or getting married." Andre chuckled. "You know we're lonely buddies." He continued laughing.

"I thought Monica was around? Boy, I know you didn't say that shit in front of her."

"Nah! She ain't over here. I was talking to her on the phone a few minutes before you called."

"Oh!" Joi giggled. "I was fixin' to say."

"Nah; it's cool. So what's been going on other than your promo? Have you spoken to D'Vyne?"

"A few days ago, but I'm not going to her house. I'm still uncomfortable with Demetric."

"Yeah, I feel you, but he doesn't live with her."

"So?" Joi retorted with intensity. She wasn't up for an argument with Andre, so she changed the subject. "Andre, I need some advice. I don't wanna hear any jokes either."

"If it's relationship advice, you should be calling Joshua." Andre chuckled. "I hate to admit it, but shit, his relationship has more harmony in it than any of ours." He chuckled.

"You ain't never lied, Andre!" Joi laughed. She knew that, as far from reality as it seemed, what Andre had said was the truth.

"I shouldn't be puttin' their business out there but fuck it." Andre laughed. "This shit is too good to keep to myself. I caught him and Jayla salsa dancing butt as naked."

"Pssh," Joi sighed. "I wish someone would salsa with me because this negro is tripping."

"My exact sentiments! Monica is cool, but she ain't got no spontaneity. None; you feel me?"

"Yeah, I feel you, but this is about my problems, punk." Joi giggled. "Major won't be intimate with me, and I called his house and I think another female was over there."

"If my man ain't fuckin' you and he had another female over there, it should be obvious what's going on, Joi. I don't even know why you're wasting your time messing with Major."

"Yeah," Joi replied with a loud sigh. "D'Vyne told me that eaten food was garbage. I shouldn't have even gone that way again." She sounded defeated.

"Yeah, that sounds like some shit D'Vyne would say." Andre chuckled.

"Hold on, Andre," Joi said after hearing a knock on her door.

She rushed to the door and peeked through the peephole. Major was on the other side of her door smiling. She opened the door and allowed him to come inside.

"Hey, baby!" She smiled and closed the door behind him.

"Hey, ma," Major wrapped his arms around Joi's waist and kissed her neck. He then kissed her lips and smiled.

"Hold on," Joi said, holding her index finger in the air. "I've got Andre on the phone." She pulled away from Major and rushed back to the telephone.

"Hello. Andre, Major just came by, so I'll call you later."

"A'ight," Andre replied. "When you play with fire, you get burned."

Joi disconnected the call and went back into the front room with her company. Major had already made himself at home. He was sitting on the love seat, so Joi slid beside him. She was happy to see him and her excitement showed in her smile.

"So what brought you by?" Joi asked.

"I felt bad about brushing you off, so I just shot right over."

"I thought you had something to do?"

"I do," Major replied with a nod. "I want you to come with me."

"Where?" Joi smiled in a girlish manner.

"Get dressed and you'll see." Major teetered his eyebrows and smiled.

Joi leapt to her feet and rushed into her bedroom. As she hustled past Major, he lasciviously slapped her behind, causing it to billow. Joi looked over her shoulder and smiled at him. Although the butt slap was mediocre in Joi's opinion, she was pleased because it was the first display of intimacy Major had shown since their reunion.

Joi wanted Major. She brushed his suspicious behavior off. Although she had sensed something earlier when she called, his arrival to her apartment had convinced her that her speculation was wrong. She knew Major was a lot of things, but he wasn't a liar. She knew Major had been loyal to her throughout their relationship—a relationship she missed and desperately desired to rekindle.

CS•BO

After speaking to Joi, Andre sat around thinking about what she was potentially getting herself into. He was concerned about Joi because he knew how naïve she was when it concerned men. He had stressed his disapproval of Joi seeing Major again, but he knew there was little he could do to prevent it from happening. He was aware of the feelings Joi held for Major, but he didn't know the true extent of the emotional constraints Major held on Joi.

After briefly pondering Joi's predicament, Andre left his home. He was meeting Monica and the people who were delivering his furniture at his new home. Andre was excited about his home being finished, but the events had not played out as he would have liked them to. Although Andre was successful and in a stable relationship, he still felt empty. He thought about his situation often and usually blamed his sense of unfulfillment on his expectations.

Andre knew his expectations of himself were high. He was also aware of the ground he had covered, but he still had a piece of joy missing. He was without something and it stagnated him from true happiness, but he was also unaware of what it was or how to obtain it. Andre's incomprehension was bothering him. He was used to putting the pieces together, but in his own life he was failing to do so. He had assumed he needed a counterpart, but the feeling of emptiness had remained long after he and Monica's relationship started.

He considered the possibility of Monica not being the right woman for him, but in essence, she was all he had ever desired. Monica had showed Andre the integrity of a great woman. She was what any man would consider worthy. She corrected Andre without bruising his ego and agreed with him without stroking it. Essentially, Monica was what Andre had always desired in a woman, but his desire was now faltering.

As Andre drove up to his new home, his lips rose into a bright smile. Monica was there with the movers. She waved to Andre as he got out of his car. Once he reached her, he leaned in and kissed her cheek.

"Hey, baby," Andre said. "Sorry I'm so late."

"It's okay," Monica replied with a smile. She then looked over to the movers. "COME ON, GUYS! HEAVY FURNITURE FIRST," she yelled, taking control of the scene.

Andre watched as Monica directed the men. He admired her motivating personality. The men marched the furniture into the home on Monica's drum. Her vision was exceptional. She delegated each of the men a responsibility. Andre was impressed. He knew Monica operated a successful company, but he had never seen her in action.

After the men left, Andre snuck behind Monica, wrapped his arms around her waist, and kissed the back of her neck. "So we break the bed in now, right," Andre whispered in Monica's ear.

"Why were you late, Andre?" Monica spun around and stared into his face. She had a reproving look in her eyes.

"Traffic," Andre replied. He was surprised by her contemptuous stare, so he walked away in an attempt to avoid it.

Monica followed behind him and stood over him, hands on hips, as he sat on the sofa.

"If that was an excuse, go with it, but it wasn't a good one." Monica playfully rolled her eyes and turned her nose up at Andre.

"Come sit down with me for a minute." Andre patted the space next to him on the sofa.

Monica sat and leaned into his chest. She sighed and looked up to him.

"You need more structure, Andre. What if I wasn't here when the deliverymen arrived?"

Andre shrugged his shoulders and said, "They may have left and I may have had to reschedule the delivery, but I would definitely have gotten my shit." He laughed and pulled her closer into his hold.

"I guess you're right, but I like being on time with some things, especially my business engagements." She smiled and snuggled into the mold that their bodies were creating.

"So, what type of shit don't you like being on time for?" Andre chucked. "For me, I think schedules should be left at the office. At home, shit should be a little more unexpected. That's what keeps relationships interesting. You feel me?" He tickled Monica gently, trying to ease the hint about her calculating and predictable way to her without any confrontation.

"Yeah," Monica replied between laughs from Andre's ticking, "I feel you, but other things keep relationships interesting, too."

"Yeah! Good sex and good communication." Andre nodded. "I feel you. Other variables come into play, but spontaneity is the adhesive that keeps couples together."

"Whatever, man." Monica giggled. "You sound like Jesse Jackson. Spontaneity is the adhesive that keeps people together." She mimicked Andre's last comment, and both of them burst into laughter.

"Well, what else?" Andre asked. He knew Monica was hinting at something she wanted him to know, just as he was hinting something to her.

"Kids." Monica smiled.

"Yeah, but that isn't an issue for us."

Monica went silent. She knew it was time to deliver the news to Andre.

"Yes, it is," Monica replied in a shy tone. She turned to Andre and smiled. "I'm pregnant, Andre."

Andre stared at Monica. He was in shock, unable to reply to what she had just revealed to him. He tried to smile, but his mouth just hung open instead.

Monica's smile vanished. "You'd better say something," she demanded sassily.

"Baby," Andre finally responded, "I'm so happy! I am, but I know it's your decision, so I don't wanna put any pressure on you."

He wanted to let Monica know he supported her in any way she chose to handle the situation, but he really wanted her to have the child.

"I'm having the baby, Andre." Monica smiled. "I thought about it. I've known for a couple of weeks."

Andre pulled her deeper into his embrace and kissed her neck. He unclothed her and made passionate love to her. For the first time since their sexual relationship began, they shared an instantaneous moment of intimacy together.

Although Andre had been having doubts concerning his and Monica's relationship, the news of her pregnancy was good for him. It was good for their relationship as well because it gave them the lift they needed to continue. As they made love to one another, Andre felt a feeling of fulfillment and Monica felt the warmth of being cherished by a loving man.

 CB•BO

Major pulled into the parking lot of a strip mall on West Seven Mile. Although he had every intention of wounding Joi deeply, he had to keep his rage hidden. He was playing a long con, a con that would rob Joi of any hope of finding true love. Major exited his car and walked around to the passenger's side. He opened the door, allowing Joi to get out as well.

"Come on, ma," Major said as he took Joi's hand and led her toward a storefront.

"What's going on, Major?" Joi was puzzled about what was going on.

Major unlocked the store. He and Joi entered the empty dwelling and he turned to her and smiled. He then slid behind her and wrapped his arms around her waist.

"This be me," Major whispered into Joi's ear.

"This is your new store?" Joi was excited for Major. She knew how hard he had been searching for a place to run his business from, so she was proud of him.

"Yeah, baby. This is it. I bought my partner out and relocated. It's official! I'm a sole proprietor."

Major was excited himself and Joi could feel his excitement because the erection growing in his pants was bulging into Joi's curvaceous mound. He was sure Joi felt his massive erection, so he purposely pressed his bulge deeper into the softness of her derriere.

"I'm proud of you."

Joi turned and touched his face. She kissed him passionately and gently palmed his manhood. She suggestively smiled at him and walked off toward the door. She locked the door, closed the blinds, and walked back to Major in a seductive sway. She was ready to seize her opportunity. She wrapped her arm around his neck, kissed him, and gently messaged his phallus.

"What's up, ma?" Major asked with a bright smile. He was sure Joi wanted some participation from him, but he didn't want a sexual relationship with her. His only interest was in humiliating her.

Joi placed her finger over his lips. "Shhh," she said.

She smiled and seductively fell to her knees. She unbuckled Major's jeans, letting them fall to his ankles. She began kissing him between his thighs as he stood above her. Joi slowly stroked his manhood. Major breathed heavily as Joi pulled on his shaft with a slow, tantric stroke, causing his erection to throb for release. He held back. He knew what Joi wanted, but he refused to give in to her. He was on a mission.

Joi kissed the crown of Major's penis. "I missed you," she said before taking the length of him into her mouth. She continued her oral pleasure with slow pulls.

Major's body betrayed his mind. His plan was lost in the act of being pleasured. He loved the way Joi performed oral sex because he had taught her. He'd molded her into what he wanted her to be and she'd obeyed him. Her sexuality was his masterpiece and he was enjoying it. His body stiffened, and his leg shook and weakened as he climaxed.

Joi swallowed and looked up to him. She wanted approval for her obedience. His body had called and she had answered. As she rose to her feet, she pulled Major's pants up as well. She smiled as she buckled his belt. She primped his shirt and kissed his lips.

"You ready?" Joi asked with a smile.

"Hell yeah," Major replied.

He knew Joi wanted reciprocation. He knew she wanted him to take her home and make passionate love to her. And he was tempted to obey the call of lust, but he couldn't do it. Not at the expense of his ultimate goal. Although he knew there could be problems after he turned her sexual seduction down, especially after her earthly display of oral erotica, he knew his plan would definitely be destroyed if he accepted.

As they drove away from the strip mall, Joi anxiously gyrated in her seat. She was sure Major would be more amazing than he was when they were teenagers. She remembered what he was like in bed and anticipated his prowess. She had shown initiative in the emptiness of Major's store. She had given him what he liked and she expected to get hers in return once they made it to her apartment.

Chapter 12

D'Vyne laughed hysterically. It had been a while since she and Joi shared a story worthy of a laugh. Their friendship had been filled with one ordeal after another, so sharing a joy-filled moment was a good turn of events for them.

"Cut it out," D'Vyne said to Joi between laughs. She could barely hold the phone to her ear she was laughing so hard. "Are you serious?"

"Yes!" Joi chuckled. "I am serious, girl. I even swallowed . . . I don't know, D'Vyne." She sighed.

D'Vyne sensed Joi's anxiety. She recognized it in her sigh because she too had been doing that a lot lately. Although they were sharing a goodhearted conversation, D'Vyne decided to turn it down a notch. She didn't want to have too much of a laugh at Joi's expense.

"So what was his excuse?" D'Vyne asked.

"He swore he had some business to take care of. He did tell me he was busy before he came by, but damn!"

Although D'Vyne tried to hold back, a faint giggle escaped her lips. She couldn't resist.

"Came by?" D'Vyne laughed. "Don't you mean came in your mouth?" She continued laughing.

"Shut up, whitey," Joi teased back.

"I'm sorry, Joi. You know I love you, but you set yourself up for that one." D'Vyne snickered. "If he was busy, he was busy. Don't worry about it. He'll finish what you started."

"I guess, but I'm worried about it, D'Vyne. I think he has someone else."

"You think? Joi, please. You know that man is fuckin' somebody else. Shit, he ain't fuckin' you! I told you, Joi, eaten food is garbage. You should have left him there."

"I'm starting to think you're right."

D'Vyne giggled. "I'm always right."

"Yeah, well, let me get off this telephone. I love you, whitey." Joi giggled.

"Whatever. I love you, too, loved one." D'Vyne hung up the phone. She shook her head, smiled, and giggled. She was feeling a lot better after speaking to Joi.

Prior to Joi calling, D'Vyne was sitting around Perceptions contemplating her next move. She and Demetric were distant. He came by her home daily, but their relationship was in shambles. D'Vyne couldn't get over Joshua's shooting. She'd tried to desperately, but the discomfort of knowing Demetric still had motive to kill Joshua wouldn't let her conscience settle. As D'Vyne's thoughts traveled, they were interrupted by the phone.

"Hello," D'Vyne greeted upon answering the phone. "Perceptions; this is D'Vyne speaking."

"Vee, this is Andre. Is Joshua in?"

"Nope; he hasn't been in all week. He put his appointments off until Sunday and Monday."

"So, I guess I don't get no heads-up, huh? I'm gonna find me another barber." Andre chuckled.

"Yeah right, nigga."

"I have a surprise for y'all. Be looking for an invitation in the mail."

"For what?"

"I thought I said a surprise." Andre laughed.

"I'ma kick yo' ass, Andre." D'Vyne chuckled. "Smart mouth butt."

"I love you," Andre said in a teasing manner.

"I can't tell. Don't nobody come to see me no more." She pouted playfully.

"Yeah; things are different though. We're all adults; everybody has responsibilities. I'm sure we all would like to get together more often, but hey, life's a bitch."

"Right," D'Vyne agreed. "I know, but damn!"

"Look, Vee. Make sure you check your mail. I need everyone to be there. I love you, D'Vyne."

"Love you, too. Bye, loved one."

D'Vyne hung the phone up. She knew Andre was holding back. She didn't know what, but she was sure he was. She knew her friends were privately discussing her situation behind her back, and she figured no one wanted to come around because of Demetric. D'Vyne's friends were her world. They had always expected her to have their backs and she did. Now that she needed the warmth of friendship and constant consoling, there was no one willing to play that position for her. She rubbed her growing stomach and smiled. She wondered what Andre's surprise was. Of course, she had an idea but she didn't want to assume.

After sitting around a little while longer, D'Vyne closed the salon and left. She now felt a reluctance to go home. She knew Demetric would be there and she didn't want to face him, especially knowing the next morning she would be betraying a code Demetric sacredly lived by.

പ•ഇ

Jayla looked up from the sofa as the door opened and Joshua walked in. He was smiling and had a gay bounce in his step. His smile was infectious, causing Jayla's lips to spread as well.

"Why are you smiling like that?" Jayla asked.

"I just left my other woman's house," Joshua replied and pounced atop Jayla as she lay on the sofa. He playfully kissed and wrestled her.

"Don't get cut, nigga." Jayla giggled.

"I got a building today." Joshua leaned upright and smiled, staring down at Jayla.

"A building? For what?" Jayla was confused. She knew Joshua was trying to put something together, but she had no idea it concerned purchasing a building.

"I'm starting my own salon."

"Why? I thought you loved Perceptions."

"And I thought you'd be happy fo' a nigga. What's your problem?"

"I ain't got no problem, boy. I am happy for you, but I can't understand why or how you could leave something you love." Jayla shrugged her shoulders.

Joshua now understood what Jayla's angst was about. He realized she was equating their relationship with his career change.

"You're trippin', Jayla! Me leavin' Perceptions ain't got shit to do with our relationship."

Jayla snapped her neck, turning toward Joshua.

"Bullshit if it doesn't!" Jayla replied. "First thing yo' friends gonna say is I'm pullin' you away. Pssh! They're probably already sayin' it!"

"Joi, Andre, and D'Vyne, they're my peoples, no doubt about it, but I don't give-a-fuck what they think. I'm up! It's that time, so fuck 'em. I gotta do me. Niggaz shootin' me and shit. Pssh! They got me fucked-up!"

Jayla touched Joshua's face with her palm and smiled. "I'm sorry, boo," Jayla said, rubbing Joshua's face. "I'm happy for you." She kissed him.

"Good," Joshua replied and nodded, "cause I thought I was gonna have to bring my Mack hand out." He stared at his palm in a pimpish manner before bursting into laughter.

Although Jayla was cautious about Joshua's sudden need to leave Perceptions, she understood the reasoning behind his decision. Initially, she was worried their relationship would have the same fate if things got rocky between them, but Joshua had convinced her differently. Jayla loved Joshua and couldn't imagine being without him. He was her shelter from the storm her life had been captured in and she appreciated him. Jayla left the living room, returned with a letter in her hand, and handed it to him.

"When did this come?" Joshua asked.

"Today," Jayla answered. She bounced her leg sassily and placed her hands on her hips. "It came while you were out with your other woman." She giggled and playfully kicked Joshua's foot.

"That's wife-in-law to you." Joshua chuckled. "This is an invitation to a party. Andre done rented one of them new houses off the river by the mayor's spot."

"Damn! Andre must be doin' good, huh?"

"Shit, that nigga still got paper he's been savin' since grade school. True story! That nigga's probably millionaire status." Joshua nodded his head, assuring Jayla he was telling the truth.

"You'll be there once your new shop opens." Jayla pinched Joshua's cheek and smiled.

"Bullshit! We gonna spend our bread. I ain't on that tightwad shit." Joshua giggled.

"I hear you." Jayla chuckled. "Shit, I ain't never seen shit I didn't wanna buy." She and Joshua high-fived.

Joshua laughed. He knew, if it existed, he had met his one true love. The synergy in their relationship was always intense. Jayla was his motivation. Joshua wanted to be worthy of the love and support she gave him. He knew Jayla held him to a high standard and he wanted to meet her expectations. Although he retained his swagger as a stomp-down player, Joshua had become a one-woman man.

"Whatchu wanna do, Jayla?" Joshua asked. He looked at her, studying her body language.

"Whatchu mean?" Jayla smiled. "We can stay home. I'll cook something."

"I'll pass on that. You know your ass can't cook." Joshua chuckled. "Nah, seriously, I'm talkin' 'bout in life. I know you don't wanna work at the supermarket forever."

"What's wrong with my job?" Jayla asked, agitated. "I'm the clerk manager. I make good money." She pursed her lips and stared at Joshua.

"That's cool, but I'm just asking, there ain't shit-else you wanna do?"

"Yeah, but you know how it is, Joshua."

"How is it?"

"I ain't that smart, so I can't go to school or nothing like that. And you know . . ."

"Know what? That you're talkin' some bullshit! I'm just sayin', Jayla if a nigga's dumb, seems like school is the place they need to be. In some way, I feel you though. I guess I just got lucky. I used to talk so much shit, everybody was like, aye, nigga, you should be a barber, so I was like fuck it. I hated going to school for that shit, but bam! Five years later, I can't imagine not doin' this shit. Seriously, Jayla, if a nigga had a callin', this is it."

"Why are you drilling me, Joshua?" Jayla sighed. "I'm cool."

"I ain't drillin' you. I just give-a-fuck."

"About what, Joshua? I ain't Joi or D'Vyne. What-the-fuck do you want from me?"

Joshua slid closer to Jayla. He was aware he had touched a sore spot with her.

"I don't want you to be like Joi or D'Vyne. It ain't about what I want from you. It should be about what you want for yourself. I talk a lot of shit and I quit on Perceptions, but I'm here for you. So if you gonna be mad at me for pushin' you, you gonna be mad often." Joshua rose and rubbed his hand across Jayla's hair before disappearing into his bedroom.

Jayla remained on the sofa after Joshua walked into the bedroom. Although she tried to keep her past out of her relationships, it always seemed to surface at some point. Whether it was her past relationships, her past lifestyle, or her childhood, it always permeated her relationships. She knew she would eventually have to discuss everything with Joshua, but today wouldn't be that day.

ଓଃ•ଌ

A federal prosecutor approached D'Vyne as she sat in the waiting area at the federal courthouse. D'Vyne was frightened when the prosecutor reached her.

"Hi, I'm Caroline Tochioni." The woman politely smiled at D'Vyne. "I'm filling in for District Attorney Daniel Pepper. The grand jury is ready for your testimony." She smiled and gestured for D'Vyne to follow her.

D'Vyne rose from her seat and followed behind the tall, lanky woman. Although she knew she was doing the right thing, she was overtaken by nervousness. With every step she took toward the courtroom, her apprehension grew stronger. As she entered the room, all eyes were on her. She was the person fulfilling her civic duty, but she felt as if she was being judged. She nervously entered the witness booth and was immediately bombarded with questions.

Although D'Vyne had been prepped prior to her court appearance, she wasn't ready to answer some of the questions she was being asked. She skated around the questions she didn't like and answered the rest to the best of her ability. After the questions ceased, the prosecutor thanked her and allowed her to leave the courtroom.

D'Vyne rushed out the room. After entering the hallway, she leaned against the wall, trying to catch her breath. The entire time she was in the courtroom, she'd felt trapped, suffocated, and unable to breathe, so leaving the stand was a relief to her. She grabbed her chest.

"Shit," she whispered to herself, panting.

D'Vyne began walking toward the exit of the courthouse. She was puzzled by some of the things she'd been asked. She wondered, for the first time, if she'd made the right decision. She loved her friend, but treacherously causing a man to spend his life in prison to protect her own interest suddenly seemed wrong. After getting home, D'Vyne pulled the invitation Andre had sent from her mailbox. She read the invitation and smiled.

"This nigga's gettin' married," she whispered to herself. She rushed to the telephone and dialed Joi's number.

"JOI," D'Vyne yelled into the phone after receiving an answer.

"Yeah," Joi replied. "What's up, girl?"

"Did you get an invitation to dinner from Andre?"

"Yes, but it's to a strange address."

"I know," D'Vyne replied. "It must be Monica's house."

"Oh yeah, it probably is, huh?"

"I think he fixin' to get married, Joi."

"At least he ain't marrying a gold digger." Joi snickered.

"She must have some paper because that's a waterfront address."

"Damn, Joi! That's all you think about."

"And you don't?"

"No," D'Vyne replied.

"All right, D'Vyne; I'll talk to you later. Love you." Joi hung up.

D'Vyne stared at the buzzing telephone, loosely holding it in her hand. She was in disbelief. Joi had hung up in her face. D'Vyne was livid. She began redialing Joi's number. Midway through, she stopped pressing numbers.

"Fuck her," D'Vyne said and threw the phone onto the sofa.

Although D'Vyne wanted to check Joi for childishly hanging up in her face, she decided to leave it alone. She was sure Joi would call apologizing later that day because she always did. D'Vyne lay across her sofa. She eventually fell asleep, but her mind was still awake with thoughts of her afternoon court appearance.

ଔ•ଔ

Jayla seductively tied Joshua's tie. After finishing his perfectly-tied Windsor knot, she smiled and gently rubbed her palms across his chest.

"You look a'ight for a square." Jayla chuckled.

"So, would you give me a loan?" Joshua asked and put on his impressive smile.

"Yeah," Jayla replied happily.

"Be serious," Joshua said, changing his pose. "If you were a loan officer, would you fuck-wit'-a-nigga?"

"I said yeah. I ain't no loan officer, but I'll loan you the money." Jayla smiled.

"Thanks, baby." Joshua leaned in and kissed Jayla.

"Shit! For another one of those, I'll give you the money." Jayla smiled and theatrically fanned herself.

Joshua leaned in and kissed her again. "There the kiss is, but Kroger's don't pay the type of bread I need. You feel me?" He slapped her behind and smiled.

Jayla snickered. "How much money do you need, Joshua?"

"About fifty racks, but I'm tryin' to get thirty from the bank." Joshua looked down toward Jayla's private area and smiled suggestively. "Unless . . . you know," he teased.

Jayla laughed. "Nigga, please, nigga, freeze! I might be a freak, but I ain't sellin' no pussy. You stupid!" Jayla punched Joshua's arm, and they both burst into laughter.

"I'm just sayin'. Mackin's still alive." Joshua playfully flinched before Jayla could strike him again.

"My pussy is yours and my money is yours. I can give you the money if you want it."

"Yeah, a'ight!" Joshua chuckled.

"Yeah, a'ight," Jayla mimicked him. "I'm serious," she said sassily.

Joshua snickered and began walking toward the door. He didn't even give what Jayla was saying a second thought because he was sure she was joking.

"Yeah, baby, I'ma keep that in mind just in case I don't get this loan. I know you got my back." Joshua chuckled and walked out the door.

Jayla smiled as she watched Joshua leave. She was sure Joshua would get the loan. She knew how much he wanted to open his own salon and she wished him the best. Jayla often wished she had a passion for something, especially after Joshua had inquired about her dreams and aspirations. When Joshua asked about her aspirations in life, she had become frustrated and combative. She felt as though he was applying pressure to her with his questions. Jayla was content with her way of life. She knew she wasn't in one of the higher echelons of black people, but considering the depth of her past, she had come a long way.

Jayla's upbringing was preparation for the abuse that was to come from Dwight. About six months after her thirteenth birthday, her mother passed away. Jayla was left with her stepfather. He was her only alternative to the foster care system, so she chose to stay. Things were fine for the first year or so, but shortly into her first year of high school, she experienced the beginning of an abusive cycle that lasted for years.

Jayla was involved with Lavar, a young man she'd known since grade school, so them finally becoming a couple was inevitable. They were the typical freshman couple. Jayla would let Lavar fondle her in any manner that he chose, but she never let him go all the way. One afternoon, Jayla and Lavar decided to ditch school for the rest of the day. They went to Jayla's home because her stepfather worked during the daytime.

Once they arrived at her house, their make-out session began. They started kissing at the entrance of the home and continued all the way to Jayla's bedroom. She led him to her bed and unclothed him. She then unclothed herself and lay across her bed. Lavar began aggressively massaging her breasts, plunging her fingers into her womanhood. Jayla moaned lascivious moans as Lavar fondled her body. She rolled on top of him and stared into his eyes. She was ready to go all the way.

Jayla grabbed Lavar's penis and roughly ejaculated him. As his erection mounted, she leaned in and performed oral on him. He grunted. The sounds that escaped Jayla's room were lust-filled and earthly. She rolled over allowing Lavar to reciprocate. He kissed her from her naval to her vaginal entry. His tongue tickled her clitoris. Jayla moaned and her body rocked and she released a thunderous scream. She was reaching her climax.

"Thump!" The bedroom door hit the wall, causing an earsplitting crash. Jayla's body tensed. She and Lavar looked toward the door and froze in shock. It was her stepfather.

Jayla's stepfather's face was menacing. "BOY," he yelled vehemently. "GET-THE-FUCK OUTTA MY HOUSE! GET YOUR CLOTHES, BUT DON'T PUT THEM ON HERE. JUST GET-THE-FUCK OUT BEFORE I KILL YOU!"

He stared at the young man from the entrance of Jayla's bedroom. Lavar nervously snatched his clothing from the floor and darted past Jaya's stepfather, exiting the room. He crashed through the door of the home, nearly breaking the hinges. Jayla's stepfather rushed to the door and locked it. He watched from the window as Lavar hustled to put his clothes on while running down the street.

Jayla was frightened. She couldn't believe she had been caught in the sex act by her stepfather. When he re-entered the room, Jayla was sure he would kick her out of his home. Her eyes filled with tears as he approached her.

"I'm sorry, Daddy," Jayla cried for forgiveness.

"Oh, don't be sorry," he said, edging closer to her. "We're gonna finish this." He began unclothing himself and lay on top of Jayla. "If anybody's gonna get this young pussy, it's gonna be me! I take care of you! You're my woman." He forcefully entered her.

Jayla gasped. She moaned violently. She was in pain, but her shock superseded her pain. She was being raped by the man who was supposed to protect her. She lay there emotionless while her stepfather made her his woman. From that day forth, Jayla continued her sexual relationship with her stepfather. She hated him for what he was doing to her, but she preferred the sexual abuse from her stepfather over the abuse of the foster care system. Although she despised her stepfather, she stayed until she met Dwight. She told Dwight about her stepfather's abuse and it seemed to fuel him. She moved from one abusive situation to another.

Later on, into her twenties, Jayla's stepfather died as the result of a work-related accident. Jayla was the sole beneficiary and was left with a quarter of a million dollars. She had spent some of the money to purchase her home, but she still had a large portion of it. Joshua had stopped the negative cycle of abuse the men in her life had given her. She loved him for that, amongst other things; therefore, she would have been honored to help him. She believed in him and hoped he loved her enough to accept her support if he needed it.

Chapter 13

Joi pulled her full, well-pressed hair behind her ear and placed a fresh flower in it. She smiled into the mirror before leaving her apartment. She walked through the hallway of the apartment building with a carefree sway of her hips. Reaching the elevator, she stood in a model-like pose and waited for the car to reach her floor. Joi was on her way to Andre's dinner party. She was sure her day would be wonderful because she would be spending it with her closest friends. As the door of the elevator opened, Joi's eyes bulged.

'Damn,' Joi thought, nervously staring Damon in the face, *'not this muthafucka!'* She sighed and her high spirits began to slowly descend. She decided to be cordial to avoid any controversy because she was sure he would win, so she led off with a smile.

"Hi, Damon."

"Hey, Joi," Damon quickly replied. He seemed to be taken off-guard because he stared at Joi in an inquisitive manner. He cleared his throat as he walked off the elevator. "I know I've been an asshole toward you lately, but can I have two minutes of your time?" His lips spread into a seemingly-sincere smile.

"No!" Joi tried to brush past him. "I'm sorry, but I'm in a rush." She was terrified to hear whatever it was Damon wanted to speak to her about. After all he'd put her through, there was no way Joi was willingly going to share a second of her time listening to him, let alone a few minutes.

Damon grabbed Joi's arm, squeezed it in a vice-like grip, and pulled her closer to him.

"Look," Damon started, "stupid-ass-bitch! I was trying to be nice, but you're a simple-ass-hoe! Play with Damon if you want to, bitch." He stared at Joi in a cold manner and suddenly released her arm, allowing her to get onto the elevator.

Joi rushed onto the elevator and pressed the button to close the door. She was petrified. Although Damon had consistently harassed Joi, he had never put his hands on her. She was shaken by his fierce aggressiveness and questioned if this was just another form of harassment, or had she been assaulted. Whichever, Joi knew she had to find out who Damon was frequently visiting so she could have them evicted. She had considered it before things got to this point, but after Major spoke to Damon, Joi had decided to let things be, but what had just happened changed everything.

Joi knew it was time for her to create some distance between her and Damon because she had seen relationship like theirs turn fatal, and that wasn't a fate she intended for herself. She rambled through her purse, pulled out her cellphone, and called Major. She wanted to warn him because he too was part of a triangle that could potentially become tragic.

"Hello, Major," Joi spoke into the phone after receiving an answer. She marched rapidly through the lobby of her apartment building, causing a panted breathing pattern.

"Yeah," Major retorted. "What's wrong?" He could hear the alarm in Joi's voice. He wanted to seem sincerely concerned.

Joi started telling Major about her run-in with Damon. She was livid and her voice carried as she spoke out. She warned Major about Damon's jealous rage. She had witnessed the aftermath of what loved-crazed men were capable of from Demetric and D'Vyne's ordeal. Therefore, she gave Major a heads-up about what he was potentially involved in.

"Fuck dude!" Major spat out. "Fear ain't my forte, but I feel you." He seemed to be unconcerned about Damon's jealous rampage.

Joi was shocked by Major's nonchalant reaction. She expected him to rush to her aid. To act as her protector, but he didn't even attempt to comfort her.

"Okay then," Joi said, "I have to go. Do you want to get together later?"

"Nah; I'm still working. I'll be callin' to make sure you're cool though."

"Okay." Joi perked up after Major's last statement. "Love you. Bye!"

She ended the call and got in her car. She wanted to call D'Vyne, but she was sure D'Vyne was still upset with her about their telephone dispute. Joi loved D'Vyne—of course she did; D'Vyne was her best friend—but she couldn't find any sympathy for her. She'd learned a lot from D'Vyne over the years and looked up to her, but after D'Vyne allowed Demetric back into her life after what he'd done to Joshua, Joi had lost a lot of respect and admiration for her. She then realized D'Vyne was no more knowledgeable about men and relationships than she was.

Although she had dodged D'Vyne for the past couple of weeks, Joi knew she would have to face her once she got to the party. In her mind, she had already had a romp with a monster, so having a run-in with D'Vyne would be a walk in the park. She was ready for any confrontation after Damon's torture.

CB•BO

D'Vyne extended her foot and fastened the straps on her stilettos. As she rose from the ottoman, she noticed Demetric quietly staring at her from the sofa. There had been a thick tension between them throughout the week. D'Vyne's caution was up. She felt uncomfortable, but unthreatened. Demetric had never shown any signs of violence toward her, so her fear of him hurting her was minimal.

D'Vyne was curious about Demetric's distant facial expressions. She wanted to ask him about his somber mood, but she didn't. She figured he would have spoken up on his own if there was something he wanted to share with her. Instead, she pretended to pay his mood no mind. She smiled and twirled in front of her wall mirror.

"How I look, baby?" D'Vyne asked, her hands on her spreading hips, primping and being silly.

"Like you're goin' to court," Demetric replied curtly.

D'Vyne gasped and her head snapped in Demetric's direction. "What?" She appeared shocked by Demetric's answer.

"It's too churchy lookin'. You're pregnant, ma. Be mannish wit' it." He smiled weak and unconvincingly. "More cleavage and more thigh."

D'Vyne's smile reappeared. "I ain't," she replied.

Her stomach settled. Because of Demetric's statement, she considered the possibility that he knew what she had done, but she refused to address her curiosity.

"A'ight!" Demetric nodded his head. "Just don't be surprised if Joi outdresses you this time." He turned back to the television.

"Fuck Joi." D'Vyne laughed. "I might smack her butt."

"Fo' outdressin' you? It ain't that serious, D'Vyne." Demetric shook his head. He knew D'Vyne was upset with Joi about something else, but he chose to be sarcastic.

"Nah, boy; for hangin' up on me." D'Vyne giggled. "She Mr. Clicked a sistah."

She continued snickering, baiting Demetric, hoping he would join her in the laughter, but he didn't participate.

"Is Joshua gonna be there?" Demetric asked.

"Yeah. Why?" D'Vyne walked toward Demetric. She was curious to know why he had inquired about Joshua.

"Tell him I need to holla." Demetric kept his eyes fixed on the television. He didn't want to make eye contact with D'Vyne.

"About what?" D'Vyne's agitation was beginning to show on her face.

"I'ma go ahead and tell 'em. Shit, you ain't, so I am." Demetric grabbed the TV remote and surfed through the channels.

"No, you ain't! We're gonna work this shit out."

D'Vyne rubbed her stomach and shook her head defiantly. She wanted to find an alternative to telling Joshua the truth, especially with her being caught into the cover up.

"Vee," Demetric said, shaking his head, "quit fakin'. Me and you both know I'm on my way to the joint. So, hell, I might as well tell the nigga and get him outta harm's way fo' it's too late."

"You're trippin'." D'Vyne grabbed her purse. "I'm going to the party. I'll be home early and we can talk when I get back because you're on some other shit right now." She walked toward the door.

"I'm trippin? Shit! I hear you." Demetric chuckled insidiously as D'Vyne walked out the door.

After getting in her car, D'Vyne exhaled deeply. She was relieved to be out of Demetric's presence. She didn't know how, but she was sure Demetric had found out about her court appearance and her testimony to the grand jury. She knew he was anti-police, and still she had chosen to snitch. Now, it was her who had betrayed him and she knew what she had to do to fix it.

D'Vyne weaved through traffic in a zombie-like trance. Her thoughts were everywhere except the party she was attending. She planned to enjoy herself as best she could, but she was definitely calling it an early night. She had damage control in her relationship that needed to be attended to. She had to justify her actions. It was Demetric who deserved an apology and bath water this time, and D'Vyne planned on delivering.

☓●☒

Joshua's latest days had been superior to any others in his lifetime. He had signed the mortgage for a building, received a loan for the whole fifty thousand he needed for extra startup capital, and his first real relationship was a puzzling success. As Joshua smiled in the mirror to check his teeth for excessive plaque, Jayla walked into his home carrying her dress. She laid the dress across the sofa and walked over to Joshua. She playfully twirled, patting her hairdo.

"You like it?" Jayla asked. She stopped and posed sexily for Joshua.

Joshua smiled, theatrically edging closer to Jayla.

"Mmm mmm mmmmm," he flirted as he wrapped his arms around her waist and kissed her. "We can fuck-it-up if you want to." He smiled and raised his eyebrows suggestively.

"Hell nah!" Jayla defiantly shook her head and pushed Joshua away. She grabbed the bag concealing her outfit, reached inside, and pulled a camel tan, one-piece, form-fitting dress from inside. "What about this?" She smiled and laid the dress against her body.

"Only if you don't wear panties." Joshua smiled.

Jayla laughed. "What? Why would you say that?"

"Because we're gonna stop at one of those parks off Jefferson on our way home and freak it off." Joshua reached around Jayla and palmed her backside.

"Boy, you are a freak!"

Jayla laughed and walked off toward the bathroom. Although she had walked away, she intended to call Joshua on his bluff. All while bathing, she thought about the types of things she and Joshua could do in the darkness of a park on the riverfront.

After Jayla disappeared in the bathroom, Joshua went back to the mirror and continued his primping. He relentlessly wrestled with his tie. He was sure Major would be there with Joi, so he opted to get suited up. He wore chocolate brown Gucci slacks, a Geoffrey Beene striped, button-up with a Burberry sweater vest, and Salvatore Ferragamo loafers. As he loosened his tie once again, Jayla snuck up behind him and slapped his behind. Joshua turned and gave her a slow once-over. He grabbed his crotch area and slightly bent his knees.

"DAMN," Joshua yelled. He was impressed with Jayla from head-to-toe. Her dress contoured her hour-glass figure.

Jayla smiled shyly. Although she knew she looked nice, she was happy to know Joshua's approval rating of her was high. She smiled and walked closer to Joshua.

"Boy," Jayla said, grabbing hold of Joshua's tie, "you fucked-that-tie-up!" She giggled and loosened his tie completely, pulled it from his neck, straightened it, and retied it properly. Afterward, she giggled and kissed him. "That's my job now." She gently touched his chest and winked at him.

"Where you pick the tie game up at anyway? Because you're cold wit' it!" Joshua fondled his tie, smiling.

"My stepdad." Jayla smiled weakly. "Come strap my shoes up." Jayla sat on the sofa, seductively lay back, and extended her foot toward Joshua. While her foot was in the air, she purposely spread her legs exposing her naked vagina to Joshua.

"Oh shit! It's on." Joshua rushed to strap her Jimmy Choo shoe boots. After fastening her straps, Joshua took Jayla's hand and pulled her to her feet. As they marched through the door of his home into the judgmental public streets, Joshua smiled a deeply internal smile because he knew he was accompanied by a beautiful woman who loved him.

Jayla was anxious to get through the dinner party. All she could think about was making love to Joshua in the park. Although she liked Joshua's friends, she wasn't interested in being in their presence the entire night. She also believed his clique talked badly about her amongst themselves, especially D'Vyne. Jayla got a bad vibe from D'Vyne. She was unaware if she and Joshua had ever been sexually involved, but her intuition assured her D'Vyne had intimate feelings for Joshua. Jayla was a sexual person, so she paid close attention to the sexual chemistry of everyone. And from her observations, she believed D'Vyne had feelings for Joshua and resentment toward for stealing him from her.

Whatever the case, whether she was right or wrong, she did not want to spend the entire night with Joshua's friends.

ಬ•ಬ

Andre watched as the caterers set up the food. Monica had decorated his ten-foot marble table to perfection. Everything was impeccable. Andre smiled. For the first time since his career had propelled, he could see the extent of his success. He had been happy several times in his life, but the feeling of fulfillment had been a stranger to him until the news of Monica's pregnancy.

Andre loved Monica, but he'd become skeptical about the future of their relationship for a while. He thought their intimacy lacked depth. He believed she wasn't right for him, but as time passed, he realized she was exactly what he needed. It was his desires that confused him.

Andre always desired to care for someone, but Monica did not need his assistance. She was already secure prior to meeting him. That intimidated Andre, especially when Monica began showering him with lavish gifts. It was the gifts that made Andre apprehensive about their relationship. He had promised himself that he would not be accepting anymore of Monica's gifts, but he never expected her to give him the gift of child.

Monica snuck up behind Andre. She kissed the back of his neck and giggled. She'd noticed he was distant and she wondered why.

"What's wrong, babe," Monica asked. "Why are you so distant?"

Andre smiled and wrapped his arms around Monica's waist. "I got lost thinking about you. I was watching the caterers do their thing and the way you set the table up. I'm telling you, baby, I ain't never seen no-shit like this. It's just fuckin'-me-up." He shook his head. "I ain't realize I had it like this, but you bring the best out in me."

"I must bring the player out in you too because that was some romantic stuff you just said."

Monica laughed and Andre joined in. As the couple enjoyed a moment of laughter, one of the caterers signaled for Andre, letting him know they were finished.

"Go ahead and get dressed, baby." Andre kissed Monica's cheek. "I'll let them out." He watched as Monica walked off toward the stairs. Afterward, he walked the caterers to the door and thanked them. As the caterers were leaving, one of them sprinted back to the porch. Andre smiled politely.

"I put y'all's tip on my charge card," Andre said presumptively.

"No," the young white man said with a slight chuckle, "that isn't why I came back. I admire your work and I've been trying to break into the business. Do you have any advice for a rookie?"

Andre was puzzled. He had a broad range of advertisements for his company, but his face was not on any of them. Therefore, there was no way the young man should know him through his company. He was sure the youngster was mistaking him for someone else.

"What do you mean?" Andre asked, curious about who the young man thought he was.

"Aren't you the Black Javelin from the *Butt Crushers* flick?"

Andre burst into laughter. "Nah, man!" He chuckled. "I wash gutters and shit." He continued laughing.

"Oh, I'm sorry, sir!" The young man rushed away from Andre's porch in embarrassment.

Andre closed the door and went to his room. He had already bathed so he began dressing. While pulling up his slacks, he burst into laughter again.

"*Butt Crushers*," Andre whispered to himself and chuckled. "Whities kill me. A nigga can't get paid without some drugs, a ball, or their dicks in their hands, let them tell it." He buttoned his shirt in amazement. It was 2008, the year of Barack Obama, and being a black man still carried negative connotations regardless of their success level. Just as Andre finished dressing, Monica rushed into his bedroom.

"My brother and his wife are here." Monica smiled and waved Andre over to her. "Come on, babe."

She grabbed his hand and pulled him along with her. They walked to the door together and Monica opened it. She smiled. "I see y'all are on time."

Monica's brother, Kamau, chuckled. "It's free food in here, ain't it?"

"No doubt," Andre replied, as Kamau and his wife, Cynthia, entered his home.

Cynthia smiled, giving Andre a quick once-over. "Kamau," she called out to her husband in a hushed tone. Kamau ignored her and continued with his sister, so Cynthia turned to Andre and smiled once again. "Andre, you look familiar." This time she turned and tapped Kamau's arm. "Baby, doesn't Andre look familiar?"

"A little bit," Kamau replied, although he wasn't paying Cynthia any attention. "I've seen him too many times to consider him familiar. Where's the food?" He looked around.

"Let's go to the entertainment room," requested Andre. He gestured for everyone to follow him. As they walked off, the doorbell rang.

"Monica, would you show them the house while I get the door? Thanks, baby."

He walked back to the door and opened it. Joshua and Jayla were on the porch. "Come on in!" Andre kissed Jayla's cheek and embraced Joshua in a manly hug. Joshua looked around. "Whose pad is this? I gotta take my shoes off?" He reached for his feet.

"Nah, dog. This be me. I just copped this; I didn't want to tell anyone. Come on." He gestured for Joshua and Jayla to follow him. "Let me show y'all around."

Jayla looked around. She was amazed by how elegantly the home was furnished.

"This is nice, Andre!" Jayla smiled and her eyes continued canvassing the home.

"Thanks," Andre replied.

He was proud as they strolled through his home. Andre had come from the bottom, so being able to custom build his home was a grand accomplishment.

"Damn, my nigga!" Joshua laughed. "I know you got some Grey Poupon in this subzero 'frigerator!"

They all laughed. Joshua was proud of Andre. He always was, and seeing his best friend doing as well as he was, was inspiring.

Andre walked Jayla and Joshua into the den. Monica, Kamau, and Cynthia were gathered around, cheerfully sipping champagne. Monica introduced everyone. Joshua grabbed the remote to the fifty-two-inch plasma television hanging on the wall and began surfing through channels. As he swiftly moved through the stations, Jayla went to the DVD collection and found something she liked.

"Let's watch this," Jayla requested and tossed Joshua the DVD case.

Jayla spent a lot of time with Joshua, so she knew about his ridiculous remote-control habits and she didn't feel up to watching him fondle the buttons for hours. Joshua looked at the disc Jayla had tossed him and laughed.

"Oh, you're trippin! Ain't nobody tryin' to watch no *Dream Girls*." Joshua leapt to his feet and gave a hilarious rendition of James Thunder Early; everyone erupted into laughter. As always, Joshua had set the partying off.

"Someone is at the door," said Monica. "I'll be back." She rose and left the room.

The entertainment room was being used properly. Everyone was conversing and getting acquainted with each other. Although the laughter was at an earsplitting level, Andre felt the cold stare of Kamau's wife. He was sure they had never met before, but she was insistent they had.

"So, Cynthia," Andre turned the direction of the conversation to her, "what type of work do you do?"

"I strip," Cynthia replied candidly.

Andre's eyes nearly flew from his head. He looked from Cynthia to Kamau. Kamau shrugged his shoulders and chuckled.

Joshua casually looked over to Jayla and smiled. Jayla sighed and gave him a "please don't" look in return. Joshua smiled again. It was impossible for him to pass up an opportunity like this.

"See, baby," Joshua chuckled, "I told you pole patrol was an honorable profession."

Everyone laughed, including Jayla. Cynthia laughed the hardest.

"I was kidding!" She pointed at Joshua. "And you're nasty."

Again, everyone laughed. Everyone in the room seemed to be enjoying one another's company. Things were going fine. Monica entered the room amongst all the laughter, followed by Joi and D'Vyne. She introduced them to Cynthia and Kamau.

Joi sashayed over to Andre and playfully kicked him. "Boy, you'd better stop keeping secrets," she teased. She looked around and smiled excitedly. "This is nice Andre."

"Yeah, nigga!" Joshua laughed. "Stop keepin' secrets."

"Whatever, dog!" Andre laughed, looked over to Joi, and back to Joshua. "You and Jayla are the ones doing the butt-naked rumba around the crib."

Everyone laughed and the attention transferred to Joshua and Jayla. Joshua looked over at Jayla. He noticed her flushed face and giggled. "They caught us sleepin', baby."

He turned to Monica with an accusing stare. "Hey, Monica! What? You done turned my nigga into some type of voyeur or somethin'?"

Cynthia snickered. "I don't think Monica had anything to do with that one."

"Nah, y'all," Andre tried to defend himself, "it wasn't even like that." He told the story as it really happened.

Joi smiled. "So," she teased, "I wish someone would do anything with me in the nude."

Everyone laughed. After drinking a few more glasses of champagne, they moved the party to the dining room for dinner. D'Vyne smiled seeing the table set up. She had been primarily quiet since she arrived. Her body was with her friends, but her mind was with Demetric. She looked over to Andre and smiled weakly.

"Andre, this table looks beautiful."

"Thanks," Andre replied, "I appreciate it, but Monica put it together. She deserves the credit."

Everyone sat, and Kamau and Joshua reached for their napkins in unison.

"Put those down!" Monica gave them a warning stare. "We're saying grace first."

Joi looked over at Joshua and snickered teasingly. D'Vyne smirked as well. Although D'Vyne was still upset with Joi for hanging up in her face, she couldn't help laughing at their inside joke about Monica.

Monica noticed the humor amongst Andre's friends. She was sure they were making fun of her, so she decided to take a shot of her own. "Joi, would you lead us in prayer? I hear you have a church background."

Joi agreed and said a quick prayer. She knew Monica had taken a shot at her with the church background comment, but she chose to overlook it. As the dinner progressed, Joi and D'Vyne made sporadic eye contact, but neither of them gave in. Joi wanted to, but she refused to because she knew D'Vyne expected her to breakdown first.

Joshua occasionally stared over at D'Vyne. He'd noticed her distance from the group. He felt bad for her, but he refused to show it. Although he had initially brushed it off, Joshua knew Dwight was telling the truth about the shooting. He was also aware D'Vyne knew because her guilt-filled aura gave her away. He realized Demetric had placed D'Vyne in an awkward situation from the beginning, but it was evident to Joshua her decision had been made.

During the dinner, Jayla's pre-party jitters settled. She was becoming comfortable with Joshua's friends. She noticed the sexual chemistry between Cynthia and Andre. She had seen Cynthia staring at Andre in a lust-filled manner on several occasions. Jayla was impressed with Cynthia's inconspicuous way of making eye contact with Andre. Kamau was unaware of his wife's trite indiscretions because he was too busy eye-sex ng Joi.

As Jayla looked on, she learned a lot about the group of friends and found them quite amusing.

"Everyone," Andre said, rising from his seat. He tried to bring a calm to the group and Monica rose and stood snugly beside him. "I've finally accomplished two of my long-term goals, and I wanted my peoples to celebrate with me. I built a house . . ." He chuckled and wrapped his arms around Monica's waist. "And I'm going to be a father in seven months." He and Monica smiled.

Joshua whistled. "I got dibs on godfather."

"Nah, player," Kamau retorted, "I've got that covered." He smiled, nodded at Joshua, and they began a friendly bicker amongst themselves.

Cynthia rose from the table. "Andre, would you show me to the restroom?" She smiled politely.

"Yeah," Andre agreed with a nod. He grabbed her hand and walked toward the stairs.

Cynthia took quick glimpses of Andre as they ascended the stairs. Once they were out of everyone's eyesight, Cynthia aggressively pushed Andre against the stair wall. She reached for his crotch area, palmed his penis, and smiled.

"I knew that was you," Cynthia said in a panted tone.

Andre was shocked. He couldn't believe what had just happened. He didn't know whether he should be flattered or offended.

"What-the-hell is wrong with you?" Andre asked angrily.

"I saw *Butt Crushers*." Cynthia looked over her shoulder to make sure no one had heard her. "Kamau saw it, too, but he was probably too busy staring at Rebecca The Body."

"You're crazy! Come on!" Andre grabbed Cynthia's hand and walked her back into the dining room. "Aye, Kamau! I love your sister, but you and your wife gotta bounce." Everyone in the room froze and stared at Andre and Cynthia.

"What?" Monica asked frantically. "What-the-hell happened?"

"I TOLD HIM I KNOW WHO HE REALLY IS AND WHAT HE REALLY DOES," Cynthia yelled angrily. "His screen name is Black Javelin!"

"Damn, Andre!" Kamau looked over to him and nearly choked on his wine. "That's you?" He stared at Andre in disbelief.

Jayla grabbed her mouth. Although the scene was entertaining, she was shocked. Joshua leaned deeper into his chair and turned his wine glass up. Joi's and D'Vyne's mouths hung open.

"Y'all gotta bounce!" Andre's eyes darkened. He was humiliated and enraged. "I wasn't bullshittin'!"

Kamau noticed the anger in Andre's voice, so he rose and took his wife's hand. He and Cynthia made their way to the front door followed by Andre. After they walked through the door, Andre slammed it behind them and walked back into the dining room. Everyone was quiet. They stared at him in curiosity. He turned to Monica.

"I'm sorry, baby. Homegirl was trippin'. She grabbed a nigga's piece."

"Oh, she's a freak!" Joshua nodded his head. "I knew it, too, talkin' all that stripper shit!" He took a sip from his wine glass and shook his head.

"Shut up, boy!" Joi tapped the back of Joshua's neck and rose from her seat. "I'm going to leave, so you and Monica can talk."

D'Vyne rose as well. "Me, too, but this was nice, Andre." She smiled unconvincingly.

"Hold up everybody." Joshua smiled. "I've got some good news, too."

Jayla's eyes darted to Joshua. She hoped he wasn't going to mention his new salon. She was sure this wasn't the time for that conversation because no one would like the idea of him leaving D'Vyne hanging.

"Another baby on the way?" asked Andre. "What's up?" He seemed anxious to hear Joshua's news.

"Nah, no shorties," replied Joshua with a smile. "I'm opening my own barbershop! I got the building and the whole nine already."

"WHAT!" D'Vyne shouted. "WHATCHU MEAN? YOU'RE LEAVIN' PERCEPTIONS?" She was upset.

"Yepper! It's on the westside." Joshua smiled.

"You sound crazy!" D'Vyne looked over to Jayla. "You done let this stupid-bitch talk you into leavin'? You're stupid, too."

"WHAT?!" Jayla yelled. She was ready to get rowdy, but she remained calm. She rose from her chair. "I'm leaving, Joshua." She rolled her eyes at D'Vyne.

"SO!" D'Vyne yelled. "LEAVE BITCH! IF I WASN'T PREGNANT, I'D WHIP THAT ASS." She turned to Joshua with hate in her eyes. "Did this-bitch tell you about Dwight making Demetric shoot you?" Tears welled in D'Vyne's eyes.

"Yeah!" Joshua nodded. "She told me! Way befo' you did!" Joshua temper flared. "You callin' my girl out her name, but she's been the only one keepin' shit one hundred! If it was left up to you, a nigga would be dead because everything's about Demetric witchu! Fuck Demetric!" He was vehemently upset.

Everyone was quiet. Joi had begun crying. She was hurt. She could not believe what she was hearing from her friends. They had been inseparable since childhood and she loved the close-knit bond her coterie had, but she was sure that, after tonight, their bond would be unrepairable.

D'Vyne spun on her heels and walked toward the door. After a few steps, she turned and looked at Joshua. "You're wrong, Joshua. I ain't never put Demetric before you or none of y'all." She turned and marched out Andre's home.

Monica eyes moistened. She was outdone. A night of friends and good times had turned into chaos. She looked around the room. Everyone was torn.

"WHAT-THE-HELL is going on?" Monica shouted, wiping tears from her eyes.

Joshua leaned deeper into his chair, took a sip from his wine glass, and rubbed his nose.

"This is some real-nigga-shit, ain't it?" Joshua's eyes roved throughout the room. "Mmm mmm mmmmm." He shook his head in disgust. "You can take a nigga outta the ghetto, but you can't take the ghetto outta the nigga." He downed the rest of his wine and rose from his chair. He kissed Joi's forehead and smiled at Monica. "Monica, I'm sorry about this."

He then turned to Andre. "Come on, walk ya boy to the door, Andre."

Andre walked Joshua and Jayla to the door. After Jayla walked out, Andre chuckled.

"My nigga," Andre began, "we gotta go to lunch tomorrow."

"No doubt! Aye, I like that nigga Kamau." Joshua laughed. "He's my type of nigga."

Andre chuckled. "Man, get your drunk-ass off my porch." He laughed and waved to Jayla as she got into Joshua's truck.

Joi eventually left. She was in disarray. All the confusion of the night was devastating for her. Andre had been accused of being a pornography star, Joshua announced he was leaving Perceptions, and D'Vyne had checked out on Jayla without reason. Although the night had started with the promise of good-hearted camaraderie, it had ended odiously.

Chapter 14

It had been a couple of weeks since Andre's dinner party. Andre had spoken to Joshua and Joi, but he was having a hard time getting in touch with D'Vyne. He wanted to speak to her. He was sure she was lonely because neither Joshua nor Joi had reached out to her.

Andre sighed as he sat at his computer. He had a lot on his plate. He was becoming a father soon, which would be another chapter in his life, but he expected things to be different at this time. The love and unity he and his friends had formed throughout the years had been destroyed by one hideous incident. Joshua, Joi, and D'Vyne were Andre's extended family and he hoped their differences would eventually pass, but he wasn't too optimistic because too much had happened. He considered the possibility of their clique being unrepairable.

Andre began typing D'Vyne an email. He wanted her to be assured that, although their group was going through some tough times, he was still there for her unconditionally. As he completed and sent the email, Monica walked into the room. Andre turned to receive an abhorrent stare from her. He could feel the hate leaping from her skin.

"What's wrong?" asked Andre with a look of concern.

"Why, Andre?" Monica asked in a calm, but cold tone. "Why did you lie to me?"

"What? Lie about what? Andre don't lie about shit!" Andre became upset after Monica's unfounded accusation.

"What is this then?" Monica dug into her purse, came out with a DVD case, and threw it to Andre.

Andre grabbed the disc from his lap and stared at the cover.

It read, "*Butt Crushers 2008*." He was sure this was the pornography video he had been accused of starring in. He laughed and opened the case.

"What-the-hell is this s'pose to be?" Andre chuckled.

"Put it in the computer, Andre! It might strike your memory." Monica's body quivered from anger. She wondered why Andre continued to play nonchalant, although he was clearly busted.

Andre put the disc in the computer. He, too, was anxious to see what everyone had seen to get them in such an uproar. Andre had thought about what Cynthia had done at the dinner party. Although she'd sounded convinced he was the Black Javelin, Andre believed otherwise. He believed Cynthia was driven by lust, which was why she'd cuffed his manhood on the staircase because he had never participated in such an immoral display of capitalism. He was a gutter cleaner, but not those types of gutters.

"Mmm hmmm," Monica hummed, seething as the movie came on. Her leg bounced erratically and tears welled in her eyes.

Andre's eyes protruded from his head. "That dirty, honky muthafucka!" He turned to Monica. He watched as she stood, arms folded over her breast as billows of tears fell from her eyes. Andre stood from his chair and approached her. "Baby," he pleaded, "let me explain."

Monica pushed Andre away. "Stop, Andre! You lied! It's over!" She turned to leave.

"I DON'T LIE!" Andre's voice boomed throughout the room as he followed behind the mother of his unborn child.

Monica stopped and turned toward Andre. "You've hurt me, Andre." Tears continued falling from her eyes. "I was good to you, Andre, but I guess I wasn't good enough or real enough, or you would've been real with me."

"That's what I'm tryin' to do, but you're trippin'!"

"Tripping? Are you serious? Tripping, Andre?" Monica insidious chuckle. "My name isn't Black Javelin." She walked off.

"Mine ain't either! Ain't that 'bout-a-bitch!"

Andre was irritated and upset. He wanted Monica to hear him out, but it was evident her mind was already set. She believed he was the Black Javelin and there was nothing he could say to convince her different.

Monica stomped through the house and down the stairs with Andre in tow. She was furious with him because he'd lied to her, and disappointed in him because he wouldn't take accountability now that he was exposed. She marched through the living room and paused at the front door. She threw Andre's house keys into the key dish and turned to him.

"Goodbye, Andre." Monica turned to walk out of the door.

"Monica! What about the baby?" Andre had desperation within his eyes.

"Humph," Monica grunted, "I took care of that yesterday." She turned and walked out the door, slamming it behind her.

Andre stood in the entrance of his home devastated. Although he was innocent of what he'd been accused of, he experienced the loss of a guilty man. He had closed the previous toil-filled chapter of his life, only to enter a new chapter of pain.

೮෮•෮෮

Joi climbed into Major's truck and smiled. "Hey, baby!" She leaned over and kissed him.

"Thanks, ma. I hope you're feelin' a little better." Major smiled and drove off.

"Yeah, I'm good." Joi smiled, although she was still crushed about the breakup of her clique.

"A'ight then! I'm glad because I know how much your friends mean to you." Major tried to sound as concerned as possible. He was hours away from scarring Joi for the rest of her life, just as she had done him.

"They do mean a lot to me, but I have to concentrate on establishing my future right now." Joi giggled. "I've been thinking about the future a lot lately." She smiled shyly.

"Like what?" asked Major. "Career? Love life? What?" He seemed curious.

Joi chuckled. "It's funny, but I'm going to be real. I'm twenty-six years old and I don't have anything to define me. I have a nice career . . . I like it, but it isn't the end all be all. I need more substance. You feel me?" She turned to Major and awaited his answer.

Major chuckled. "It seems like you have somethin' to say or ask, but you're tryin' to do it in a roundabout way." He smiled devilishly. "What? You feelin' old?" he teased.

"No, boy!" Joi laughed and playfully punched Major's arm. "I want a husband and some kids. I want to come home every day to people who love me."

"Yeah, that would be nice." Major's hate toward Joi softened after her last statement. "I get lonely sometimes, too, but I'm confident with who I am as an individual. I don't need a woman or kids to define me. Besides, I believe it takes death to define someone's lifetime experience because the man I was yesterday can't measure up to the man I am today."

"Okay." Joi smiled.

She liked what Major was saying. They always shared good, meaningful conversation, and that was one of the reasons she cared so much for him.

"I guess you're right. I shouldn't be so anxious. Hell, I might be in the truck with my husband." She smiled.

"I ain't the marrying type." Major chuckled. "You would marry me?"

"In a heartbeat." Joi giggled girlishly.

"The night isn't over," Major laughed, "but let's take it one day at a time before we come to that conclusion."

They cruised through the Windsor/Detroit tunnel. Joi had never been to the dog races, but she was sure she would have a good time because she was with Major. Major had a way of relaxing Joi. He had consoled her when Damon humiliated her and he was uplifting to her now. During the months of Major's return, he had been Joi's rock and she was appreciative of his comfort.

After arriving at the Windsor Raceway, Joi and Major shared more intimate conversation and placed a few small wagers. The energy the greyhounds expended impressed Joi. She paid close attention to Major's comfort level. She wondered if he was a regular gambler at the tracks, or if he was simply a fan of the sport. Whichever it was, she could see he was intrigued because he was slouched deep into his seat with a tranquil smirk on his face and a mysterious shimmer in his eyes the entire time they were there.

After the race, their moods seemed to simmer. She knew it was getting late, but she didn't want their evening to end. As they pulled away from the race track, Joi giggled and leaned onto Major's side of the truck.

"I'm not coming back here." Joi laughed lightly. "We couldn't even hit!"

Major shook his head and chuckled. "I hear you, but I come for the noise, the excitement, and the people."

As Major drove away, he was having second thoughts about going through with his treachery. After spending the evening with Joi, his opinion of her had changed. He realized for the first time since their reunion that Joi had evolved just as he did. She had transformed into a woman, just as he had become a man, and he was impressed with her maturity. He considered actually giving her a chance. Joi had slightly pierced his armor, but his vengeance was still alive.

As Major pulled into the parking lot of the Renaissance Center, Joi glanced over to him and smiled.

"I thought we were going to Bistro's?" Joi asked.

"I changed my mind. Let's get a room. We can order room service."

"Okay."

Joi tried to hide her excitement. She was ready. It had been months since she'd had intercourse with a man. Of course, like any woman, she loved her vibrating Bullet, but she knew a warm body was a greater pleasure.

They entered the Marriot and Joi stood by in the mezzanine while Major checked them into their room. After receiving the key card, he and Joi rushed off to their suite. Opening the room door, Major stepped aside and allowed Joi to enter first. She gasped and held her mouth. Major slid behind her and wrapped his arms around her waist. He kissed the back of her neck.

"You like this?" asked Major.

Joi spun and cupped his cheeks. "Thank you!"

She kissed him while the candles that filled the room silhouetted their bodies. They continued kissing, their feet aggressively sweeping across the floor, shuffling the assorted rose petals that had been scattered throughout the carpet. They began savagely unclothing one another and fell to the floor. Joi's juices flowed from her vaginal cavity. She was dripping wet and her moans matched her libidinous desire to be entered. Petals clung to her perspiring body as she and Major passionately rolled around the floor.

Major decided to slow things down. He swept Joi off the floor and gently laid her across the bed. He laid his naked body atop hers and smiled into her eyes.

"Joi, I want you to do something with me." Major sat up and Joi followed. He sat into a Buddha like position. "I want you to sit like I'm sitting."

Joi obeyed Major and sat into the same position as he sat. She wondered what she was participating in. She wanted to be with Major, but his request had made her cautious.

"I want you to look at my body," said Major, as he intently surveyed Joi's beautiful anatomy.

Joi's eyes slowly browsed over every chisel of Major's muscular body. She was clueless to what type of erotic foreplay she was participating in. Joi felt weird and wonderful at the same time. She had never been in a sexual situation like this, but she was enjoying the view of Major's masculinity.

"Now, I want you to close your eyes and tell me what you want this to be." Major moved closer to Joi as she closed her eyes.

Joi's emotions poured out. She spoke demands in panted whispers. Major kissed her and laid her body down. Joi sprawled across the bed in submission as she continued her sexual instructions. Her body wasn't hers; instead, she'd given herself to Major, and she told him as much.

"Do whatever you want with me," Joi panted in an erogenous whine.

She had reunited with her first love. After everything she'd been through, she was finally receiving her piece of joy. She was consummating her desires. She was with the man she loved. She passionately groped his chest and genitals, passionately kissing, licking, and sucking his body.

"Oooh," she shrieked a sound of joy as Major's finger pierced her vaginal entry.

Major kissed from Joi's clavicle to her womanhood. He pushed her foreskin back causing her clitoris to surface. He gently sucked, licked, and tickled her clitoris with his tongue, causing Joi to release boisterous sounds of passion. He cupped her breasts and massaged them roughly.

As Major massaged Joi's breasts and tickled her clitoris, her body stiffened. Her legs shook and she clasped Major's face. "Oh," Joi moaned, then she climaxed. "I love you, Major." Her breathing was heavy and perspiration was over her entire body.

Major turned Joi onto her stomach and gently rubbed her back and derriere. He spread her legs apart and pushed her feet to her buttocks. Joi's panting returned as Major mounted her. He entered her, causing a thunderous yelp. He pounded deep into Joi, causing her to shriek sounds of pleasure. He then flipped her over into the missionary position and lay atop her. He kissed her neck and placed her legs over his shoulders. He palmed her shoulders into a forceful lock and penetrated her anal cavity.

Joi shrieked violently. "STOP!" She wiggled and twirled trying to shake loose from Major's strong hold. "NO, MAJOR STOP! YOU'RE HURTING ME," she cried as Major pushed deeper into her.

Major pulled out of her. His eyes were darkened. He looked enraged as he smiled sinisterly.

"What's wrong with you?" Major laughed an insidious laugh.

"What's wrong with me?" Joi eyes welled with tears. "What's wrong with me, Major?! What-the-fuck is wrong with you? I don't play that shit! That shit hurt!" Joi was frantic.

Major laughed. "Hurt, huh?" He continued laughing. "Just like you hurt me. Bitch, get-the-fuck outta my room!"

Joi was appalled. "What?"

Tears fell from Joi's eyes in a way they had never fallen before. She couldn't believe what was happening. She wished she was in a dream, but reality was everywhere.

"Get-the-fuck-out! Bounce, bitch! Remember those words?" Major grimaced and pointed to the door. He was pleased with what he had done. He had taken Joi into the clouds and dropped her to the pavement without a parachute.

Joi began dressing. After getting dressed and gathering the rest of her things, she walked to the door and spun around. Her eyes were filled with hate—not only hate for Major but hate for every man who would follow him. She gave him a vehement stare.

"Nigga," Joi said between sniffles, "you're gonna rot-in-hell with Osama and all the rest of those sick muthafuckas."

She opened the door and ran into the hallway. Joi had finally reached her boiling point. She angrily stormed through the hallways and the lobby of the hotel. After getting outside, she hailed a cab and got inside.

"Just drive down Jefferson," she demanded, and the cabbie drove off.

After Joi left the suite, Major lay across the bed with his hands folded over his eyes. He realized he had made the wrong decision. Although hurting Joi started off as a high, it ended as a low. After all, she'd done what she had to do to become the woman she wanted to be, but what he'd done had been done solely out of hateful revenge.

03•80

Andre was sprawled across his sofa in an emotionless state. He couldn't believe his luck. Monica had left him and had implied she'd terminated her pregnancy. He clenched his fist at the thought of her killing his unborn child. Was what had happened reason enough for her to act so irrationally? He wondered how he could have been so easily manipulated into Bill Young's sordid game of treachery.

Bill Young had deceivingly tricked Andre into believing he was having an erotic romp of kinky sex with the wife of a voyeur husband, but in actuality, Andre had starred in a pornography movie. He knew the whole dinner had been purposely set up by Bill and Rebecca for their sexual purposes, but he'd had no inclination he'd been deceived to the degree he had been. He'd had no idea he would become a pornographic celebrity.

After sulking for hours, Andre decided to call Monica again. He grabbed the telephone from its receiver and dialed the number. The phone rang continuously, but there was no answer. He let it ring several times before finally giving up. This had been a recurring scenario. Each of the other twelve or so times Andre had called Monica, he hadn't received an answer. He had left several messages, but she hadn't returned any of them either. He understood Monica's rage. She had every right to be upset, but Andre believed he had a right to explain what really happened.

Andre surfed through the channels on the television, but he couldn't find anything interesting to watch. He tossed the remote onto the cocktail table and slouched deeper into the sofa. Just as he got comfortable, the doorbell rang. He leapt from the sofa and rushed to the door. He was sure Monica was returning to talk about what had happened between them earlier. He knew she would eventually come to her senses. Once he opened the door, his optimism disappeared.

"Hey, Joi," Andre greeted Joi, examining her tear-drenched face. "What's wrong?" He wrapped his arm around her shoulders and welcomed her into his home.

Joi was sobbing profusely. She looked broken. Everything that had been going on in her life had finally come to a head. She had been tormented by man after man, but the ultimate betrayal was the betrayal she had done to herself. She had let Major burn her twice. She had been warned against dealing with him, but she'd allowed this to happen. Now, as she entered Andre's home, all she could do was shed tears.

"He hurt me, Andre," Joi finally managed to reply between sniffles. She curled into a fetal position on the sofa and continue to sob. She felt as if she was near death. The hurt was deep and painful.

"Who?" Andre asked firmly. "Major?"

"Yes." Joi nodded and buried her face into a couch pillow. "HE SODOMIZED ME," she yelled in pain.

"What? Where is that-nigga?" Andre was livid. He was ready to destroy Major for what he had done to Joi.

"No, Andre!" Joi shook her head in protest. She knew Andre was ready to go after Major, but she didn't want to bring his world down just because hers was shattering. "I just want to take a shower and go to sleep."

"Okay," Andre replied.

He rushed to the bathroom and ran Joi some bath water. He went to the linen closet, got fresh towels, and put them into the bathroom. Afterward, he went back to the sitting room, where Joi was still curled into a fetal position.

"Come on, Joi."

He took her hand and walked her to the bathroom. After getting Joi settled, Andre left the bathroom and rushed to the telephone. He called Joshua.

"Hey, Joshua," Andre started after getting an answer. "I need you over here, man." His voice was stern and demanding.

"What?" Joshua retorted. "What's wrong?"

"It's Joi, dawg. Get over here, bruh!"

He hung up the telephone to assure Joshua of his urgency. After hanging up on Joshua, he immediately called D'Vyne, but didn't get an answer.

"I'm about to get some aggression off on this nigga," he whispered to himself, thinking of all the ways he would like to hurt Major.

Andre had warned Joi on a few occasions against following through with her and Major's courtship. He knew second-chance relationships were prone to disaster. He had known Major just as long as Joi had, so he was well aware of Major's unmanly and cunning behavior. He was sure Joi knew as well; therefore, he couldn't understand how a woman as intelligent as Joi had fallen for Major's unscrupulous game.

Joi walked into the living room wearing Monica's robe. Just as she entered, the doorbell rang.

"I'll get it," Joi said, and walked to the door. She opened it and smiled. "Hi, Monica." Joi's lips spread into a weak and unconvincing smile.

Monica's face grimaced. She couldn't believe what she was seeing. Joi was wearing her robe! Not to mention, she was naked beneath it! Monica could tell because of the way the silk material clung to Joi's shapely body. Monica had come to talk about things with Andre, but the rage she'd felt after seeing the pornographic video returned after seeing Joi running around Andre's house nude.

"ANDRE," Monica yelled, furiously roaming through the house.

Andre heard Monica's voice. He instantly leapt to his feet. The despair that had overtaken him turned into hope after hearing Monica's call. He was sure she had come to work things out with him. As he moved toward her, she and Joi entered the living room where Andre was.

"Baby!" Andre smiled and moved toward Monica. He was ecstatic to see her.

"You're fucking your friends now, Andre?" Monica's face was angrily contorted as she stared at Andre. "I hate you!" She turned to run out the house.

Andre darted behind her and grabbed her hand. "You ain't runnin' out on me this time, Monica. I can't handle this shit! Sit down," he demanded, pointing to the couch.

Footsteps traveled through the house startling everyone. Suddenly Joshua was entering the living room. He was breathing erratically.

"What's wrong?" Joshua asked curiously. He had worry in his eyes. "Is Joi okay?"

He looked around for her. As his eyes roved the room, Jayla walked in followed by Joi. Jayla stood beside Joshua, and Joi sat on the floor and leaned against an ottoman.

"Joshua, go lock the door," Andre commanded. "Everyone else, sit down." He turned to Monica. "You, too! Especially you."

"What's goin' on?" Joshua asked after returning to the room.

Andre released a deep, empathy filled sigh. "Joi was raped."

Joi perked up. "No, I wasn't!" She shook her head defiantly. "I didn't say that."

She went on to tell everyone what Major had done to her. No one seemed to be offended as she told the story. Not even Monica and that was surprising. It made her question if she had overreacted to what had happened.

Joshua's face softened. "Yeah, the nigga shouldn't have said that shit or put you out, but umm . . ." He giggled and looked toward Jayla. "Me and my baby like to get a little freaky every now and then."

"Nah, dawg," Andre said, shaking his head in disagreement, "I don't even get down like that, my nigga."

Monica's neck snapped sassily and her eyes shifted toward Andre. "Psssh! You just don't know when to tell the truth."

She turned to Joi with a contrite look on her face. "I'm sorry for what I said about you, but I just found out my child's father is a porn star."

"Joshua, do you remember the white couple I told you about a few years back?" Andre asked. He was searching for a cosigner to his story.

"Yeah," Joshua replied candidly. "Them freaky muthafuckas." He laughed, then it dawned on him. "Aw, hell nah! That's the tape? The one her husband recorded?"

"Yeah." Andre nodded. "They got over on me."

"I told you yo' ass is naïve!" Joshua laughed. "You remember Candice at the Palace?" he teased.

"Joshua, this ain't the time; Joi is hurt. This is about her." Andre tried to steer the attention away from himself.

"My butt hole hurts, but my feelings are unfazed," Joi lied. "Fuck him."

Jayla chuckled. "It'll be all right in the morning," she said and smiled.

"Monica, can I speak to you upstairs?" Andre asked and held his hand out to her. She took his hand and they walked away. After entering his bedroom, he embraced her. "I'm sorry, baby."

He kissed her and explained what had taken place with Bill and Rebecca Young in detail. Monica's tear-drenched face assured Andre of her forgiveness and understanding. She hugged him.

"I love you, Andre," whispered Monica as they passionately held each other.

CB•BO

D'Vyne rubbed Demetric's chest as they lay in his bed. She had been staying over his house the last week or so. D'Vyne loved her man and planned to stand by him. She understood Demetric and he understood her.

After D'Vyne left Andre's dinner party, she had lost all hopes her life would return to normal. She came into her home defeated. Demetric embraced her, causing an overflow of tears and words to spill from her. She told him about visiting the courthouse, and just as she believed, he was already aware of her indiscretions.

Demetric knew D'Vyne had committed a carnal sin for a hustler's girlfriend by speaking to the police about street business, but he still allowed her to vent. Although he didn't condone what his girl had done, he understood her reasoning. He was aware of D'Vyne's deep love and commitment to her friends, so what she had done wasn't shocking to him.

As D'Vyne rubbed Demetric's chest, she noticed clusters of flashing lights glaring through the window. She rose and looked out the window. There were dozens of police cars in front of Demetric's home. Demetric reached beneath the sofa and came out with an AK47 assault rifle, equipped with a grenade launcher.

"GO TO THE BASEMENT!" Demetric demanded with a fierce yell. "VEE, GO TO THE BASEMENT!"

As D'Vyne ran toward the basement stairs, she heard a loud thump hit the front door. Thunderous gunshots followed the thump as Demetric let off multiple rounds from his rifle. Two police officers fell to the floor by the entrance door. Demetric kicked the door back shut, dropped the blinds, and ran to the upper level of his home. The police fired an arsenal of gunshots into the home, but Demetric had already barricaded the crawl space in the attic of the house. Demetric launched a grenade from the assault rifle, causing the police SWAT van to go up in flames.

Demetric was sure the police would be coming to his house to pick him up once Dwight had snitched on him. He had known Dwight to be a coward, but desperation had made him go against his intuition. His financial situation had caused a lapse in his judgment.

Demetric met Dwight while he was still in the dope game. They made a few moves out of town during early 2000 and everything was official, so when Dwight offered Demetric the chance to participate in a major robbery, Demetric was all in. He needed the money and he had a subtle comfort doing business with Dwight. Although he believed Dwight was a coward, he was sure his business acumen was official.

Dwight had plugged into a heroin ring out of New York. He moved from them for a few months before he decided to take over. Since the Cartel's team was so small, he and Demetric decided to execute all of them. There were two houses that needed to be hit, so they each took one.

The robberies went down without a hitch. Afterwards, they switched pistols. They were supposed to bury the other's weapon to assure solidarity amongst them, but Dwight's arrogant greed caused him to sell Demetric's pistol. The buyer of the pistol was caught by the police and turned Dwight into the law.

Dwight believed he could beat a murder case where there were no eyewitnesses and no motive. As he predicted, he beat the murder charges, but unfortunately, he could not escape the life sentence. Dwight was found guilty of complicity to commit murder in the first degree. He had sealed his fate with his compulsive greed and he sealed Demetric's with his testimony to the grand jury.

Now, after being snitched on, Demetric illusively scrambled through his home in a bloody standoff with the police.

D'Vyne kneeled in the corner of the pantry. She was afraid and knew Demetric's death was inevitable. As shots rang out throughout the upper levels of the home, D'Vyne now knew why Demetric had been so down lately. She realized he was attempting death-by-cop, rather than death in a prison cell. This was a time she really needed the comfort of her friends, but she was sure everyone had written her off.

ᏬᏞ•ᏮᎢ

Joshua kicked his feet up in Andre's recliner and smiled. "Andre, you and Monica are some real hospitable people." He chuckled, pointed the remote at the television, and began surfing through the channels.

Monica chuckled. "I bet it took a lot for you to say something like that, Mr. Sarcastic." She smiled.

Joshua shrugged his shoulders. "I'm used to asshole or son of a bitch, so Mr. Sarcastic is cool wit' me." He laughed. "Ms. Bourgeois Bombshell."

Joi snickered underneath her blanket. She'd pretended to be asleep, but she was very much awake. She was still disbelieving of how Major had treated her at the hotel. She wasn't as upset with him about attempting anal sex with her as she was about him cursing her and throwing her out the room for not participating. She was aware of Major's spoiled character, but she refused to allow him to violate her dignity by performing degrading sexual acts with him.

Jayla sighed as she lay across the floor watching Joshua continuously browse through the television channels. Although D'Vyne had attempted to degrade her the last time she was around Joshua's friends, Jayla felt awkwardly comfortable with them. She was confused about a lot of things that were going on within their clique. She wondered how a group of friends who were so close knit and so successful, have so much drama within their circle. That puzzled her, but with all the drama that she had been involved in over the years, she began to feel at home with them.

Andre slouched deep in his recliner with Monica sitting between his legs. He was becoming irritated with Joshua continuously flipping through the channels. Although he had been through enough confrontations for one day, he couldn't take it any longer.

"JOSHUA!" Andre yelled." Give me the remote, nigga."

Joshua chuckled. "I'm tryin' to find the news. Monica, rub dude's balls or somethin'. Calm the nigga down, 'cause he's trippin'."

Monica laughed. "Jayla, how do you put up with this cat?" She continued laughing.

Jayla smiled. "I ignore his ass," she teased.

Joshua finally found the local news station. "Damn! They say some nigga's shootin' shit up over on Lake Point," Joshua said, intently staring at the television.

Joi rose from beneath the blanket. Her eyes bulged from her head. "LAKE POINT?! THAT'S WHERE DEMETRIC LIVES!" She rushed over to the television.

"THAT'S HIS HOUSE, TOO," Joshua belted. "CALL D'VYNE, ANDRE."

Andre sprinted to the telephone. He dialed D'Vyne's cellphone but didn't get an answer. He then rushed back into the living room.

"She ain't answering," Andre said in a panic-filled tone.

"Get y'all's shit!" Joshua commanded everyone as he rose from the recliner. "We're smashin' through there."

Everyone obeyed Joshua and scrambled for the things before racing out the house. Monica jumped into the car with Joshua and Jayla, and Joi got into Andre's car.

Joshua sped off wildly. Although he and D'Vyne had been feuding since the dinner party, D'Vyne was still his best friend. Joshua loved her and hoped Demetric hadn't done anything to harm her.

"I hope Demetric ain't hurt her," Joshua said. His tone was enraged. "I swear, I'll bury that nigga." He was tormented by the thought of Demetric doing to D'Vyne what he had done to him.

"Baby, ain't that the guy Dwight tried to have kill you?" Jayla asked in a shaken tone. She was sure anyone associated with Dwight was capable of the worst of anything. Therefore, she was afraid D'Vyne's life was in jeopardy.

After hearing Dwight's name, Monica's ears went up like antennas. She was familiar with someone by that name. Akil, her ex-boyfriend's, death had been plotted by someone name Dwight. Monica was sure the names were a coincidence rather than concrete, but she continued listening in just to be sure.

"Yeah," Joshua replied to Jayla's question, nodding.

"Yeah, that's him. I'm tellin' you, baby . . ."

Joshua turned onto Lake Point. Police were everywhere. They had the entire block barricaded. Shots were ringing out from both sides of the situation. As they looked on from nearly a block away, Joshua's cellphone rang.

"Hello," Joshua answered, hoping he would hear D'Vyne's voice on the other end, but it was Andre instead.

"She ain't here, Joshua." Andre's voice was shaky. "You have to tell someone she could be in there with Demetric." He was distraught.

"A'ight," Joshua said and ended the call.

Joshua hastily exited the car and headed toward the barricade. Jayla and Monica followed. He leapt over the barricade and sprinted in the direction of the mayhem. As he neared the block where the shooting was taking place, an officer came from nowhere and tackled him.

"MY SISTER'S IN THERE WITH DUDE," Joshua shouted, tussling with the officer. "THEY HAVE TO STOP SHOOTIN'!" He continued to struggle with the officer. As Joshua wrestled around in the grass with the policeman, Jayla and Monica appeared.

Jayla rushed over to them. "GET OFF HIM!" she screamed angrily, watching her man being restrained.

Monica walked over to the scene just as Joshua was being handcuffed. "May I speak to whoever's in charge?" she asked an officer. She began explaining why they were there. The officer kept Joshua restrained and took Monica to speak to someone.

 As they moved closer, the shooting suddenly stopped. Jayla shook from fright. She didn't want to catch a stray bullet. She turned to an officer and asked, "Is the shooting over?"

Just as she completed her sentence, the officer tackled her to the ground, shielding Jayla from harm. She heard SWAT yelling, demanding Demetric to drop his weapon.

Joshua was furious as he watched what was happening. Demetric bolted from his house carrying an AK47. Demetric's eyes briefly canvassed the surrounding area as he opened fired on the police. The tactical officers returned fire, riddling Demetric's body with slugs. Joshua knew Demetric had chosen death-by-cop, which made him believe the worst had happened. He was almost positive Demetric had killed D'Vyne before signing his own death certificate.

As Demetric's lifeless body lay across the lawn filled with lead, the officer who had tackled Jayla turned to her and smiled. "Ma'am," the officer said, "the shooting is over now."

ఇ•ఏ

Andre weaved through traffic en route to Demetric's home. He feared that, if Demetric hadn't hurt D'Vyne, she would catch a stray bullet from the police during the shootout. Although Andre wasn't a religious man, he had said a few prayers for the outcome as he sped through traffic.

Joi was distraught. Her day had begun with the pleasure of a truck ride and a dog race, which had changed into a sexual assault and a possible death threat to her best friend's life. Her eyes moistened. She cursed God for allowing bad things to continuously happen to her and her friends. She considered herself and her friends to be good people, and she just couldn't understand why they were consistently confronted with misfortune.

"WHY?" Joi screamed crazily. "WHY DO WE HAVE TO KEEP GOING THROUGH SHIT?"

Andre ignored Joi and continued driving. He knew she was making a statement rather than asking a question, so he let her vent. As he reached Demetric's street, his heart dropped to his stomach. There was a morgue wagon and a few ambulance trucks parked near Demetric's house. The lights glaring from the emergency vehicles nearly blinded Andre. Seeing so much medical assistance assured Andre there was more than one injury or fatality. Andre's blood boiled at the thought of D'Vyne's body being hauled away in the meat wagon that was parked in front of the scene.

As they reached the barricades, Joi leapt from the car and darted pass them. She yelled for Joshua as she approached the police and medical vehicles. As she frantically yelled for him, she noticed his head peek from inside an ambulance. Joi rushed toward him.

"Is D'Vyne in there?" she asked erratically.

Joshua embraced Joi. "Yeah, she's in there wit' Jayla. Come on; you can ride wit' me. She wants Jayla to ride wit' her so they can talk."

Andre approached them and Joshua filled him in; he was relieved. After briefly speaking to Joshua, Andre walked off to find Monica. He found her sitting on the curb crying.

"What's wrong, baby?"

Andre was sure Monica was fed up with the drama he had brought into her life. He sat next to her and wrapped his arm around her shoulder.

Monica embraced Andre and cried. She loved him, but she doubted she could handle the chaos of his world. She lived a humble and conservative lifestyle, a lifestyle free from drama, and she intended to return to it.

Chapter 15

D'Vyne's face wrinkled into a pain-stricken frown. Doctors and nurses surrounded her. Joshua held her hand and Joi coached her. Andre stood back, recording the birth of D'Vyne's child. D'Vyne pushed as she released violent, almost inhuman, screams. Her breathing was heavy as she grunted. Joshua's face brightened as the baby's head burst through D'Vyne's birth canal.

"MY GODBABY!" he yelled excitedly. "PULL IT OUT!" He smiled as the baby came forth screaming.

The doctor pulled the baby from D'Vyne's womb and smiled. She turned the child toward D'Vyne. "It's a girl," she said.

"PUT IT BACK IN THERE!" Joshua yelled jokingly.

Joi pushed Joshua. "Shut up! She's beautiful."

Andre passed Joshua the camcorder so he could cut the unbiblical cord. He cut the cord, walked the baby over to the nurses, and smiled as the nurses cleaned the baby. Andre knew his time to enjoy fatherhood would be coming soon. D'Vyne was exhausted. She wanted to hold her baby girl, but she was too weak to make the request.

It had been months since Demetric's death. Although he'd been D'Vyne's world, she was recovering remarkably. Her friends had been by her side throughout the entire ordeal. Andre, Joi, and Joshua had consoled her. They forgave her and understood why she'd made the decisions she had. Her love for Demetric had caused a lapse in her judgment, but her clique was forgiving and steadfast in their support for her.

Joi sat on the hospital bed with D'Vyne. She gently rubbed D'Vyne's back. Joi was happy for D'Vyne and she admired her strength. She was sure D'Vyne missed Demetric and needed him during a time like this. Although Demetric had done some treacherous things that had nearly destroyed the cohesiveness of their group of friends, Joi wished he could be with them today. She wished Demetric could have shared the birth of his child with D'Vyne.

As she sat snugly next to D'Vyne comforting her, Joi's thoughts turned to Major. It had been months since she'd seen him and she missed him. Although Major had degraded her at the hotel, Joi had learned to forgive him. After contemplating the ordeal for months, she realized Major had returned to Detroit with vengeance and malice in his heart. She'd come to the conclusion that his love for her was no more than a ploy. Major had wanted to pull her in and destroy her, mentally and emotionally. Although he had initially stunned Joi, she quickly recovered. In actuality, Joi had escaped Major's retaliation because her emotional stability was still intact.

D'Vyne squeezed Joi's hand. "I miss him, Joi," she whispered faintly.

Joi combed her fingers through D'Vyne's hair. "I know." She continued raking through her friend's hair.

೮•ಬ

Monica lay across her sofa feeling drained. She had gained nearly forty pounds during her six-and-a-half months of pregnancy. She and Andre's vacation was coming up soon, but she was unsure if she would be going with him. Of course, Monica loved Andre. He was everything she desired in a man, but there were surrounding factors that made her question the destiny of their relationship. She was positive Jayla's ex-boyfriend and D'Vyne's child's father were the culprits behind Akil's murder. Knowing that, Monica believed she was disrespecting her late boyfriend by consorting with acquaintances of his murderers.

Earlier in the day, Andre had called Monica and told her about D'Vyne's water breaking. Monica was unmoved and assured Andre she wouldn't be coming to the hospital. She was sure her attitude was smug and equally as sure Andre would want to know why once he arrived to her home from the hospital. Monica sighed a deep and heavy sigh. She knew it was time to tell Andre about Akil, and what Demetric and Dwight had done to him.

Akil's death was simple, but brutal. After being tied to a chair, he was shot in the back of the neck, exploding his medulla oblongata. He died an instant, painless death, but it wasn't painless for the people who'd survived him, especially Monica.

Andre came into the house. "Monica," he called out from the entrance. He walked into the living room where Monica lay across the sofa. "Hey, momma." Andre sat next to her and rubbed her swollen stomach.

"Just being lazy." Monica smiled and forced a chuckle.

"Why didn't you wanna come to the hospital? You were tired?" Andre smiled and continued rubbing Monica's belly.

Monica used her elbows to lean upward. "I don't want to be around D'Vyne or her baby," Monica replied nastily.

"What?" asked Andre. He was confused by what Monica had just said to him and her tone of voice. He wondered why she was being so cold. He had heard the glibness in her voice earlier when he called from the hospital. He'd assumed her attitude had something to do with her hormones, but he now realized it was something more.

Monica grabbed Andre's hand. She looked at him with gentleness in her eyes. "Demetric and Dwight killed someone special in my life."

Her eyes began moistening. The anxiety that had consumed her was being released. She began telling Andre Akil's story. Although Monica was carrying Andre's child and she loved him, a piece of her heart housed the undying love and loyalty she had for Akil. She had withheld this story from Andre throughout their relationship because it had no relevance, but after finding out about the ties Andre's friends had to Akil's murder, Monica could no longer keep it from him.

Andre gave Monica his devoted attention while she told him about her ex-boyfriend. He was sure she expected him to be offended, but he wasn't. Andre understood her gripe, but he didn't agree with her. He knew losing someone you loved was traumatic and could cause a person guilt for trying to love again, but he didn't agree with Monica's anger toward Jayla and D'Vyne.

"Monica," Andre interrupted her, "I understand your pain, but I don't understand why you're upset with D'Vyne and Jayla. Shit, if anything, you should embrace them. Think about it. The cats who killed ol' boy and bought drama into your life, brought drama into their lives, too. Demetric tried to kill Joshua, and

Dwight pressured him into doing it. D'Vyne and Jayla didn't do shit!"

"But they loved those guys," Monica whined. "D'Vyne loves Demetric just like I love Akil. You don't see a conflict of interest in that?"

"Yeah," Andre agreed, "but what good is gonna come from you resenting them for somethin' they didn't have shit to do with? Just think about it." He rose, kissed her forehead, and left her home. He wanted to give Monica some room to think and hopefully reconsider.

Monica sulked after Andre left, but she was amazed by his understanding and compassion. Those were two of the many reasons she loved him, but as she sat alone pondering the myriad of things that wedging into their relationship, she doubted the possibility of them weathering the storm.

 C3•ЯD

Joshua walked into Perceptions and dropped his hat on the floor.

"Everybody," Joshua called out, "y'all better put somethin' in this hat fo' my goddaughter." He smiled as he received "negro please" looks from everyone.

Rashaad chuckled. "It's a girl," he teased because he knew how much Joshua had wanted it to be a boy.

"Yeah, nigga!" Joshua grimaced playfully. "You gotta problem wit' that?" He intently stared at Rashaad.

"Nah, but I gotta problem with you comin' up in here tryin' to shake us down." Rashaad walked over to Joshua and kecked his hat across the floor. The entire salon erupted in laughter.

Joshua waved his middle finger at Rashaad, picked up his hat, and walked toward the back of the salon. Although Joshua had started his own upscale barbershop on the other side of the city, he was still partial owner of Perceptions, so he was running both salons while D'Vyne was on maternity leave.

The months that had passed after Demetric's death had brought D'Vyne and Joshua closer. Although Joshua was sure their friendship needed more time to completely heal, he had forgiven her. He still loved D'Vyne and knew the upkeep of Perceptions was only a fraction of the support she would need. As Joshua thumbed through the mall, he ran across a letter from the United States District Attorney's office. He knew the letter wasn't business related, but he was curious, so he opened it.

Joshua's eyes widened as he read the letter.

The United States of America would like to thank you for your testimony in the case against Damon Frisk and Joi Valentine. Your future cooperation will be needed at trial. Damon has already been apprehended and we plan to bring Joi into custody soon. Once again, thank you for fulfilling your civic duty.

Joshua tucked the letter into his shirt pocket and rushed toward the exit of the salon. As he reached the door, he turned to Rashaad.

"You have to lock up tonight," Joshua said and walked out.

He was astounded by what he had read. After getting in his car, he called D'Vyne's hospital room. He knew this was a bad time to be grilling D'Vyne, but what else could he do.

"YES!" Joshua yelled into the telephone after receiving an answer.

"Yeah! Why are you yelling?" D'Vyne retorted.

"What are you testifying against Joi and Damon about?" Joshua was immensely curious.

"What?" D'Vyne asked. She was confused by Joshua's question. "Joi didn't have shit to do with that!" D'Vyne began telling Joshua about what Damon had done to her and Joi, and about her testifying to the grand jury.

Joshua listened to D'Vyne's story in puzzlement. He wondered if he was really part of their clique because they hadn't told them anything about their trip to Miami.

"WHAT-THE-FUCK?" Joshua shouted into the telephone.

He was pissed about them being so secretive. That trip could have cost them their lives, and could still potentially cost Joi her freedom.

"I'ma check up on Joi because these people talkin' 'bout lockin' her ass up!"

Joshua told D'Vyne what the letter said before hanging up. He tried to call Joi, but she wasn't answering, so he decided to go by her apartment.

ᘓ•ᘔ

Joi joyfully wrapped the gifts she had purchased for D'Vyne. She had bought the gifts months ago but had been unable to wrap them because of all the drama that surrounded her at the time. Now, she had a clear mind that was free of drama.

Major's stunt had helped Joi more than it had hurt her. After he degraded her, she began looking at herself for answers to her relationship dilemma. Joi wondered what was in her they saw to make men want to hurt her. She was convinced that men saw vulnerability in her character they considered exploitable. Joshua had teased her throughout their friendship about being naïve. Now, after all she had experienced with men, she wondered if his assessment of her was true.

Joi smiled as she wrapped the presents. She was proud of herself and proud of the progress she had made healing emotionally over the months since the incident with Major. Joi knew she was far from being completely whole, but she was sure she was on the right path. Although her path was lonely, she was content with it. She was free from men and the strife they had brought into her life.

Joi's telephone rang, bringing her out of her personal thoughts. She reluctantly rose and went to the telephone. As she reached it, it stopped ringing. She looked at the caller ID and saw Joshua's cellphone number.

"Pssh, he doesn't want anything," Joi whispered to herself.

She placed the telephone back onto her desk and walked back to the presents. Joi was anxious to finish wrapping the gifts so she could return to D'Vyne's bedside. She knew D'Vyne was lonely and needed company, especially since she'd lost Demetric.

D'Vyne was always Joi's confidant and counselor during her time of need, and Joi wanted to return the favor. As Joi fumbled with the tape dispenser, she heard voices at her door. She rushed to the door to see who it was. She peeked through the peephole and noticed two strange men casually talking to one another. She opened the door.

"Excuse me," Joi interrupted the men's conversation, "the noise is bothering me." She smiled politely.

One of the men smiled at Joi. "Joi Valentine?" he asked firmly.

"Yes," Joi replied and stared cautiously.

The man reached into his jacket pocket and showed Joi his badge. "I'm Parker Russell and we're with the FBI. We need to speak with you."

"Please, come in."

Joi moved aside to let the men inside her apartment. She was curious about their visit. She had no idea what they needed to speak to her about. She wondered if Joshua or Andre had been harmed or caught-up in some way. All sorts of things traveled through her mind.

"No," one of the agents said. "We need you to come with us."

He pulled handcuffs from his waist and read Joi her rights, cuffing her. The agent called someone and told them Joi's home was free for search. They closed the door to her apartment and walked Joi toward the elevator. As Joi was being marched out the building, her humiliation peaked. The woman she had given the verbal warning to a year or so back glibly smirked at her. Joi was sure Andre had caught up with Major and assaulted him, possibly killing him, causing her to be an accomplice.

ଔ•୧ଠ

Joshua pulled into the parking area of Joi's apartment. He was too late. He watched as the federal agents walked Joi to their vehicle and drove away. He wanted to make his presence known by protesting her arrest, but he was sure that acting a fool would only cause him to be arrested as well, so he just looked on as their car disappeared with Joi inside.

Joshua drove away after seeing the agents leave with Joi. He wanted to get some advice, so he decided to go to Andre's office. Joshua knew Andre hated to be bothered at his office, but he felt compelled to fill him in about what had happened to Joi. He was sure Andre was tired of bad news, especially with him doing so well in life, but it was imperative he knew because Joi was his peoples.

As Joshua walked into Andre's office, Andre dropped his pen and looked up to him. Joshua sighed.

"Andre, man, I know how you feel about niggaz fuckin' with you while you're at work, but Joi is in jail."

Andre's face stiffened. "What? She said she was cool! What, she done killed Major?"

"Nah, dawg."

Joshua shook his head and began telling Andre about what had happened to Joi and D'Vyne. As he spoke, he could see the wear in Andre's eyes. Andre was silent for a few seconds, rubbing his thick goatee.

"You might as well sit down. It ain't shit we can do until she calls. I'll try to put some money together for her bail and an attorney, if she needs one." Andre's voice was emotionless.

"What about D'Vyne? She's still in the hospital."

"Man, listen." Andre sighed. "I done had enough of hospitals, shootin's, and this jail-shit. In fact, I done had enough of D'Vyne, too." He retrieved his pen and began writing.

"WHAT?!" Joshua asked angrily. "AIN'T YOU THE SAME NIGGA WHO ASKED ME TO FORGIVE HER AND UNDERSTAND HER, AND ALL THAT TYPE-OF-SHIT?"

"Joshua," Andre said sternly, "this is my business. You'd better lower your voice. Yeah, I said that and I meant it. I understand D'Vyne and I care about her, but I care more about my life and my future."

"And you think Vee would do some shit to hurt you intentionally?"

"Just because it isn't intentional doesn't mean it's less painful. Shit! Would it have hurt less if she'd pulled the trigger instead of Demetric?" Andre stared at Joshua briefly before answering his own question. "HELL NAH!"

"Now you the one getting' loud."

"I'm just tired of all this shit! D'Vyne's done caused too much shit and Jayla has too!"

Joshua became offended by what Andre had said. He thought Andre liked Jayla because he was never the type to put on a façade for anyone. Andre had never liked Demetric and he'd never pretended to. Joshua stared into the ceiling.

"Look, bruh," Joshua shook his head in disappointment and sighed, "I'ma bounce befo' I say some shit I don't mean." He rose from his chair.

"Joshua," Andre called as Joshua turned to walk out, "sit down, man."

He then told Joshua about what was going on between him and Monica. He explained his position about the situation. Andre was caught between his lifetime commitment to his friends and his commitment to his woman and unborn child. He really liked Jayla and he loved D'Vyne deeply, but he felt obligated to put his family first.

Joshua heard Andre out. He understood Andre's plight, but he believed Andre was oversimplifying the situation. Andre thought alienating himself from his friends would bridge the gap between he and Monica, but Joshua knew better. He knew what Andre was considering could be catastrophic to his friendships and his relationship to Monica. Joshua shook his head in disagreement.

"I feel you, but, my nigga." Joshua shook his head again, "you're wrong about this one. Everything you're mad at D'Vyne and Jayla fo', you're about to do. If you love Monica," he shrugged his shoulders, "love her, but love yo' friends, too, because at the end of it all . . . we're all we got. I'ma go ahead and pull out so I can find some change to help Joi."

He gave Andre a pound and walked out.

C3•80

Joi lay silently across the cold cement floor of her holding cell. She believed she had experienced the worst in life after what had taken place with Major. She thought Damon had tortured her to the edge of death, but this was worst. Joi had definitely seen the pit of hell, but after being arrested, she realized its depth had no end. As she lay weak and motionless, she asked herself the question she had continuously asked since being arrested.

"Why?"

Although Joi had done everything required of a person to succeed in life, she had failed. She acknowledged her failure, but she did not know where she had gone wrong. She rose to her feet after hearing keys at her cell door and an officer came in.

"Ma'am," the officer called for Joi, "you can make another phone call because tomorrow you'll be transferred to the federal detention center."

Joi agreed to make a call and followed behind the officer. After reaching the telephone, she called Andre.

"Andre," Joi spoke softly into the telephone. "Did you all find out why I'm in here?"

"Yeah," Andre replied, "we know, but the attorney we retained for you advised us not to discuss it with you over the jail telephone."

"What? What-the-hell is going on, Andre?"

Joi was afraid. She was sure the charges were false and she would be released, but it had been three days since her arrest and she was becoming hopeless.

"Joi," Andre tried to calm her, "don't trip. Be patient and be honest. I don't give-a-fuck if they wanna know what color panties you have on, be honest."

Joi's eyes moistened. "I'm scared, Andre." She didn't like being held captive, especially without knowing the reason. She panted and gasped as tears sprang from her eyes.

"Yeah, Joi; me too." Andre's tone was sincere. He was afraid for Joi. "We'll know what's up come tomorrow."

"Okay; bye, Andre."

Joi hung up the telephone and was escorted back to her cell. Because of the reality of her luck, Joi dreaded to see what would come of the false arrest. She wondered why everyone was being so secretive about the nature of her drug charges. Joi despised drugs. She hated everything about them, from the smugglers to the users. And now, she sat in a jail cell, charged with conspiracy to deliver multiple kilos of heroin and cocaine.

ଓଷ•ଞ

Jayla stood in the doorway of Joshua's bedroom. She watched as he stared at the empty computer screen. She and Joshua had not spoken much since Joi's arrest. She could see his hurt, but she felt as if it was interfering in their relationship too much. She wanted to spend some time with Joshua, so she snuck up behind him. She began massaging his shoulders.

"Joshua, what's wrong?' Jayla was concerned.

"Everything! Shit, it's fucked up! Niggaz do everything they're s'pose to do to come up outta the hood, but the hood always follows you." He continued his void stare into the computer screen, as if he was unmoved by Jayla's company.

"Yeah, but it'll be cool."

Jayla wanted to remain optimistic. Joshua was already pulled down by the situation and she did not want to drag him down any further.

"What?" Joshua asked. He seemed to be upset with Jayla's assessment of Joi's situation. "Cool! My girl's locked up, facin' space-age time fo' some shit she ain't even know about! What's cool about that? Cool my-muthafuckin-ass!"

"Joshua, I know you're upset, but Joi is a grown-ass-woman and she's smart. She's gonna pull outta this little bullshit. She ain't done shit, so she'll be okay."

"Yeah, right! I just got through paying all the bills fo' Perceptions and Crisp's, and my account is damn-near depleted. I can't even afford a bond if she gets one tomorrow." He shook his head and banged his hand against the computer table. "What difference does it make anyway? The justice system doesn't give-a-fuck about niggaz being innocent! Shit, look at Dwight!"

"FUCK DWIGHT!" Jayla shouted. She was getting upset. "He wasn't innocent! I've got money, Joshua. I told you that. If I have it, we have it, so Joi's going to be all right. You don't have to keep hollering and cursing at me. I didn't send her to jail!"

Joshua's mouth hung open and he stared at Jayla vehemently. He'd thought she was kidding when she told him she had enough money to loan him to open Crisp's. He scratched his head.

"Oh," Joshua said, "now I see it." He grunted. "You done ran off wit' that-nigga Dwight's bread. You peeled the nigga and he thinks I been regulatin' his chips, so he tried to have me smoked." Joshua's tone was cold. "All this time, I've been fightin' fo' you and you done ripped this dude off."

Jayla was outdone. She couldn't believe what she was hearing or seeing. Tears filled and profusely fell from her eyes. Everything she'd thought about Joshua had been diminished by his last statement.

"You ain't any different than Dwight!" she spat out at Joshua. She wanted to hurt his feelings just as he had hurt hers. "I can't believe you, Joshua! I ain't stole shit from him.! My stepdad left me some money!"

Jayla spun on her heels and tried to run out of the room, but Joshua caught her arm before she could. Joshua held her by her waist and pulled her to him.

"Jayla, I'm trippin'." His tone was contrite. "I didn't mean to say that."

Jayla turned to face Joshua. Her face was drenched with tears. Her emotions turned like a roller coaster and bent like a contortionist. Joshua had accused her of trading her integrity as a woman for money.

"No, Joshua," Jayla wiped tears from her face, "you said it because you meant it! You wanna know what-the-fuck I went through to get that money? Huh, Joshua?"

She started by telling Joshua about her nonconsensual relationship with her stepfather. She'd known her truth would surface eventually, but she hadn't wanted it to come out in the midst of a heated argument between her and Joshua.

Joshua was taken aback by Jayla's story. He couldn't believe such immoral sexual acts were going on in the black community. He was upset with himself for jumping to conclusions without asking. Jayla was trying to be helpful to Joshua and his friends, but he had disrespected her with his presumptuousness. Joshua looked at Jayla's tear-soaked face.

"I'm sorry, baby." Joshua pulled her into his embrace. "I'm just goin' through so much shit right now. It ain't no excuse, but I'm sorry."

Jayla smiled softly. "You'd better have apologized 'cause I was gonna Tae Bo your ass." She had forgiven him.

Joshua pulled her deeper into his arms and smiled. He was relieved he still had his girl because he loved her.

⋘•⋙

Andre's feeling of emptiness had returned. He and Monica had been at odds ever since she'd found out about Demetric and Dwight's participation in Akil's death. Although Andre was a fighter, he was no longer willing to fight for Monica's love. He doubted if he wanted it any longer . . . or if it was worth it. Andre took into account that he and Monica were using their unborn child as a crutch in their relationship. He knew his love for her was unstable without the help of other variables, especially Monica's pregnancy. Monica was weak in Andre's eyes because she was willing to give up so easily. He also questioned his ability and willingness to carry her emotionally, especially knowing she carried the emotional weight of another man.

Andre figured he was receiving the backlash of Akil's mistakes, and he was uncomfortable with it. He was sure Monica had a reason to point the finger of derision at his friends for Akil's death, but her cause had no merit. Andre was a firm believer in accountability, and therefore, he considered Akil a culprit in his own murder because of his career choice. Not only did he hold Akil accountable, he held Monica responsible as well because unlike Joi, Monica condoned what Akil was doing. As Andre sat around pondering the whole situation between him and Monica, he knew today would be the day he revealed his true feelings about her and the situation that had caused the trouble between them.

After speaking to Joshua at his office, Andre realized he had lost a lot of himself adjusting for he and Monica's relationship. His truth had become a lie. He'd become what he thought he had to in order to make his relationship work. He'd been willing to sacrifice his friendships for his relationship until he realized how cowardly that decision would have been. Now, after hours of lying around contemplating his situation, he heard Monica enter his home. He sat upright as Monica entered the den where he was waiting for her.

"Hey, Monica." Andre's tone was nonchalant.

"Hi, Andre," Monica greeted and sat next to Andre. "I'm sorry about how I've been acting."

"Yeah, me too. I'm sorry about how I've allowed you to make me act." Andre was glib.

"What? Man, I'm trying to be nice," she warned. "You'd better stop tripping." Monica seemed to be upset.

"Tripping?!" Andre chuckled. He was outdone. "You're right; I should stop." He laughed.

Monica rubbed Andre's head. "We can't be arguing like this, especially with our vacation coming up." She smiled.

"I ain't going. I'll give you your money back, but I ain't going nowhere until Joi gets outta jail."

"What?! So the-hell with our trip, huh, Andre? It's always something with them! If it ain't D'Vyne and her lunatic boyfriend, it's Joi! What about me? What about us, Andre?"

"Us?" Andre laughed. "Monica, you don't want nothing you can't control. I don't know what you're used to, but I ain't Akil." He chuckled. He was through playing second fiddle to Monica's dead boyfriend and he wanted her to know it.

"I'm leaving, Andre!" Monica rose from the couch and looked down to Andre.

Andre chuckled. "I'm not chasing you, Monica." He mimicked her voice. "You know what? Leave my keys, too." Andre got up and walked her to the door. "A'ight then."

He watched as she walked away before he closed the door. Although he was losing the woman he wanted to love, he felt a great burden lift off him.

೧•೩

Joi waited at the bus station for Joshua to come pick her up. Although she had experienced the worst weekend of her life, she was elated about it. She'd had no idea what she had been arrested for until she spoke to the federal prosecutor.

The prosecutor explained the mix-up with her arrest. After D'Vyne testified before the grand jury, the prosecutor had issued a warrant for Joi's testimony, but the warrant had come out as a warrant for her arrest. Initially, Joi was furious, but after a moment of thought, she realized she had been given the opportunity to put the dagger in Damon's chest for the way he had tormented her.

While awaiting Joshua's arrival, Joi felt at ease for the first time in months. She had finally escaped the grasp of Damon's hateful antics and Major's attempt to destroy her. Being released from jail had given Joi her first piece of joy.

For ten years, Joi had believed her happiness would come from the comfort of a man loving her. She'd searched for the perfect man, believing he would bring serenity into her tumultuous love life. Now, after being released from jail, she realized her true love came from freedom. Freedom from men, freedom from drama, and freedom to enjoy her life to the fullest and never settle!

Epilogue ~ Two Years Later

Andre was ecstatic about his new relationship. Monica had stolen a lot of Andre's peace, but his true love had returned it. He was a great father, and he and Monica had a civil relationship as parents. Although she was surprised by Andre's new love, Monica knew she could never love him the way his new love d d. Andre smiled as his woman walked into the bedroom carrying a breakfast tray. He pulled her onto the bed and kissed her.

"I love you, D'Vyne."

Andre pulled her deeper into his embrace.

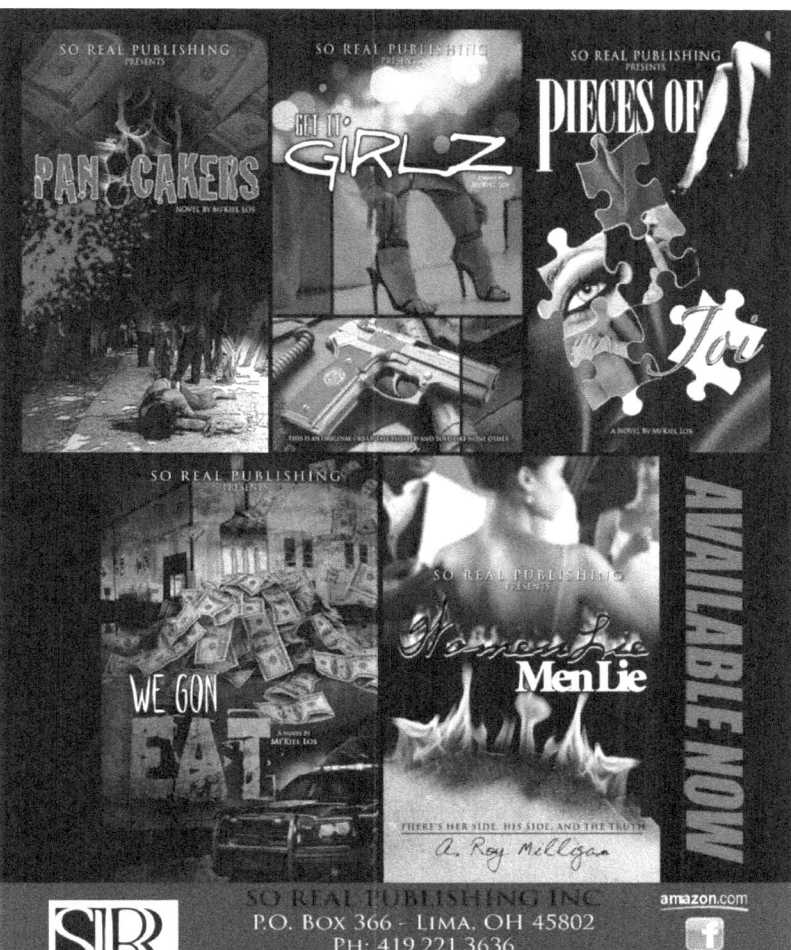

www.ingramcontent.com/pod-product-compliance
Lightning Source LLC
Chambersburg PA
CBHW071247170626
46809CB00001B/117

* 9 7 8 0 9 8 4 0 2 1 6 0 4 *